'Laying bare our twenty-first-century weaknesses and dilemmas, Carver has created a highly original state-of-the-nation novel' *Literary Review*

'Arguably the most original crime novel published this year' *Independent*

'At once fantastical and appallingly plausible ... this mesmeric novel paints a thought-provoking if depressing picture of modern life' *Guardian*

'Unlike anything else you'll read this year' *Heat*

'A powerful look into the abyss of a psychopathic personality' *Publishers Weekly*

'Wickedly fun' *Crime Monthly*

'One of the most compelling and original voices in crime fiction' Alex North

'A gripping novel laced with humour and cutting character insight ... a thrill from start to finish' Sarah Pinborough

'Equally enthralling and appalling ... unlike anything I've read in a very long while' James Oswald

'Creepy and brilliant' Khurrum Rahman

'Reminiscent of *The Shining* ... a creeping and perfectly crafted novel tinged with dark humour and malice' Victoria Selman

'A masterfully macabre tale' Louise Mumford

'Magnificently, compulsively chilling' Margaret Kirk

'Fans of Chuck Palahniuk will adore Carver ... he is utterly brilliant' Christopher Hooley

'Will Carver's most exciting, original, hilarious and freaky outing yet' Helen FitzGerald

'Thrilling and completely original ... deserves to become an instant classic' Kevin Wignall

ABOUT THE AUTHOR

Will Carver is the international bestselling author of the January David series and the critically acclaimed, mind-blowingly original Detective Pace series, which includes *Good Samaritans (2018), Nothing Important Happened Today* (2019) and *Hinton Hollow Death Trip* (2020), all of which were ebook bestsellers and selected as books of the year in the mainstream international press. *Nothing Important Happened Today* was longlisted for both the Goldsboro Books Glass Bell Award 2020 and the Theakston's Old Peculier Crime Novel of the Year Award. *Hinton Hollow Death Trip* was longlisted for the *Guardian*'s Not the Booker Prize, and was followed by the literary thrillers, *The Beresford, Psychopaths Anonymous, The Daves Next Door, Suicide Thursday* and *Upstairs at the Beresford*.

Will spent his early years in Germany, but returned to the UK at age eleven, when his sporting career took off. He and his partner run their own fitness and nutrition company, and live in Reading with five children and a tortoise.

Find Will at www.willcarver.co.uk and follow him on X and Instagram @will_carver.

Also by Will Carver and available from Orenda Books:
Good Samaritans
Nothing Important Happened Today
Hinton Hollow Death Trip
The Beresford
Psychopaths Anonymous
The Daves Next Door
Suicide Thursday
Upstairs at the Beresford

KILL THEM WITH KINDNESS

WILL CARVER

**ORENDA
BOOKS**

Orenda Books
16 Carson Road
West Dulwich
London SE21 8HU
www.orendabooks.co.uk

First published by Orenda Books, 2025
Copyright © Will Carver, 2025

A catalogue record for this book is available from the British Library.

ISBN 978-1-916788-38-1
eISBN 978-1-916788-39-8

Typeset in Garamond by Elaine Sharples
Printed and bound by Clays Ltd, Elcograf S.p.A

For sales and distribution, please contact info@orendabooks.co.uk

'Near the gates and within two cities, there will be two scourges. The likes of which have never been seen. Famine within plague. People put out by steel. Crying to the great immortal God for relief.'

Nostradamus

Live. Laugh. Love.

Anonymous

For those who care more about seeing than being seen.

THE
END

HAIRDRESSERS IN IPSWICH

They're lining up around the block to collect their dignity pills. A mixture of diazepam, morphine and phenobarbital will eliminate any pain and cause a sleep that eventually falls into a deep coma. The digoxin and amitriptyline will induce cardiac arrest within that coma condition so that death is comfortable.

That's the best way to go.

Better than any war in the Middle East.

Better than any famine in Africa.

Better than any plague made in China.

The government has allocated sixty-seven million of these pills, for free. One for every person in the country. Old. Young. Sick. Healthy. They have been distributed to every doctors' surgery in the land. People are queueing in the streets for their own death.

Waiting for their one pill. Their ticket away from this hellish mortal coil. It's the same pill for women as it is for children, which is the same as it is for men.

It'll work.

It will be more dignified than the bleeding and blisters and gagging and choking that has been shown on the TV screens and shared across social-media channels. China no longer has the largest population on the planet, they say.

This is the end. Every country with nuclear weapons could wipe themselves out, but that's not as kind as the dignity pill. Some arsehole marketing guru gave up that gem of a name to take some of the edge off global euthanasia.

It's not the suicide pill, it's the comfort pill.

Nobody wants to give their kid a 'top-yourself tablet' or a 'coma capsule'. Much better that they take their 'composure pastille' or their 'integrity lozenge'. Pepsi are running a campaign getting people to swallow it down with their drink. Still making millions as the world implodes.

There's a pill set aside for the prime minister and one for Doris who works at the Job Centre in Macclesfield. The queen has one if she doesn't think the bunker will hold. Librarians in Telford don't have a bunker. Neither do teachers in Yeovil or hairdressers in Ipswich.

The government suddenly seems to care about the homeless situation and has called on volunteers to deliver blister packs to as many cardboard jungles as possible.

Every class, race and sexual orientation has an equal right to end their own life before the plague sweeps in from across the ocean. Nobody should suffer. It may be the end of the world, but that doesn't mean it can't be a pleasant experience.

This world. Where countries face growing health issues because they are eating too much while others die of starvation. Where man thought the best way to stop all wars was to build the biggest bomb. Where every one of the seven hundred gods is unresponsive to the prayers of their worshippers. Where religious disagreements go back so far that nobody knows what they're fighting for now. Where restaurants deplete the seas to feed people who no longer talk to one another at dinner.

The pill is the only answer.

It is too late to fight. To save.

The horsemen have arrived.

War. Famine. Pestilence. Death.

The only thing left is to give up.

And all people had to do was find some genuine compassion. All they had to do was be kind. And mean it. And maintain it.

STAY AT HOME

It was only a month ago that the first test was carried out. It was a Sunday night, around the time when most people are starting to dread the fact that their weekend is over and they have to go into the office the next day. The same time that many people are flicking through the channels on their televisions, frustrated that there's nothing on, and finding themselves watching *Antiques Roadshow* for the twentieth week in a row.

If ever there was a litmus test for the kindness of humanity, it is *Antiques Roadshow*. You can judge the mental state of the collective consciousness by comparing the percentage of people who want an item to be worth a lot of money against those who hope dear old Gladys from Wolverhampton hasn't noticed that the R on the Rolex watch passed down through generations is, actually, a B. And it's worth nothing.

But you also can't blame people for being a little cantankerous on a Sunday evening, when there's nothing else on TV and they have to return to the call centre in twelve hours.

It was one of those nights. Kenneth Hargreaves, a war veteran, had brought in a jewel flower to be appraised. The expert was examining the piece, floating the possibility that it was a botanical study by Fabergé. If so, it might be worth seven figures.

That's when the alarm sounded.

The first test.

Millions of mobile phones across the country suddenly started blaring a siren noise. Some people were waiting eagerly by their phones to see what would happen, others were startled, having forgotten it was scheduled. Many missed the expert's final appraisal as they waited for the piercing tone to desist.

The idea behind the test is that the government has the ability to warn people *en masse* about dangerous incidents. Local flooding, for example. But also things like terrorist attacks. When an unexplained World War II bomb was discovered in a garden in Plymouth, the alert was used to inform local people to evacuate the area until the possible threat had been neutralised.

If an enemy state launches a nuclear bomb at the UK, the alert will tell people to flee the target area or say goodbye to their loved ones. If Mother Nature decides she has had enough of us polluting the planet and sends a five-hundred-foot tsunami, the alarm will sound, telling coastal townsfolk to seek higher ground.

Of course, there are so many things to think about with blanket campaigns like this. What about people in abusive relationships who hide secret phones that they don't want their partners to see? What if they start sounding and are discovered? What level of abuse could follow such a revelation?

So the government had to release instructions on how to disarm the warning:

Go to 'Settings'. Find 'Emergency Alerts'. Turn off 'Severe Alerts' and 'Extreme Alerts'.

Everyone in the country needs to have the alert on because they are days away from the arrival of this biohazard. This gas. These insects. Whatever it is that is ravaging its way across the sea to wipe out civilisation. If the wind doesn't take it in a different direction, if the military don't find a way to stop it, the people need to know when to take their pills.

Of course, there will always be a small percentage of people who don't like to do as they are told, who are happy to take their chances at surviving. And there are some who simply choose not to believe.

They've been lied to before.

They were told to keep their distance.

They were told to stay at home.

They were told to get vaccinated.

And they don't want to be told when to kill themselves.

So they turn off the alert and they don't collect their pill and they know just how much that Fabergé flower is worth.

THE LIFEJACKET PROTOCOL

It's Wednesday. The world ends tomorrow.

On a Thursday.

Who thought that was a good idea?

The weather guy on the BBC points at part of the country and tells everyone that it's raining there. It's raining everywhere. That it's colder up north. He waves an arm and says something about a cold front and pollen levels and pollution around the bigger cities. And then he points at some yellow, blurred blob below Svalbard, over the Barents Sea, and says that it's moving towards us. That it should arrive by dinnertime tomorrow.

It's all very British.

He doesn't say that everyone will be dead, he just lets people know that there is an opportunity for a last supper. Maybe the kids can have dessert first. Maybe the vegans can gorge on foie gras. Maybe forget the food, and drink so much champagne that you won't need the dignity pill.

There is no mention that it will be his last weather broadcast, but it is. He had been working in Acton for years until the studio relocated to Salford. His mother, sister and two nephews live in Dorset. They are planning to spend the day together. They're not doing anything in particular, just staying in the house. Talking. Cooking. Letting the kids play in the garden.

Maybe they will stay up all night and reminisce. Maybe they will imagine what the world could have been if they had believed the scientists or tried harder to listen or been more present for other people.

The plan is to live, love, possibly even laugh. Just like the canvas on the hallway wall says to do.

Others will choose to loot. The entitlement that got us here in the first place will remain until the bitter end. They will steal cars they could never have afforded and drive them at speeds that will no longer get them arrested because the police are off duty.

The end of the world can act like a purge. There will be murder and rape just because someone wonders what that will feel like. And they're going to die anyway. On a goddamned Thursday.

The alarm will sound on their mobile phones. If they have small children, they have to administer their pills first, like the lifejacket protocol on a crash-landing plane. Because they shouldn't have to see their parents die and then be devastated by the ensuing plague. Even if they're going to die either way.

Some parents will panic and forget. Some children will have to be brave enough to do things themselves. And others will have to see it out. Because they won't be able to take the pill. They shouldn't have to. They're kids. It's not their fault. They were brought into this world and left in front of their screens. And their idols were brainless. And their teachers were overwrought. And their health service was strained. And their leaders morally bankrupt.

Somehow, they have lost the ability to fight for themselves. Resilience is all but extinct. Kids are fragile, and parents are scared of upsetting them.

Maybe it's better this way.

Start over again.

On Friday.

A MIDNIGHT APERITIF

The alarm sounds just after seven. A little later than was originally anticipated. The Met Office staying true until the end by not predicting things quite right. Many hoped the poison would blow right past and not hit land until Florida, where most of the residents are already dead in some way.

One hour until impact. Prepare your families. May God be with you.

That's all it says. The extreme alert sounds more like bidding someone an interesting cruise.

In Croydon, a new mother cries as she crushes one of the pills into a powder to add to her baby's milk. She looks into her child's eyes as they guzzle the warm formula. Oblivious and innocent. And trusting. She and her husband had tried so long to have a baby. He has already taken his pill. Couldn't stand the pressure. He was anxious. Didn't want to see his family perish so went peacefully and selfishly in his reading chair after lunch.

In Oxford, eight students have been drinking since breakfast. They have taken their pills and have paired off for one final moment of intimacy. What a way to go.

Families barbecue on the beach in Cornwall and dance until the drugs kick in. They can die on the sand and be collected by the high tide. There will be nobody around to bury them, anyway.

Many churches and temples and mosques are filled with parishioners who still believe in God's great plan. They are expecting a last-minute rapture or they have just given in to His will. They are some of the least scared. Many are almost excited about their next chapter. What is it they have been fighting about all this time?

Not everyone is so calm and stiff-upper-lip about it. There are people who have measured the area of the encroaching gas, or whatever it is, and figure that, if they get in their boat and go south of the Isle of Wight, they will be out of harm's way. They can come back and claim the land as their own. Rebuild the country that once dominated the globe.

The über-rich have fuelled whatever vehicles they have to get out of there. The airports might be shut down, but the runways are still there. Private jets are still there. There's no control tower so it might be a case of Russian oligarchs flying into each other and exploding, but they are going to die, anyway.

The helicopter on the roof that was once a status symbol, an attempt at peacocking, now seems to have some practical application. Hover above the gas. Witness the destruction and chaos. Slowly lower back to the roof in time for a midnight aperitif.

It's moving in. And it's not going to stop.

Still, despite the warnings from the government and the military and the scientists, and the photographs and videos of the devastation in China, there are people who don't believe it. Who call it fake news. Who create conspiracies about nanotechnology and propaganda. They don't think we went to the moon in '69. They say Lee Harvey Oswald was a patsy. And they are so convinced, they didn't queue around the block for their dignity pills.

Because they see no dignity in killing themselves for something that is not their fault. Their ideas might not fall in line with the majority, but they have their own faith. They think it is always right to question rather than following blindly.

And they don't all get together. They are mostly alone. Dotted around the country. Risking their skin flaking away and their eyes being eaten out of their sockets and throwing up until they can no longer breathe.

There's a refined chaos in that final hour. People realise that, in death, they finally have the ability to make their own choice about their fate. And they realise this because they are selfish and self-absorbed and solipsistic. Because, if their realisation was that there was a world beyond themselves, that kindness, compassion and considered thought was a superpower, that benevolence and generosity was a gift, they wouldn't be lying in a coma, in bed with their children, not noticing that they are already dead from a heart attack.

That nobody had to die.

THE
FIRST
SCOURGE

ONE YEAR EARLIER

ONE YEAR **EARLIER**...

THERE IS MOULD IN THE PETRI DISH

Knowledge, research and experimentation are huge parts of scientific discovery, of course, but blind luck and chance have been responsible for some of the greatest finds in the history of medicine.

Edward Jenner, developer of the first vaccine, stumbled upon a cure for smallpox. Speaking with a milkmaid who had contracted the irritating, though not deadly, cowpox – a hazard of the job – she remarked that people who had cowpox never seemed to get smallpox.

Jenner injected a young boy with cowpox from the sores on the milkmaid's hands. A small dose. He grew feverish but was otherwise healthy. Weeks later, he injected the same boy with a small dose of smallpox, a deadly disease causing many fatalities. The boy did not contract smallpox.

Vaccinations were born.

Of course, the method was unethical, but progress was made that saved millions of lives.

Without the misfortune of Fleming, the idea of antibiotics, which are so readily available and relied upon now, may have taken much longer to discover and develop.

A petri dish of staphylococcus bacteria, which Fleming was studying, became contaminated, growing mould inside. Instead of throwing the sample away, Fleming examined it, noticing that the areas around the mould were clear. This showed that it was lethal to the bacteria. He had discovered penicillin. Still a vital antibiotic to this day.

Dr Haruto Ikeda is about to have such an accident.

A discovery that could change the world.

He has a special mind when it comes to virology, but he struggles with things like emails and syncing his calendars. Apart from Candy Crush, his favourite app on his phone is Messages. He can write documents easily enough and he is something of a natural with a spreadsheet. But he can never find the files he wants when he needs them.

He hits save and then doesn't know where they go.

It is late in the lab. He has cleaned and sterilised the space he has been working in today. Somebody, recently, helped him figure out how to monitor the mice he experiments on through his mobile phone. It took some getting used to, and he didn't really want a fifth app clogging up his home screen but it is part of his job and his study, so he pushed past it.

In his office, at his desk, he scrolls through one of the drives, looking for a spreadsheet that he was only using this morning.

Why does it not just save everything to the same place? he asks himself.

He clicks one folder and it's not there.

He tries three others that all have names that are too similar to be useful.

Ikeda has the highest level of access in the building. His key card will get him through any door and his computer login will get him into any folder, which is the opposite of what he really needs.

He eventually finds a folder that looks as though it could be the right one and opens up the spreadsheet inside. It is not the one he is looking for but it is no less interesting. The doctor sighs, at first, then his eyes narrow as he moves closer to the screen.

It's not his file.

But it is his work.

There are references to his discoveries concerning the SARS-CoV-2 virus that was found in the cave. There are mentions of the experimental mutation that would have proved so deadly it had to be steamed out of all existence. There are notes that seem to have been taken verbatim from his own musings. And theories that he only posed to himself.

One word sticks out.

Tau.

The Greek letter assigned to the variant of the virus Ikeda and his small team have been working with. The one that was found in the cave. The one they are testing and trying to develop a vaccine for, even though it is not known by anyone outside of the Wuxi Institute.

And there are dates:

When the Tau virus was discovered.

When it was mutated – into something the scientists referred to as Ypsilon.

When that mutation was eradicated.

The original virus is called Tau by a handful of people in the world who have knowledge of its existence.

That makes sense. It's all true. Ikeda has a similar list on the file he made that is hiding in some other folder in the cloud.

There's a future date that says the Tau vaccine is ready. Ikeda assumes this is some kind of deadline that he has not been made aware of yet. It's not uncommon – there is a lot of US funding, and they love a deadline.

Then another date, just over a year from now:

First Tau infections.

This makes no sense, at first. The virus is aggressive but it is contained. It is isolated within the labs.

Then a date a few months on from that:

Phase one – vaccine rollout.

He contemplates what he is seeing.

It hasn't clicked yet, but this is serendipitous.

There is mould in the petri dish.

It's a timeline of events that are yet to occur.

Most people would shut down a file upon realising that they had not created it, but Haruto Ikeda spends a great deal of his time, each day, extrapolating data. It is something he has to be good at otherwise everything would take twice as long. And he is a stickler for detail.

Everything in the spreadsheet seems correct apart from the dates, and that makes it seem purposeful. Working in scientific research is rewarding, at first, but the presence and power of the large pharmaceutical companies can leave even the greatest idealist a little jaded.

He scans the document again.

Scientific vocabulary. Calculations. And those dates.

One is the proposed deadline for the vaccine, though it is surely a guide, because these things cannot be rushed, they must be tested and retested and tested again.

Then it comes.

The virus is to be released once the vaccine is ready.

Both have a date.

Ikeda's mind does not work in a politically strategic way. He cannot understand the motive behind such a thing. He assumes that large amounts of money are probably involved. He has seen the effects of this virus. It is highly contagious and fast-acting.

This is not the same as accidentally discovering the effects of insulin or fortuitously creating the X-ray. But Dr Haruto Ikeda has, through his own technological inadequacies, uncovered a potential plan that could cause a global catastrophe.

But blind luck steps in and shows that information to the one man who can stop it. The one man with the knowledge and experience to save millions of lives.

He doesn't want to make any changes to the file and he knows that he will never find it again, but the search window on his screen shows the trail of folders he clicked to get to where he is now.

He copies it down onto a Post-it note, so that he can come back to the correct folder, if he needs to. And he sticks that note inside a *Lonely Planet Guide* for London – somewhere his wife would like to spend some time one day.

The deadline is real.

Somebody wants to release this virus.

They want to infect innocent people for months.

And then they want to vaccinate them against it.

But why?

There is no time for Ikeda to sit and cry at the futility of existence and the dishonour of man.

The situation may call for him to do something unethical for the first time in his illustrious career.

Sometimes, progress can only be made by subjecting somebody to a deadly disease.

It is a complicated discovery but, to Haruto Ikeda, there are two solutions, both of which are simple. He could spend the next year testing and developing a vaccine that will eventually save millions from this deadly virus. That's what he does, and he is great at it.

But there is that second option. One in which he releases his own virus. A more effective virus. In fact, he could release a virus that will make people better.

FOURTEEN WEEKS
TO PLANNED RELEASE...

A WORLD IN WHICH THEY ARE STARS

Nobody is watching them. And nobody cares.

This is the great misconception under which today's youth labour: they think everybody is looking at them. They are constantly online, uploading images of themselves or videos where they dance or kick a ball or cook a pie. Or whatever.

And there's that small hit of dopamine every time they are notified of a like. And they are watching everybody else's videos and comparing themselves and scouring the comments sections and double-tapping their hearts (and minds) away.

So, they think that everybody is watching them.

But, of course, they are not. They are only interested in themselves. In their own little world that they have created with their own online personas.

Haruto Ikeda worries about the younger generation. He is watching them, for science. Nobody else seems to care.

Yet he notices that teenagers are suddenly more anxious about going out shopping with their parents in case somebody they know sees them. They don't want to get a part-time job in the town where they live because they could be spotted.

And many parents don't understand these new pressures because, when they were the same age, they had to go to school even though the idea of putting their hand up in class brought them out in hives. They didn't know what anxiety was. Nobody in their school year was coming out as gay or trans. Gender fluid was something that was produced when you had sex.

Things have progressed in that sense. There is greater understanding and more tolerance. That's a good thing. It's not the issue. Not for Haruto Ikeda.

The issue is one of misplaced power, disillusionment and the loss of self.

The current batch of teenagers are being told that they can be whatever and whomever they want to be, but they are not being provided with the tools to make that a sustainable reality. They have been empowered but they still require a guiding hand. They're still kids. They're still learning.

But the technology that was supposed to liberate them is preventing their parents from providing that guidance. It's making these kids believe they are the stars of their own reality show. They think that people are interested in their chia-seed breakfasts and buddha-bowl lunches. They think they can make money from recording make-up tutorials or pool-table trick shots. They have created a world in which they are the stars, they are the centre of their own universes.

So, of course they think that people are watching them and judging them for going shoe shopping with their mother or bowling with their father. It's no wonder they are anxious and embarrassed about being spotted behind the till at the local supermarket.

But that isn't the issue, either.

Not to Dr Haruto Ikeda.

It's that, through the social-media boom, there seems to have been a systematic removal of compassion.

A million people, every day, post something like 'Be someone's sunshine when the skies are grey', and another million people hit like, even though the sentiment is utterly saccharine and disingenuous.

Others push the schmaltz to a Hallmark-card level. 'Kindness is a passport that opens doors and fashions friends. It softens hearts and moulds relationships that can last a lifetime.' The message is one of positivity but it's still too sickly to get behind.

Even when something appears more thought-out – 'Unexpected kindness is the most powerful, least costly, and most underrated agent of human change' – it is disregarded. People put it out there because it makes absolute sense – it's so true – but they do not act in this way. It's too difficult. And, if nobody else is doing it, somebody is going to stick out. Someone is definitely going to be seen.

It is like Gandhi said: 'I like your Christ, but I do not like Christians, for they are not like your Christ.' Posting an inspirational quote about kindness on a social-media platform does not make a person kind. It makes them unoriginal.

The people talking about kindness are, most often, not kind.

Kindness requires action.

But something else that Dr Ikeda has discovered through his research over the past few years is that humanity triumphs in the face of adversity. We deal with horror in a way that brings out the best in us – for a short time, at least.

So, in fourteen weeks, when a contagion is scheduled to be released – a contagion that will spread through Wuxi, killing thousands, before being allowed onto aircrafts to be transported around the world, forcing countries to shut down and close their borders. When hospitals are overrun. When people are struggling to breathe. When everybody knows somebody who has died.

Will humanity, once again, step up?

And will it be worth the loss of all those lives?

Could catastrophe get the world back on track?

This is something that Haruto Ikeda contemplates. He has been thinking about it for almost a year. And, because he is so focussed on everybody else, it doesn't even enter his mind that he is the one being watched.

A POTENTIALLY DEVASTATING BIOWEAPON

When faced with the spread of any coronavirus and with possible pandemic-levels of infection similar to those previously seen with SARS, which reached every corner of the globe, touching millions and killing hundreds of thousands, the person to turn to would be Dr Haruto Ikeda. The world's foremost expert in this area.

He would know what to do.

How to contain it.

He would be able to develop the first test in his lab.

Ikeda studied virology at Hokkaido University in the early

nineties, where he developed a fascination with animal coronaviruses and how they can become true human diseases with a high likelihood of sparking epidemics. This was not part of the syllabus, but Ikeda was drawn to it.

By his mid-thirties, Ikeda had risen to a senior position at Kyushu University, an establishment that receives billions of yen in funding for medical research each year. There, Ikeda studied the evolution of viruses. He worked with pig farmers who had developed encephalitis and camel racers who were affected by MERS. His research even suggests that the common cold may have originated in camels.

But it was not until he focussed his attention on animal coronaviruses in bats that his findings would set him apart from anyone else researching in this area.

And this would take him to China.

Specifically to the Wuxi Institute of Virology. A foundation backed by US money. Dr Ikeda spent his first three years investigating viruses similar to SARS found in bats located at a mine in South China. Several of the mine workers had died due to respiratory problems. This was, of course, kept quiet.

The American funding allowed further investigation and experimentation, but it was the work of British scientist, Raymond Task, that provided the researchers with the means of testing the effects of the viruses they were discovering, or indeed creating. Task's innovation was to inject albino mice with genes that would allow them to develop vascular systems that were similar to humans'. Viruses similar to SARS could then be injected into the mice's nostrils, and the effects monitored.

Ikeda did exactly that with a cocktail of the virus that had been found in the South China mine. Eighty percent of the mice died.

He realised the implications of his research. That, while the focus of his experiments was to gain an understanding of these types of viruses and eventually develop a universal vaccine against them, there was always the possibility that his findings could be obscured, and used to produce a potentially devastating bioweapon that could be targeted towards humans or food crops and result in dire consequences for civilisation.

This epiphany altered the doctor. He became more contemplative. More insular. More secretive. His work continued, but he was momentarily disillusioned. He wanted his work to make a difference for good, for positive change. He looked to Buddhism, Taoism and Confucianism for solace. He read the philosophies of Laozi, particularly his thoughts on compassion. That the more we care for others, the greater our sense of personal wellbeing.

That was three years ago. In fourteen weeks, a new coronavirus will be leaked: first, to the population in Wuxi, from where it will spread across the world. And it will happen with or without the backing of Dr Haruto Ikeda, and whether he knows about it or not.

Today he is short-staffed because three of his scientists are seriously ill and off work. One of them has a vulnerable parent who has also been taken sick. The doctor has ordered everybody in the lab to wear a mask that covers their nose and mouth for the entirety of their day at work.

And they listen.

Because with the spread of any coronavirus pandemic, the person to call on for answers would be Dr Haruto Ikeda. Especially as the virus has probably been created in his laboratory.

THE MAN IN THE PERFECTLY PRESSED SUIT

The kids are wrong. They are not being watched. Nobody cares about the dance routine they have learned or what skin care product has given them that glow. But, if you show any indication that you are going to go against the laws and policies of your country, if you intend to attack or even think about harming citizens, somebody will be listening. Somebody will be watching.

In China, there are a lot of people to listen to, which is why information needs to be contained. So that misinformation may be monitored.

The ECHELON spy system picks up certain words in phone conversations or text messages or email communications. Certain phrases get flagged as potential threats. Every country has them. These are monitored by the various intelligence agencies around the globe.

You don't have to email the word 'Jihad' or call a friend talking in a code that the NSA laughs at because it's so easy to crack; you could be marked for buying three components of a nail bomb on Amazon.

You could type 'assassinate' or 'UFO' or 'Supreme Assembly of the Islamic Revolution in Iraq' and it will be gathered by ECHELON. But the same is true if you write 'steak knife' or 'Goldman' or 'Harvard'.

And there are private-security firms who operate on behalf of the government but also outside it. Most of them specialise. And they are well funded. It is prudent to ensure that these private companies are employed on a retainer to observe companies involved in major technological advances and it would certainly be wise to listen in and look over any facility researching viruses that could be harnessed and used as a bioweapon.

Haruto Ikeda has been monitored on several occasions. So has his wife. And Dr Bauer. And Zhu Jian, the minister for science and technology. And the billionaire Waylon Taggart. And Ikeda's college friend and nanotechnology expert, Xiang Lao. And, of course, the British prime minister, Harris Jackson. But, for now, the man in the perfectly pressed suit with the immaculate hair and porcelain skin is merely watching with interest. He does not become a danger to anyone until somebody on that list steps over the line.

HIGH CHANCE OF AN OUTBREAK

Stefan Bauer's father is dead. The old man had struggled with asthma since he was a kid. Stefan had left the Wuxi Institute of

Virology with a dry cough and high temperature two days ago. The same as the other two scientists on Ikeda's team. The kind of symptoms that are difficult for a mutated albino mouse to describe.

Stefan's father was old but fit. He walked every day. He tried to stay active. The exercise gave him time to think about his wife, who had died a few years before – she had paid a man to paint her bedroom wardrobes and the idiot painted one of the doors shut. When Mrs Bauer forced it open, the door hit her hard in the ribs and caused her to fall. She contracted pneumonia in the hospital and didn't last the week.

Mr Bauer seemed healthy, but there were underlying conditions that meant a visit to his ailing, highly contagious son, who had been accidentally infected with the Tau virus, proved to be the final attack on the old man's respiratory system.

Stefan is still struggling with his illness and now has the grief of his orphanhood to keep him company when he comes around from his feverish bouts of sleep.

Dr Ikeda had warned of this. He knew of over thirty labs working with these kinds of viruses. He had told his superiors that, one day, there was a high chance of an outbreak somewhere, that something would eventually escape.

It was inevitable.

Even with the strictest safety and sterilisation procedures, things can leak. It's been less than a year since Ikeda found that file that alerted him to a possible deliberate outbreak. This time it was an accident, but people are sick and now somebody has died. And it's worse because Ikeda's team is so close to a Tau vaccine.

Whoever made that file is not looking for Ikeda and his team to develop a universal vaccine; they want a new kind of weapon and they want an antidote to be developed alongside the disease. It's not a new idea. The business of pharmaceuticals is so broken and corrupt, it makes the World Boxing Organisation look like a church fête tombola stand run by nuns.

Bauer calls Ikeda to update him on his illness and inform him of his father's passing. 'We're screwing around with nature,' he says. The Tau virus was contained deep within that cave. There was no need to disturb it. But part of Wuxi Institute's job is to discover potential threats and create vaccines against them, should they ever find their way into the world naturally.

Ikeda doesn't want to lose Bauer from his team. He's pragmatic and meticulous and thoughtful beyond the chemistry and biology of what they do every day. Ikeda sees himself in the young scientist – sees that he is exhibiting the same questions and disillusionment that Ikeda suffered years ago.

'Stefan, I struggle with the same thing, both ethically and philosophically. But this is going to be examined in one of the labs, so our focus has to be on vaccination. There is always a risk of exposure with our work.' It's a risk for Ikeda to talk this way, particularly over a telephone line that could easily be monitored. It's not a secret that Ikeda has been more insular in recent years. Everybody can tell he is different, but he still functions and he gets the work done and the people above him are satisfied with his progress and results.

'I hear you have everyone in face masks,' Bauer laughs.

'How did you hear of that?' If trivial information is seeping from the building, Ikeda worries about what else is getting out.

'Jensen sent a text to see how I was doing. I asked her how things were without me and she told me about the masks. Go easy on her, it's not like she was sharing state secrets.' Bauer coughs. When he comes back to the phone to say something else, he coughs again, and can't stop for the next twenty seconds. It sounds painful. 'Sorry about that.'

'Stefan,' Ikeda interrupts, 'I'm terribly sorry to hear the news about your father. Please take the rest of the week off, you sound awful and you need time to process what has just happened.'

There's a silence.

Stefan starts to cry.

Then he starts to cough again.

It goes on for almost a minute, and Ikeda hangs up.

He returns to his work. Looking into a microscope, he sees the virus – yellow irregular circles with green spikes around the outside that give the coronavirus its name. Corona. A crown. The king of all infections.

Royalty among cruel, harmful influences.

But this is not the same thing that took Bauer and two of his colleagues out of action. It's not the thing that killed Bauer's father. This is new. It has nothing to do with the vaccine. It's a new mutation of the Tau virus.

This is Ikeda's.

He is calling it CompX. But that is not being recorded on any computer. It is only in Ikeda's head. And, if he can get it right, it could be the cure.

He moves across his station, captures one of the white, modified mice, and injects into its nostril. He does this another seven times.

And then he waits.

There is a knock at Bauer's door. He's not expecting anyone. He doesn't have anyone anymore. And that's perfect. He's alone. He has had everyone taken from him. He is questioning his place in the world. But he is also college educated. He has a degree and some expertise in both chemistry and biology. It also helps that he speaks more than one language fluently. He fits the profile perfectly.

MAYBE IT WAS FATE

Both his parents died when he was nine years old. His father had been drinking and thought it would be okay to get behind the wheel and drive home. It wasn't such an issue back then. Nor was wearing a seatbelt.

It wasn't that far to the house.

They would hardly be on the road.

It turns out that he was right – he was a little over the limit but not enough to impair his judgement. He talked with his wife about the party, and she placed her right hand on his hand until he had to change gear, then she moved it to his leg. Just as she always did, whether he had been drinking or not.

And when the driver who had been drinking way too much hit their car at speed, she didn't even have time to try to hold on to her husband before she was thrown through the windscreen.

It was a mess. Glass everywhere. Blood. Smoke. Steam. She was dead. He was hurt. The drunkest driver was screaming for help. He had recklessly endangered anyone in his way that evening, he had killed Harris Jackson's young mother, and he had the audacity to call for help.

The only person around was Jackson Senior, who could see the mangled, twisted body of the woman he loved. He was not going to help.

A ball of rage and confusion and blame and guilt, the pain in his legs and chest disappeared as he got out of that car and strode over to the struggling drunk murderer.

Jackson Senior yanked the door open to find the whisky-soused wife-killer writhing around beneath his seatbelt, which had somehow managed to sever an arm and then get stuck. Jackson Senior didn't want this scum to survive, but if he did, he was not going to feel whole again. Jackson Senior took the hand of the arm that was no longer attached, pulled it out of the footwell, ran towards the edge of the bridge and hurled the limb thirty metres down the River Thames.

It made him laugh.

It was an odd time to do such a thing, with his wife contorted on the road behind him. He knelt beside her until the ambulance and police arrived at the scene.

The paramedics loaded the drunk, one-armed man into the ambulance. He was screaming, 'That fucking psycho threw my arm off the bridge.'

The policeman approached Jackson Senior. 'Sir, is what he's saying true?'

'You think I threw some stranger's arm off the bridge? Some drunk driver who hit my car head on and killed the love of my life? I think he's so drunk, he's forgotten that he only has one arm, don't you?'

There's a long pause while the policeman fully digests the situation.

'You know ... I think you could be on to something. I mean, when I arrived, he definitely only had one arm, so maybe it was always like that, I don't know.' He wants to smile or wink, but it's not appropriate. He says it with his face, though. 'Look, I'm going to need to take some details from you now, but we can get a full statement tomorrow. You got kids?'

'A son. He's nine.'

'You'll need to go home to him tonight. Come down the station tomorrow. Okay?'

Jackson Senior nods. He obliges the police officer and gives him all the information he needs. More officials turn up. They cordon off the area, they take pictures and they bag Mrs Jackson and take her away.

'I can take you home,' the police officer assures Jackson Senior.

'You know, it's just up there,' he points, 'we almost made it back. A minute either side and she'd still be here.'

The police officer doesn't know what to say.

'It's fine. I'll be fine. I can walk.'

And he does.

Jackson Senior walks all the way back to his house. It takes him around twenty minutes. They could have walked from the party. They should have. Maybe the drunk driver would have ploughed them down on the pavement. Maybe it was fate.

He lies to the babysitter about his wife and says that she will be coming along shortly after. He doesn't ask how his son is, whether he behaved. He doesn't even go up to see the boy. He tells the young girl – the daughter of a friend – that he needs to go into the study to fetch some cash to pay her. He says he is very grateful for her help.

She waits in the hallway.

Jackson Senior goes into his study, walks around the back of his desk, opens the top drawer, where he keeps a cheque book and some cash, takes out his hand gun, places it against his temple and pulls the trigger.

The sound startles the babysitter and wakes up his son.

Harris Jackson's parents died in tragic circumstances. He could have become Batman. Instead, he went the other way, towards something darker, and became the country's prime minister.

HIDDEN BY THE APPARENT CHAOS

Two days later, Bauer's father is not the only thing that has died. Four of Ikeda's mice have perished. Those are not great odds of survival but they are better than they have been.

Ikeda knows he is not quite there yet – the virus is scheduled for release and the vaccine can't be too far behind. The pressure is on. He feels the weight of his responsibility to save people.

Fifty-percent survival is not good enough, but to Ikeda, it is not the dead mice that concern him, it is the behaviour of the mice that survived that are of interest. Scientifically, of course, but also zoologically. He can see that not only have they survived, their behaviours have also altered. He can't quite ascertain what is so different, but he will monitor them while performing tests on another batch of innocent rodents.

He leaves a camera running on the cage and lets himself out of the sterile lab to return to his office.

It is a stark contrast to the clean, straight-lined, seal guarantee of the testing area. Ikeda's office is a mess. The bookshelf behind his desk is filled with the many medical books he has had to read through his training and subsequent career. A framed PhD certificate hangs wonkily on an adjacent wall with reams of medical journals and psychology texts piled on the floor beneath, creeping higher and higher.

The bin next to his desk is overflowing with crumpled pieces of paper and prepared-sandwich packets. Ikeda never makes his own lunch. There are clothes on a chair in the corner. A tracksuit, neatly folded on top for when he feels like going out for a run to clear his mind, and a smart jacket hung over the back that he hasn't worn since the last time somebody important came to the institute.

There's a stack of papers on the desk. To look at Ikeda's office, you would think he was a disorganised slob. But he knows where everything is, and the room is, actually, this way by design. He doesn't want anyone snooping. Everything he is working on is in plain sight but hidden by the apparent chaos.

There is a picture frame on his desk but, instead of containing an image of his family, the frame houses a quote from the Dalai Lama dated 1995: 'An openness to the suffering of others with a commitment to relieve it.' Anyone who comes into his office might assume that it is Ikeda's life mantra, because he works on vaccinations, he wants to help, to cure, to relieve suffering. And that is true, but this quote is related to his new mission.

Mixed in with his papers is a copy of *American Behavioral Scientist*. It is folded over on an article by Kano et al titled 'Compassion in Organizational Life'. In the margin, he has scribbled the words, *Noticing, feeling and responding*.

Beneath his tracksuit is another article from 2009 by Gilbert. Ikeda has written six bullet points above the title.

Sensitivity.

Sympathy.

Empathy.

Motivation.

Distress tolerance.

Non-judgement.

Beneath a copy of Freud's interpretation of dreams – a red herring if ever there was one – is a more recent article by Pommier. The words 'kindness,' 'mindfulness' and 'common humanity' have been highlighted. Another scrap of paper simply says 'equanimity of patience'.

It's all there to see.

To Haruto Ikeda, the problem is not the greed of the men in power or the population cull from a devastating pandemic that is scheduled in fourteen weeks, it's the apathy. That, along with the Western Black Rhino or Pinta Island tortoise, human compassion appears to be extinct.

And he may believe that nobody is watching and nobody cares but, as the date on the file he found draws ever closer, he finds himself feeling more paranoid. And that maybe he's got it all wrong.

A SEAT AT THE TABLE

Jackson is late for the meeting.
He's always late.

It comes across as disrespectful and entitled and arrogant, but nobody says a thing because they all want a seat at the table. They can't jeopardise their personal wealth or the prosperity of their own country. So they tolerate the insufferable bore.

'Sorry, gents. Traffic was an absolute bloody nightmare. The congestion charge hasn't freed up the roads at all. Then again, it wasn't really supposed to, was it?' He laughs at his own comment and winks, nudging the Russian with his elbow as he sits down. The Russian leader seems to be able to take Jackson's crap more than the other nations, so he always draws the short straw in the seating plan.

A small price to cultivate the *special relationship*.

There are seven people in the room. All of them men. There used to be eight, but the representative from Türkiye died in a jet-ski accident and was never replaced. It's a cabal of Western influence. Three leaders from the UK, US and Russia and four senior-ranking officials from Australia, Germany, France and Brazil who do not necessarily agree that their current political chiefs are representing their countries to the greatest potential.

They have to meet in person to avoid information leaks or

recordings. This time, the meeting is being held in a remote London location.

There are no real leaders of the group but the prime ministers and presidents certainly command the most respect, and they decide the focus of discussions. They fully believe that there is a group just like this in the Middle East, and another that includes China, Japan and maybe South Korea.

The Russian can be a hothead. The American is pragmatic. And Harris Jackson is exactly who he always is, full of bluster. But he's greedy and he wants his country to remain a force. And, despite his idiot persona, he is something of an entrepreneur. It was his idea to release a virus.

'So, what did I miss?'

It's going to be a boring meeting but it's necessary. The rollout of the Tau virus is scheduled to start in a little under fourteen weeks. But you can't just throw a virus into the world then deal with it as towns are being decimated by an unknown disease. It's a logistical nightmare.

There are protocols in place for earthquakes and terrorist attacks. Nobody is getting near the royal family or the pope. If any country in the world decides to press their button that releases a nuclear weapon, a chain of events is set in stone to protect the ones who need protecting while defending the liberty of the targeted country through cataclysmic retaliation.

But there is very little in place for a bioweapons attack.

This is a laborious meeting about how to deal with the airports, especially Heathrow. Because there needs to be a period of time for air travel in order to transport the infection across the globe, but then there will need to be a halt on all flights. And how will that affect the tourism business? And how will the government subsidise things to prevent companies from failing or having to offload their staff?

Full country lockdowns are likely. What happens to the high street? What will be the economic consequences? This is the kind of information that seemingly flies over Jackson's head, but he's not really an idiot. It's a persona. A character that he plays. He's a loudmouthed party boy, of course, but he understands politics.

He does drift off at times, throughout the meeting, thinking back to the real reason he was late. He was screwing a young social climber. Again. He has two children with his wife and one with a mistress that the tabloids found out about.

It wasn't the result of investigative journalism – the girl wanted column inches and maintenance payments, and maybe a slot on a minor-celebrity reality show about dating or camping in a jungle or singing while obscuring her identity with a mask.

She received a small sum from the newspaper for the scoop and monthly instalments from Jackson. His wife forgave him. She stuck by him. And strangely, so did the public. Jackson has the ability to do what he wants and get away with it. His list of fuck-ups has become so outrageous that the stories are almost unbelievable, now. It's almost as if he is trying to outdo himself each time so that he can get caught out. It's psychopathic.

Essentially, Jackson is a social researcher. He keeps on throwing out these straw polls, seeing how the public react to his screw-ups and how far he can push his favour. It bodes well for him that whatever path he chooses when this contagion is released, he'll have the backing of the majority of people, if not his own party.

And, even though Jackson has half an eye on his phone, he still seems to take in all the information. Travel. Hospitality. Health services. All will be impacted, in all countries across the globe. But this group is primarily concerned with the West, and Jackson is obviously most interested in how this will affect the UK.

The public will panic because the worst they have had to deal with here was a swine flu that called off a few local farm shows. But, just to be certain, plans are in place to leak stories of shortages in certain products. Hand sanitiser and toilet paper to begin with. And baked beans.

These powerful men fully expect the public to assume a mob mentality. They will take care of themselves, first. They will buy up what they can, spreading fear on their way.

'And are we any closer to a vaccine?' Jackson asks, not looking up from his lap until the last second. There's a silence. The rest of the group are shocked that he has been paying attention, even though they've seen him do this before. 'I mean, we can't very well release this thing without knowing that we can slow it down at some point.' He seems concerned, but none of the other men in the room could even hazard a guess at what that concern might be about. 'How long do we wait before we offer some hope? How many have to die? Have we thought about how the Chinese will react when we throw the blame on their lab and this chap, Ikeda?'

It becomes clearer. Jackson is not concerned for the welfare of his nation, of his constituents, he knows that they have to set things in place and do the whole political thing, but that is secondary to how he is going to cover his back when things hit and the best way to spin it so there is no swing when it comes to election time.

The American answers each question in turn, keeping things concise. That's his way.

'I'm assured the vaccine is weeks away. A million seems like a nice, round number, don't you think? Let's wait until half a million before mentioning the possibility of a vaccine. I wouldn't worry about the Chinese – they will push it onto Ikeda, who is Japanese. He can take the fall and we can take his vaccine.'

It's cold. Like he's deciding what to order off a restaurant menu. Maybe it's easier for him if he removes emotion.

'Well, it all seems in hand,' Jackson responds, 'as long as we don't have to close the bloody pubs, eh?' He nudges the Russian again, perpetuating his party-boy image, pretending he is stupid, but nobody in that room is buying it. They've seen Jackson at work. He's loud but he's shrewd and, as long as he is out in the limelight, taking up column inches and drenching the social networks with his image and antics, nobody would ever believe that a gathering such as this would take place.

Jackson may not be able to control his libido but he can control the electorate. If his parents' death taught him anything, it was how to take care of himself. But all the men in that room are the same. They feel invincible because they get away with everything they do, no matter how heinous.

They're drunk on power.

And people do stupid things when they are drunk.

Like release a deadly virus into the world.

Like believing they can control a living weapon.

Jackson's phone vibrates with the arrival of a picture message that takes the blood from his brain and sends it straight to his pants.

'Well, seems like we have things under control.' Jackson makes his excuses to leave. He says something about the home secretary and heads off to make another mistake.

SUSCEPTIBLE TO SUGGESTION

In the 1940s, in Mattoon, Illinois, residents complained about the smell of gas that was then followed by nausea, fainting and, in some cases, paralysis of the legs. These symptoms were temporary and nobody was hurt. There also seemed to be no medical explanation for what they had experienced.

Still, word travelled and the rumour morphed into horror story – that a 'mad gasser' was lurking around the town and anaesthetising people.

There were no solid leads and nobody could describe the assailant. But the number of cases grew, and the local news jumped on it, treating the tales as fact. This pushed the people of Mattoon towards some kind of hysteria. Not only were they worried about a local madman, but this fear manifested in a sociogenic outbreak.

Mass hysteria.

More and more people were developing the symptoms. They said that they could smell the gas but they never saw the person who was allegedly spraying it.

With no evidence and no biological reason for the symptoms, it was concluded that the response was psychological. Psychosomatic, in fact. The brain told the body that it was sick when it wasn't, and the body acted accordingly.

There are cases of this throughout history. In the Middle Ages, people across Europe began involuntarily dancing until exhaustion. In 1892, schoolgirls in Germany began shaking uncontrollably while writing. The following year, the same thing happened across Switzerland. And, in 1962, at a textile mill in America, workers complained of a sickness that they believe was brought on by the presence of a mysterious insect. Some broke out in a rash. It was later concluded that no such insect existed but that the anxiety about it could produce flu-like symptoms.

They believed it in their minds, and their body reacted as though it was real.

Harris Jackson and the other members of his group know that it's even easier to create mass hysteria now. With the prevalence of social media and its ability to disseminate information – whether true or fabricated – in an instant, it is the perfect tool to create a sociogenic outbreak that affects people across the globe.

The fear of the unknown created by a coronavirus pandemic will make people more susceptible to suggestion.

Which can make them easier to control.

It is not about the death toll, it is about the power.

In America, research has been undertaken in this regard, and the results show that there could be a degree of success around Tourette's Syndrome. Some videos have billions of views. Putting these in front of the younger generation during the time of uncertainty would almost definitely result in a widespread epidemic of ticking, involuntary movements and outbursts of swearing.

It will act like a nocebo. Where a placebo – a sugar pill instead of actual medication – has proven to cure symptoms, a nocebo does the opposite. People have a negative effect based on their expectation. If they believe a (fake) pill is real, they start to feel better. If they are watching these videos that are being fed to them, they may start to feel anxiety that manifests itself in the replication of the involuntary movements they are seeing.

And that is the simplest form of control – making people physically spasm.

If that test works, what else can the government do? Could they cause groups of people to spasm mentally? Could they divide a country's opinion? Could they start a war? Could they aim specific messages at specific groups to make them do specific things?

The concerns of the time will play a huge role in the success of such an online sociogenic sickness campaign. But if it works, it would affect many more people than the virus itself.

The virus causes the fear. The fear makes the subjects susceptible to manipulation. And the internet is the perfect highway for the message, for misinformation.

That's how they maintain their hold, their power.

It's how they each got elected.

The virus may kill a million people before the vaccine is finally released, making the governments and Dr Haruto Ikeda heroes of the time. But it's the online effect that will make one million seem like an insignificant number.

To count to one million, one second at a time, would take around twelve days. To count to one billion would take thirty-one years. If the virus kills a million people, the vaccine will suppress lots of that fear. But, if the psychological impact can stretch around the world and affect a billion people, the fallout could be disastrous – this excites the Russian leader.

The clean-up will not take twelve days.

Not for a billion people.

Potentially, it could destroy an entire generation without actually making most of them sick.

Just tell them that they are and they will be.

It's almost too easy.

This is how you affect the most amount of people.

Ikeda understands the strength of mass hysteria, he just doesn't have the technical know-how to implement it. Not everyone is watching, but everyone is certainly talking.

What if this was used for kindness? What if a million people suddenly became more compassionate overnight? Would this have the same potential? Could it be the sugar-coated pill that would then affect a billion more?

It's exactly what Dr Haruto Ikeda hopes.

A SPLIT-SECOND OF HUMANITY

Wuxi airport has been serving Wuxi, Suzhou and Changzhou since 2004. Terminal One will take you to (and from) Hong Kong, Macau and Singapore, while Terminal Two is for internal flights around China, to Guangzhou, Nanning and, most importantly, Beijing.

Beijing is key. There are almost twenty-two million people there to infect, of course, but, from Beijing, the virus can be transported to Dubai, Frankfurt, Paris, London, Doha, Istanbul, Amsterdam, San Francisco, Abu Dhabi, Madrid, Rome, Sydney, Nagoya, Brussels, Geneva, Stockholm, Athens, Cairo, Copenhagen, Vienna, Baku and Kathmandu, to name but a few of the corners the contagion will reach.

A million deaths suddenly seems a conservative estimate.

Now, Ben Ziegler is taking the evening flight directly from Beijing to Boston. He flies to China once every quarter to inspect the factories that are manufacturing the LCD screens for the monitor division he directs.

Four times a year, he flies to the capital, wines and dines the people he has to keep sweet and wanders the factory floors, pretending to care about the working conditions. He attends a few meetings that would have worked just as well as emails. And, for two days, he cheats on his wife with a woman he knows in Wuxi, who is always happy to accept his generosity.

Ziegler walks through the door heading towards the departure lounge. He lets it swing shut behind him. Not looking. Not noticing Wen Tsou walking a few feet back.

Not caring as the glass flies back towards her face.

Not knowing that when he returns in twelve weeks for his next work inspection and two-day dalliance, he'll be at the epicentre of an outbreak that will be felt around the world. And he will be leaving ground zero with more than just an itch in his pants.

Wen Tsou doesn't like Americans. She finds them brash and impolite, but they are still the best tippers. She huffs as she pushes through the entrance into the airport behind the loud white guy in the expensive suit. No doubt she'll be serving him his pre-flight cocktail soon. He'll call her sweetheart. She will smile as though it means something to her, and he will drop a few extra dollars in the tips jar to thank her for being something pretty to look at before he has to sit in the same seat for the next fourteen hours and forty minutes.

But what would it have taken for him to just hold that door open for her?

The airport had an overhaul for the 2008 Olympics. Wen works in one of the first-class lounges. She collects plates, sometimes, or clears tables, but mostly, she is making drinks. Tea and coffee for the early flights and alcohol for the late travellers who want to sleep things off on the way back home.

Anyone flying in coach would not be allowed on the plane if they look even a little intoxicated, but the rules are different for travellers who turn left when they enter the aircraft. They will start with a complimentary can or bottle of something from the Yanjing Brewery before making back the money they pay for the privilege on cognac and after-dinner brandy.

Wen Tsou is on shift for twenty minutes before she hears Ziegler's obnoxious tone creeping down the corridor. She wants to roll her eyes but she has more composure than that.

A white man, whiter than most – Scandinavian white – sits on a table by himself, his head in his hands, a plate of half-eaten dumplings between his elbows, which rest on the table, a large glass of red wine ahead of him.

He looks exasperated. Like all he wants to do is get on that plane and get back to wherever he is from so that he can sort out his problems.

But Wen has misread. As she approaches to see whether he would like his plate taken away or his glass refilled, she sees his eyes. Red. Redder than most against his almost translucent skin. He has been crying. And Wen cannot help herself. She should leave it alone, not get involved. Her job is to pour and wipe and collect and serve, not act as counsel.

But Wen Tsou is not in control of her compassion.

It is just there.

It's not something that you can simply switch on.

You feel it, or you do not.

'Sir, is everything okay? Is there something I can help you with?'

The man takes his hands away from his ears and lifts his head but doesn't say anything. He just stares at Wen.

'Sir? Do you need something?'

'If you have the ability to travel back in time or to erase the memory, I would gladly take it.' His words are softly spoken. Wen detects a possible Swedish twang. She sees people from all over the world, every day – she can differentiate between accents.

'The first part is tricky.' She comes back at him so quickly that he half smiles at her response. 'If the wine isn't cutting it, I can make you something stronger to help forget.' And Wen smiles back.

The man exhales and sits back in his seat.

'Alas, it is not *my* memory that needs deleting.' He looks her dead in the eyes. 'But please, feel free to take away these cold dumplings, and perhaps upgrade this middling cabernet to a triple Scotch of your choice. Neat. I could try to forget that I want her to forget, I suppose.'

She does as he requests. It's her job. She hasn't saved the stranger.

And drowning his sorrows isn't going to help, but she showed that she cared. And they had a moment. A split second of humanity.

It seems like nothing.

But it is everything.

A million split seconds would add up to a week of compassion.

A billion would be over a decade.

It makes a difference.

Behind the bar, Wen's co-worker asks her what the hell she was doing talking to that guy. That he has been sitting there for ages, drinking and crying.

'And nobody spoke to him? Checked on him?'

'How is that any of our business, Wen?'

'Are you not a human being, Yina?'

'A human being who buses tables for the one percent. They don't care about my mental health, I assure you.' She starts to untie her apron.

'You're missing the point...'

'No, Wen, I'm missing my train. Enjoy the rest of your shift. I'll see you again tomorrow.' Yina kisses the ends of two fingers and points them towards Wen. 'Be nice to the Americans.' She laughs.

Then, 'Excuse me, sweetheart. Can I get a beer?'

Wen turns away from her friend, takes a deep breath, and walks towards the man who let a door slam in her face. Yina picks up her jacket and runs out the door.

A butterfly flaps its wings.

There are still plenty of people in the airport. It's a quieter time of day, but still a lot of eye contact for Yina to avoid. Her head is down, she wants to get the airport express train into the city centre. It's the quickest and cheapest way home. But when she arrives on the platform, the queues are six people deep and they're all either reading or wearing headphones. They're all somewhere else and they're all ahead of Yina.

She arrives at the back of one of the queues, rests her hands on her knees as she bends over and breathes heavily. The train arrives. People get off. People get on. It's filling up.

The man in front of her is in his fifties, double the age of Yina. He hears her panting and he sees the train carriage getting busy. So he steps aside, a novel folded around one hand, his other ushering Yina into his place.

'Are you sure?' She doesn't understand why he would do such a thing. Surely he, too, has to be somewhere.

'You want to be on there more than I do, I think. I'm very happy where I am.' He holds up his book. And he smiles.

Yina steps onto the train. The doors close and she watches the older man disappear behind his book as she pulls out of the station. For the next twenty minutes, nobody offers her a seat. Men stand too close to her. They stare. She feels self-conscious and not as safe as she should.

The old man waits twelve minutes for the next train. He notices a couple snickering at him for reading a book. They are young. Disrespectful. Another young person nudges him in the back as they arrive in the city, and he almost falls out of the train. A car hits a puddle too fast and sends rainwater over his legs. And when he arrives home, his wife is annoyed with him for walking into the hallway with wet shoes.

She spent forty minutes on the phone, earlier, trying to get through to somebody who could give her the results of a test she has been waiting to hear about for the two weeks since her hospital procedure.

The surgeon who performed her procedure lost a patient today. He meets friends for a drink and they find it difficult to empathise, because he earns more money than they do and feel it should be an expected part of his job.

And the other 21.53 million people in Beijing have also experienced some of the rudeness and greed and squalor and lack of joy that the world has on offer today. Things are awful. Tech-zombie kids and pollution and corrupt politicians.

This is how things will remain for the next fourteen weeks.

Only the occasional act of kindness.

They have no idea how lucky they are.

SHE NEEDS COLE PORTER

Listening to somebody else's problems can be draining, no matter how compassionate the listener. Kimiko Ikeda has made a career out of this very skill, but she still feels the weight of certain clients' issues and realisations.

Breakdowns and breakthroughs.

She allows herself thirty minutes between patients in order to decompress. It can be difficult to separate your work life from your home life when your office is a part of your house, but Kimiko does well. She has a routine.

After her first patient, she leaves her office room and sits in the kitchen with a pot of herbal tea. She doesn't speak or sing or hum. She doesn't watch television or look at her phone. She sits and she listens. But not to people who are dealing with grief or an emotional break-up. She just listens to the world as it is.

Birds singing. Rain against the window. Even the traffic or the bell on somebody's bike is a welcome distraction. She can go into her next client afresh and ready to give her undivided attention.

After her second, she likes to speak with Haruto, whether that is on the phone or simply via a text message. Nothing naughty – though occasionally she will be cheeky – just a note to say that she is thinking of him. Or she will send him a video of something that he may find amusing because, with both of their jobs, it is important to spend time that is not too serious.

Kimiko takes a little longer at lunch. Perhaps she will tidy some of the house, though she usually stays on top of things in that department, but most days she will take her husband's Rubik's Cube and twist it around in many directions for thirty seconds or so. She will leave it on his pillow or his bedside table. When she gets into bed at night, it has always been solved. She never sees him do it. It has become something of a game between the two of them, but she knows that her husband likes to solve puzzles. He can't resist. She loves that about him. Even the Candy Crush game he plays on his phone. There have to be these breaks from their very serious worlds.

Mental health.

Psychosis.

Deadly disease.

Her next break, she listens to music. She loves the songs of Cole Porter. 'Night and Day'. 'Every Time We Say Goodbye'. She can sing along to these. But she loves 'You Do Something to Me'. It feels magical to her. It transports her to another time. Another place. She needs that. Her last client struggles so much with self-esteem that he thinks the world will be better off without him. He has been highly medicated for years but he still thinks that nobody would miss him if he was dead. Kimiko digests it all. She takes it all in and she supports him.

But then she needs Cole Porter. She needs to sing. She needs to dance around her living room.

Her last clients are a couple struggling with their marriage. She knows the woman has found somebody else. She is urging her to admit it. To end the farce. It feels like a mental workout.

Her final break is the best.

Because Haruto comes home. He will have his second shower of the day and he will somehow fix the Rubik's Cube without her noticing and he will talk, and she will want to listen. He is the only person she can listen to and not need a break.

It doesn't matter what he says, she will support him. It is what she does best.

Whether there is a dead body in the boot of Haruto Ikeda's car or he says that he wants to cure the common cold, Kimiko is by his side. And Haruto knows that he would not be able to deal with either of those things if she was not there.

He needs his wife if he is going to save the world.

ALL THE MICE ARE DEAD

Dr Ikeda lives in Suzhou, which is around seventeen minutes away from the lab by train, but today he takes the bus. It's more expensive and it takes four times as long.

He wants the commute. Some time alone to process his thoughts. And he wants to watch the people who think that everybody is watching them.

The clock is ticking.

The people orchestrating things have an ideal-case scenario in which the vaccine will be ready when the disease starts to roll out, but it's not necessary, it's just for their own peace of mind – it's more of a logistical issue than a medical one. Ikeda has set his own deadline. They want it in fourteen weeks, he will be ready in twelve.

He has to be.

Stop after stop, the doctor watches people, how they act when the bus is full and how that differs from when it is empty. Who heads to the back and who will not sit next to another person at any cost.

A university student wearing headphones seems lost in his own world, but he offers his seat to a woman who is heavily pregnant. She turns him down with a scowl, as if to say, 'It's not a disability, boy.' Ikeda wonders how that interaction will affect the young man when confronted with the same opportunity in the future.

He sees three people run to catch the bus. They all make it.

The pace of the passengers seems a little slower than those who ride the train. They are more considered and, perhaps, more considerate. Mothers with children, the elderly, men in suits, women in suits, students, and a doctor of virology – it's a decent cross-section of society, existing together harmoniously. Quietly.

If one person infected with the Tau virus got on the bus in Wuxi, a hundred people would have it by the time it arrived in the next city.

If only goodwill was able to spread in the same way, Ikeda thinks.

He arrives at his stop. He thanks the bus driver before stepping off. He doesn't need to do that but it is something he always did as a schoolboy. It's polite. He doesn't even have to mean it. It's a reflex. And it does no harm to anyone.

It has been raining, but Ikeda has always liked that. He thinks the streets look more beautiful. They have more character. Headlights reflect off the puddles and the traffic has a different sound when tyres pass over wet tarmac.

He walks the streets for a while. Slowly. His hands in his pockets, his face towards the sky, kicking an imaginary stone along the path. He's not an overly religious man but Ikeda considers himself a Buddhist. He believes that everything in life is impermanent and ever-changing. He also believes in people but feels as though many have given up, that they are concerned with material things rather than intrinsic reward.

Ikeda trusts in his work and he believes that he can make a positive change to the world. But he is troubled by it, too. He looks up, not towards a god, but to the rain, to nature, to science. He looks out in order to look within.

There's a coffee shop a few minutes from his house. He could drink something when he gets home, but Ikeda is still deep in thought. He wants to observe. To people-watch. To make sure that what he is doing is the right thing. That the world needs to change in order to be saved.

It's the kids. They are not a part of their own world, the real world, because they spend so much time viewing the false and often unattainable world of others. Everything is a trend that they have to be a part of. He sits down with a ginger tea and looks at a table of four girls. Teenagers. Dressed similarly. Made up. They are drinking iced coffee. No teenager requires caffeine like that. Ikeda assumes there has been some online influence.

They laugh and smile and talk to one another while also tapping away at their phone screens. They seem happy. Together. Thriving in their group.

Two tables from them is another girl around the same age. Dressed similarly. Equally made up. Drinking the same coffee. But she is on her own. She is not smiling or laughing with anybody. There's no way to tell from looking whether she is thriving or not. Does she feel lonely? Is she sad? Is she better off?

These are the questions that haunt Dr Ikeda. A medical man. A clinical man. Obsessed with human psychology. He wonders what it would take for the group to reach out, to welcome another, to even acknowledge her. It's not cruelty, it's apathy. And Ikeda believes that it will kill many more people than his little coronavirus could. Because there is no vaccine for not caring.

The last half of the tea goes cold as the melancholic doctor watches the tables slowly empty. The music playing through the speakers is just noise to him. He wants to know everybody's story. He wants to know whether all these people, a couple of months away from chaos and potential tragedy, are worth saving.

His mobile phone vibrates in his jacket pocket. He doesn't want to look at it but he knows that it will be his wife. Worrying about him. He sends a message back to say he is a few minutes away and, as he is looking at his phone, he logs in to the cameras overlooking the cages in his laboratory.

All the mice are dead.

EVERYONE WILL BE SHUT AWAY

For the clandestine group of government leaders, the plan is simple. They release the Tau virus. People get sick. Economies collapse. There's a shortage of products. Health services are strained. They can usher their people into line like herding sheep into a pen.

These leaders know how dangerous the virus can be, but they don't want to go into immediate lockdown because it will dampen infection rates and that kind of a strict and regimented approach causes panic. And fear is different to panic.

In order to be cultivated into power fear needs to be slower.

So each member state will keep things open for longer than they should, but then they have to respond in a way that fits their own culture.

They agree that Germany will be the first country to go into a full lockdown situation because it will look suspicious if their economy hasn't already begun to recover by the time other countries have even realised that people are sick and follow suit.

The UK will hold out on closing pubs and bars. The French will refuse to shut their restaurants. Brazil will focus on encouraging people to exercise at the beach. And the US and Russia will assume that they are too big and powerful to be affected by some stupid virus that probably came from a Chinese dog. They will take the minimum preventative measures and will opt for a more reactive approach when things turn a little uglier.

The leaders assume that, in the East, China will take a measured approach whereas Korea will act similarly to the Germans.

Eventually, everyone will be shut away, and a vaccine programme will roll out. And the governments that spread the disease will be praised for curing it.

They have the strength of their positions and the financial means of implementing their simple plan.

Ikeda is one man.

Fighting against the world.

To somehow save it.

Yet he is the one being watched.

He must continue working as normal with his team, trying to finalise the vaccination against the Tau virus he knows is due to be released. He can't draw any attention to himself. He can't raise any suspicions. But he also can't allow this virus to leak without knowing that there is a way to counter it.

He must develop his idea for CompX on the side. Alone. Away from his team. If successful, he will release it before Tau has an opportunity to do damage. If he is unsuccessful, in order to minimise the cost to human life, he will risk his position by announcing that the vaccine is ready before anybody wants him to.

By performing his job, he knows that he can do well.

By going against his ethics, he could, actually, do some good.

IT'S A VERY HUMAN RESPONSE

A mouse is not a man. Even a genetically modified mouse with a human-like respiratory system. It's similar. But it's not exactly the same. It's like a human, but it's not.

Ikeda can't test this type of thing on humans.

Of course, that isn't entirely true. In 1932, the US Public Health Service and Tuskegee Institute wanted to monitor the natural effects of syphilis in black men. Three hundred and ninety-nine men were told that they were being treated but not a drop of penicillin was actually administered. Instead, the effects of the disease were being recorded and the men were offered free meals and burial insurance – a possible clue to the outcome of their 'treatment'.

There were no humanised mice back then.

There are now.

But there are also men. Men who have been subjected to the virus and its effects. Four men. One is already dead – though there were some pre-existing, underlying conditions that may have exacerbated the effects of the disease. The other three are exhibiting similar symptoms and, if last week's batch of mice are any indication of mortality, it is likely that one out of the remaining three will also perish.

It was accidental but that makes it no less useful as a case study.

Dr Bauer is sick but he is also overcome with grief at the passing of his father. It's draining. The virus has taken his energy. He is coughing whenever he lies down, but he needs to lie down because he hasn't been able to keep any food in his body for a day or so. Drinking water makes him gag, but it's the only thing that helps.

He's losing weight and is all cried out about his father. But the virus won't kill him.

The other two scientists, who have quarantined themselves inside their homes, are also struggling with the same heavy cough as their colleague. Moorcroft is Canadian, mid-thirties, athletic. He is strong. His mother has asthma but she is also overweight. Chen was born in Shanghai. He's a similar age but smaller in stature. There's no history of breathing problems in his family, but his father struggled with depression and his grandmother battled with a crippling case of racism.

They won't die, either.

It's not that the virus isn't deadly – it is. And just because half the mice died, it doesn't mean that half the people will die each time. Another four people could have been infected and they would all be worm food.

It's lucky. These people will be back in the lab in a week, searching for the answers to the vaccination question. They're heroes in the making. Loyal to the cause. They're not privy to the same information as Dr Ikeda. They are just doing their jobs. Examining viruses. Coming up with ways to eradicate or contain them. It's a job. It's science. No political agenda.

They're foot soldiers. To them, this is a hazard of the job. It was an accident. Bound to happen at some point. They are innocent, no idea what it is that they are really working on. It's not like they're in a room tinkering with a nuclear warhead every day.

The plan is not to strap a bomb to somebody's chest and have them walk into a busy shopping mall before detonating themselves. It is not to arm a lonely teenager and have them blow away half of their chemistry class, including the teacher. A plane is not going to be hijacked and flown into a building. No landmines, exploding vehicles or snipers.

The future is cybercrime and bioweapons.

It's quieter and more hands-off. It's faster and broader reaching.

And it is still terrorism.

The thing about terrorism is that, once the perpetrator is known, once somebody takes responsibility, it becomes one-hundred percent ineffective in weakening the intended enemy. Tragedy galvanises people. It's a very human response. And it's better to have a common enemy.

The virus will have the same effect.

But nobody will ever own up to the terrorism of releasing it. People can only aim their hate at the virus itself. And that keeps them weak.

PHILOSOPHY AND SCIENCE

Mrs Ikeda is also Dr Ikeda. Haruto himself would admit that she is much smarter than he is. They are both quiet, thoughtful. He may have had an epiphany a few years ago that sent him down an ethical and psychological rabbit hole, but she has been living in that world for twenty years.

She's a psychiatrist, and her current patient is feeling particularly troubled. It's Haruto, home from his bus journey and his cold oolong tea, and he is lying on the couch, hoping for some free counselling from a woman who is annoyed that the dinner she lovingly prepared has been ruined by his lateness.

Kimiko Ikeda puts aside her own irritations because she understands her husband. She will return to them at some point, but she can tell that he needs to offload. Nobody would ever choose to use the bus if they did not have to.

'Haruto, what is it? I bought wine. Would you like wine?'

'I would like wine and to talk.'

Neither of them says any more than they have to. It is efficient and it works. They are loving in their own way. Supportive of one another.

'Did something happen at work?' she asks, sitting in her chair with her own glass of wine, looking like the most unprofessional shrink in town. But this is pro bono work, the same rules do not apply.

'A few of my guys have been taken ill, but it's not that.'

'You're not worried?'

'Of course I'm worried. I care. What I want to know is why do I care?'

'What do you mean?'

'Why is it that I am affected, but others around me are not?'

'You're a good man. A compassionate man.' She takes a swig of wine. 'A late man. But a good man.'

'And I am this way through my environment, right? My parents and my friends and the books I read...'

'Of course. You understand that. And, in a biological sense, you have developed the part of your brain that deals with that emotion. What is it, dear? You are pensive because you care?'

Haruto Ikeda does not know how to explain things to his wife. What is he going to say? That he knowingly mutated a virus that came from deep within a cave of bats? That exposure to the original Tau virus has already killed his colleague's father? That it will be used as a weapon? That it will be used as a weapon for population control? To reduce, instil fear, and exert power over people? That he strangely sees the logic behind the decision but that he thinks there is a better way?

That he is nowhere nearer to finding a way to vaccinate against the outbreak than he was three months ago?

That all the goddamned mice are dead again?

Yes.

That's exactly what he says. They are a partnership. And he knows that she is much smarter than he is. She will know what to do.

'How long have you been keeping this to yourself, Haruto?'

'A year.'

'A year? This is why you are looking so thin. It has aged you, my dear.'

Haruto Ikeda shuts his eyes for a moment. He feels great shame. His wife is duty-bound to report the things that her husband has told her. He has put her in a difficult position. A dangerous one, too. Because these orders have not come from the Chinese government or their own Japanese government. It's from a place that is outside government. Darker. More nefarious and self-serving.

If Kimiko Ikeda goes public, there is a chance that she and her husband will wash up somewhere along the Yangtze River or float to the surface of Taihu Lake in a week.

They drink the wine and sit together for a reheated dinner of General Tso's tofu with pak choi. There are long silences, but they are not awkward. The Ikedas are considering their options.

'So, do you have a plan?' Kimiko asks.

Haruto takes his glass, fills his mouth with wine and nods.

'And what is your intention?'

He swallows the wine, places the glass back on the table and looks at his wife. His eyes do not move from hers. 'I think it is clear that I have only one option, my dear.' He places a hand on hers. 'I'm going to have to save the world.'

'Well, that sounds very thought-out and comprehensive. And how exactly are you going to save our world, Haruto?'

'With the two things that I hold to be true. Philosophy. And science.'

'My God, we're doomed.'

'It is starting to feel that way, my dear. It is starting to feel that way.'

Kimiko smiles at her husband. A knowing and mischievous smile saved only for him. She lifts her glass. He lifts his. And they tap them together.

'Well, I think the dishes can wait, this evening, don't you,' she says, and he agrees. 'We have a lot of work to do.'

Philosophy and science.

TREATMENT IS BETTER THAN TESTING

The Ikedas never had a child of their own. It was, of course, a disappointment to them both that this would never be the case. They considered adoption for a while, but Haruto found himself in a dark pit, deeming the world to be a cruel place to raise a child in anyway. He and Kimiko buried themselves in their work and in each other.

They would love one another with increasing fervour and continued understanding. It would be a quiet passion but an undying devotion.

Then Haruto's brother got his wife pregnant. The Ikedas would have a niece or a nephew whom they could dote on, they could love. And they could hand them back at the end of the day, put their feet up and share a bottle of wine.

The Ikedas would be the greatest aunt and uncle of all time. Though they could have felt jealous or aggrieved, that is not their way. This was going to be a positive experience.

And then the baby was born. A little boy. Haruto and Kimiko went to visit, straight away. This may not have been in the way they had hoped, but their family had grown.

The baby started spitting up even though it hadn't been fed recently. A seizure. Then a rising fever and dropping blood pressure. At this rate, the newborn would not make it through another day. The hospital rushed him through an MRI but found nothing.

The baby's mother explained that she'd had a cold while pregnant, but the hospital said that was not relevant because the baby was healthy when it was born. The best diagnosis was an infection of some sort, so the doctors placed the baby on powerful, narrow-spectrum antibiotics, specifically vancomycin and aztreonam, for the most resistant bacteria.

There was a brief period of respite before the child's kidneys started failing. The doctors suspected that one of the antibiotics were the cause but couldn't say which one. So the baby was temporarily taken off both until a clear diagnosis could be formed, until they could test further.

The newborn baby was being treated for nothing while the hospital deliberated, and he died.

The family was destroyed.

Ikeda's brother was so ashamed that he disappeared. One day he was there, the next he wasn't. Haruto did not believe that his brother had killed himself, it was more likely that he had exiled himself. There are companies in Japan that can help with that sort of thing: take you away in the middle of the night and give you a whole new identity elsewhere. It was one way of dealing with shame.

After the baby's death, an autopsy showed heart damage. Doctors believed that the antibiotics would not have worked, anyway, as it was likely to be echovirus 11, a condition that is relatively harmless in adults but deadly to newborns. Intravenous immunoglobulin can sometimes help to bolster those with a weakened immune system.

But it was too late.

Dr Haruto Ikeda took a lot from the entire experience. The grief over losing a child. The shame of his brother and his subsequent disappearance. The fragility of life. The cruelty of disease. The damage a virus can do.

But the thing that really resonated with him, that has stuck with him until this day, is that treatment can be better than testing. The hospital were so worried that the wrong diagnosis would have killed the baby that they seemingly forgot that no treatment would have the same outcome.

Of course, you cannot take a risk with the life of any human being, but no treatment and the wrong treatment have the same outcome.

The right decision is often the hard decision, but no decision at all is a waste of time. And there isn't always time.

Like now. It's coming. It's on a schedule.

So, Ikeda can test and test and test, hoping he finds a way to vaccinate against the Tau virus, or he can do something else. He can develop CompX and treat the virus that already exists in society. The one that makes the world a cruel and apathetic place.

In the open, he will work with his team to complete testing on a vaccination for the Tau virus. In secret, he will create CompX. Not a vaccine but a virus. A different virus. A virus that will act as a treatment for the selfishness and apathy that is doing more damage to the world than Tau ever could.

Haruto Ikeda is going to make people care.

It's a good thing.

But there are still people who are going to want to stop him.

THE BRAIN CAN BE REWARDED

There is no time for philosophy. In fact, the opposite is true. There is too much time for philosophy. Hume and Nietzsche could talk around a subject until the end of days. Agreeing. Disagreeing. And calmly agreeing to disagree.

Instead of placing a painted canvas that says 'Live, Laugh, Love' on the wall in the entrance to a home, self-kindness could be something that is taught from an early age. Mindfulness would not be something associated with Tibetan monks or wheatgrass-swilling hippies whose clothes are made from hemp.

It is understood there are six attributes that underpin the human capacity for compassion: a motivation to be caring; a sensitivity and attention to the needs of others; an ability to be moved to action by the distress of others; also the tolerance for difficult emotions; empathy, of course; and not to act in judgement or condemnation.

These philosophical building blocks are all very well, but Ikeda doesn't know how to make people care about other people's need for hand sanitiser. To him, the line that says human life is worth more than crude oil is obvious. But is there even a way to encourage those in power to truly consider the needs of the many over the ambitions of the few?

A knowledge of philosophy is key in order to theorise a better outcome, but science is the thing that is going to get him there faster.

The same part of the brain lights up when humans feel personal pain as it does when they empathise with the pain of others. It makes no difference to the layman if this is the middle cingulate cortex or the subgenual anterior cingulate cortex. The science is for Haruto Ikeda to manoeuvre. The psychology is for Kimiko Ikeda to teach.

And quickly.

If a person suffers an injury to the frontal lobe of their brain, it can have a disastrous impact on their ability to empathise. But that person can still learn the practice of compassion. The brain can be rewired. It may not 'feel' empathy, but the person can learn to become compassionate.

There is hope.

There has to be.

Being kind can boost oxytocin and dopamine and serotonin, which helps to regulate mood. This is important. Oxytocin is released through touch and emotional warmth. It's the thing that makes people feel love and trust and has been associated with sexual arousal. It can also be increased through the food that is eaten. Plenty of vitamins C and D and magnesium.

The Ikedas have everything they need. The Tau virus is scheduled to go out into the world and spread. They possess the knowledge of the brain, how the presence of oxytocin, and the fact that personal physical pain and empathy act in the same way.

This is the key.

These are the ingredients to create CompX.

The plan to save the world is in motion. Kimiko has to return to her patients tomorrow, holding on to the knowledge that a pandemic is possibly imminent. And Haruto must get to his lab and initiate a vital phase: keeping all the mice alive.

AN AMICABLE EXISTENCE

The Earth keeps spinning.

In the three weeks since the Ikedas set out to save an uncaring world, countries continue to struggle with famine as others try to tackle obesity. Some don't have enough while others are taking way too much. There was an earthquake in Indonesia and a volcano erupted in Iceland. Further unrest in the Middle East. Another six school shootings in the US as the NRA repeat the diatribe that 'guns don't kill people, people kill people'. And still, nobody on the left has cottoned on to the fact that this is exactly what they are saying, too, because they are too busy punching down and muddying the message.

And in the UK, one tabloid newspaper leads with the headline, 'Waxin' Jackson Lunch Break'. And they think they are being clever or funny because it seems that a young woman in a junior political position has been fellating the prime minister during his lunch hour, and he is wishing a deadly coronavirus could be released now to distract people from another alleged infidelity.

The article says that a source within parliament leaked the information, but Jackson knows that the woman in question did it herself. He can't be annoyed. He's in the wrong. But he's not annoyed. He can either confirm or deny it, or he can dance around it. Either way, for every female voter he loses, he picks up a male voter who thinks Jackson is a hero.

None of this is on Ikeda's radar. Information is controlled in China. He's busy. Working. If *they* want him to develop a vaccine alongside their virus then he feels it is only fair to develop his own virus alongside the vaccine.

There have been two more successful trials that have seen a sixty percent survival in the CompX mice. It's beginning to feel a lot closer.

Working concurrently with the job he is being paid to do, Ikeda has been monitoring the territorial nature of male mice. It's instinctive in them. And it is immediate. A male and a female results in mating. But two males equals fighting.

Ikeda is doping them to see the levels of oxytocin required for an amicable existence. Success in this is difficult to quantify because there seems to be a trade-off. Mice are not smart. Their actions are often instinctive. Too much and they become docile. Zombie mice. That's not the answer. What he wants is to gather information and then use that information to alter the virus so that the initial symptoms are there – shortness of breath, lethargy, coughing, sickness – but the result is a secretion of oxytocin that is heavy enough to alter the way a person acts.

To force them to be kind.

To care.

To live, laugh and love.

It would also be ideal to reduce the deaths to zero. No mice die and no people die. It sounds too fantastical but he has to try. He is the best in the world at what he does. If anybody can pull this off, it is Dr Haruto Ikeda.

And he believes.

He has hope.

He is moving closer.

But he is also clever enough to understand that there will come a point when the mice won't do. He will have to become unethical, like Jenner, and test on humans.

IT'S A RACE AGAINST TIME

'You piece of shit. You embarrass me like this again.' Helena takes a Delft plate off the wall and throws it in Harris Jackson's direction.

'Jesus, Helena, you'll wake the kids.'

'Fuck the kids. Oh, wait, you already did. How old was that twinky little aide who was sucking your dick under your desk while you were munching on the fucking BLT I made you?'

She's furious. Not because he has been sticking his parliament member into any hole that presents itself, again, although that isn't ideal, it's that it gets plastered over the tabloids and makes her look like an idiot. She knows what she let herself in for. She was charmed by Harris in much the same way as these other women. Power and prestige can be an aphrodisiac.

'Just because it's in the papers, doesn't mean it's true.' He's trying to wriggle out of it.

'Oh, come on, Harris. So you didn't lie about how much money the NHS are given? Your private-sector chums aren't getting all the lucrative contracts? She sucked your dick on your lunch break and you know it. And I know she wanted to for whatever reason. You didn't force her to. You don't have to. You've probably already got your next bimbo lined up and you don't care that it makes me look like a mug, that your kids will see this one day, and that your parents would roll over in their graves if they knew...'

He turns.

Harris doesn't want anyone to talk about his parents unless they are saying how in love they were, how tragic it was that they were taken so soon.

'Don't you dare talk about them.' Harris takes a step towards Helena. She is afraid but she doesn't budge. 'You didn't know them.'

'Neither did you, Harris. What happened was horrible for any kid. I just don't know why it made you this way. I'd have thought you'd want to be better.'

'Better than the prime minister of one of the most powerful countries on the planet?'

'A better person. Faithful. True. Honest. Honourable. A leader.'

'You have no idea of the pressures I'm under, Helena.' He backs down. Walks away.

'You're right. I don't. But you don't have to relieve them into the mouth of your goddamned secretary. Jesus. Such a cliché.'

There's a moment of silence. Not the comfortable kind that the Ikedas have, this is not that kind of relationship.

'You're right.' He's quiet.

'What?'

'You're right, okay. I fucked up again. Again. I'm just ... The world is about to change, Helena. And I need you beside me. I need the kids here. We ... we need to be a family.' What he is thinking is that they need to look like a family. For the cameras. They need to appear to be strong. Unbreakable. How many eligible bachelors have been elected to lead their country?

But he has also calculated that, if he can get her to stay another couple of months, she'll have no other choice but to remain after that when the country locks down.

Harris Jackson was born into a loving family, to parents who were so perfect for one another that the idea of continuing life without the other person was worse than death. Jackson's mother was taken too soon. It was an accident. An avoidable accident. And his father, so overcome with grief, didn't think twice about blowing his brains out.

People have always tried to comfort Harris by telling him that they are together now. He doesn't believe any of that. What he does believe is that while they were alive they were more together than any two people have been.

Harris Jackson wants the same. It may seem as though he thinks that there are three billion women out there and that he's in a race against time, but all he wants is a relationship like his parents had. He wants somebody that he would shoot himself for. All the power, money and lunchtime blow jobs won't fill the hole left behind by their passing.

'A family? How much were you thinking about your family when that whore was on her knees beneath your desk?' Helena punches him in the chest with the fleshy part of her clenched fist. She's frustrated and embarrassed and wants to hurt him.

It goes on. She calls the woman every derogatory term she can think of while also trying to emasculate her husband, questioning his sexual prowess and stamina. Harris takes what she has to give. He doesn't shy away. And when she has howled at the moon for long enough, he pulls her into him and holds her tight. She pretends to fight it but Helena is exhausted.

'You're going to have to work hard at this, Harris. And you start by telling the truth. A conference, an interview, I don't care. Set it straight. Say that it is true. Don't let her have the fifteen minutes of fame that she wants. Be genuinely sorry. The public will respect that more.'

Harris Jackson has to bite his tongue. He wants to say, 'Couldn't I just drop a bomb on Syria or something? That would stop people talking about our private lives.' But he doesn't. He assures his wife that he will do as she asks.

The only problem is that he has been a politician for so long, he's forgotten what the truth looks like.

He kisses the top of his wife's head in an attempt to comfort her, but he's thinking, *God, this epidemic can't come soon enough.*

TRUST

Bauer is back at work. He dropped almost ten pounds while sick with the virus. He looked gaunt and grey when he returned. But he has buried his father since then, and the weight is slowly creeping back on. He's starting to look like himself again. Healthy.

But he is not the same.

He's more pessimistic than he ever was and he seems to get angry quickly. Ikeda has noticed. Bauer has always been one of his best and his brightest. But he seems … ruined.

Bauer knocks on the office door of Dr Ikeda, who is having his usual pre-packaged sandwich. He's a creature of habit. He waves Bauer to come in.

'You wanted to see me?'

Ikeda beckons Bauer closer and swallows down a mouthful of food.

'How do you know where anything is in this office?' Bauer smiles. Something he doesn't do as much as he used to. He flicks through a few out-of-date medical journals and shakes his head.

'It's ordered chaos, I assure you.'

'I trust you. You're the genius.'

Ikeda is pleased that Bauer trusts him. He could do with an ally.

'How are you?'

'How am I? You mean since I was sick or because my sickness ended up killing my father?'

'I wonder whether you came back too soon, perhaps.'

'It's nice that you care, Haruto, but I'm fine. My father is buried in a graveyard and I'm buried in my work.' Bauer is investigating another SARS-like virus. A level-three lab, like Ikeda's. Sometimes, viruses seem to spring up spontaneously and have to be studied after they have taken effect. But a lot of work is done on viruses that already exist and are suspected to mutate into something worse in the future. This area of study is important to limit the impact of such an event.

It's not uncommon to work on more than one thing at a time. Both of Bauer's projects are above board.

'Your glibness is a worry.' Ikeda is a man of few words but he makes sure they all matter.

Bauer fidgets on his chair. 'I definitely came back too soon. I don't think there's a time limit on grief, though. Honestly, it's helping me. Sitting around in my apartment would send me insane. But if you think that's what's best, I trust you.'

There it is again. That word. Trust.

Ikeda has always seen the good in things. He even sees beauty in a single cell affected by a virus. He wants to believe that somewhere, deep down, people care, that they want the world to be a better place. That nobody wants war or animal suffering or hunger and homelessness. It is, at once, his greatest weapon and the harshest of flaws.

His world changed three years ago when he was given a much deeper insight into the shadowy regions where the pharmaceutical industry and governments meet. So, whereas in the past, when someone showed trust in him, Ikeda would have reciprocated, now he has to keep his guard up. He has to be suspicious.

Bauer has used the word 'trust' twice already but he is also riffling through articles in Ikeda's office. He's different. Of course he is. His life has been thrown upside down, maybe he is looking for somebody that *he* can trust, maybe that is what Bauer needs.

'I'm just looking out for you, Dr Bauer. What you have been through, what you continue to go through, is not something usual. If you say it helps, then I shall put my own trust in you.'

Am I right to do so? That's what Ikeda wants to ask. He needs a friend in that building. There are too many suits wandering the halls. People he doesn't know peering through windows and cracks in doorways. The whole institute now feels sinister. Anyone not in a white coat is suspicious. If they're dressed smart, they're watching.

'How are *you*?' Bauer asks.

'I'm sorry.'

'You seem quiet. Quieter than usual. You're still experimenting with the Tau virus, right?'

'Who told you that?'

'I caught something here and my father is now dead. I've been looking around. You know I still can't taste food? I'd probably even enjoy that sandwich you bring in every day.'

'It's a coronavirus. It attacks the respiratory system with violence.'

'How bad is it?'

'It could be worse.' Ikeda doesn't say a lot but it's enough to pique Bauer's curiosity.

'Is there worse? Did you make it worse? Did you manufacture something?' Bauer is caught up emotionally because his father died as a result of a virus that came out of the institute.

Ikeda says nothing. Ypsilon was worse. But it's gone.

'So it could be a weapon. Jesus. If it's contained, you could blast it. Destroy it. Nobody is going down into that cave by choice.'

The government couldn't take the risk. Ypsilon was too virulent. It was not the type of virus that could be examined after the fact, and Ikeda knew that. So he did what he had to do.

'I already blasted it. It's gone. What you were exposed to was the Tau virus.'

'Well, there needs to be a vaccination.' Bauer stumbles, he knows Ikeda is always working on other things but his father's death has him on edge. Ikeda just thinks he is still upset.

And this is where he takes a risk. He conducts a test. On Bauer.

'You've done great things. The team has worked well. The vaccine works well. I've tested it.'

'What? You haven't said anything?'

'The sooner there's a vaccine, the sooner there's a weapon.' He lets it hang for a moment. This is it. He is not giving Bauer any concrete information. In fact, he's not telling the entire truth about the vaccine – it's not quite where it needs to be. But if Ikeda can arm his colleague with potentially damaging information and it finds its way to the wrong person, Ikeda will know where it came from, because Bauer is the only person he has spoken with about this. Ikeda would know that Bauer cannot be trusted.

'So what are you doing with it?'

'Experimenting. Making it better. Making it good.'

'You're making the vaccine ... good?'

Dr Ikeda shakes his head and takes the last bite of his sandwich.

'The vaccine is already good. The virus is not.' Ikeda stands up and thanks Bauer for coming to see him. He says that he is glad that work is giving him some purpose and a more positive focus.

He has given Bauer enough information, cryptic though it is, to chew over, to decide whether it is worth sharing with anybody else at the Wuxi Institute of Virology. If anything comes back to Ikeda, he can deny or divert attention with the vaccine. But he will know that Bauer is not one to be trusted.

Again, he just has to wait.

A PLACE TO POINT THE FINGER

Animal-borne diseases that are contagious to humans can transmit in various ways. If you're not keen on a dog or a cat or a hamster and want a slightly more exotic pet, there are a plethora of risks. If you find fish boring, don't worry, turtles can carry salmonella.

Maybe you have a few drinks one night and decide that you've always wanted to play the drums. Maybe you'll start with some bongos. Maybe those bongos use goat skin that has been imported from Guinea. You just want to see what it sounds like when you hit it with your hand, but you are unaware that the skin carries a naturally occurring anthrax. Now you wish you hadn't let your kids play with it.

Or you bought a rug or a carving of some kind, and now you don't feel so great.

If you're in the south-east of England, you may frequent the fortnightly farmers' market because you want fresh cheese, and the kids like to see the pigs being paraded around or the chickens running about. They are roaming around freely even though there's still a chance they have swine flu or bird flu or foot-and-mouth disease.

In China, they have something similar called a wildlife market. There's one in Wuxi. It's huge. There are open-air stalls filled with fruit and vegetables and all kinds of seafood, but it's a great place for fresh meat.

So fresh that it will be slaughtered on site.

There are, of course, risks to this. Cramped conditions for the animals. Lack of cleanliness. All the blood from the butchery. Contaminated water from the sea life. All havens for bacteria and infections.

In many wildlife markets across Asia, there is also a desire for the more exotic meats. Snakes and crocodiles, beavers and even porcupines. Sometimes, you may see things like badgers, bamboo rats and bats. It is thought that HIV and Ebola have been spread from such places.

But Wuxi is regulated. What they call 'bushmeat' is rarely seen. These things still make their way there, although much of it is now sold online because that's tougher to control. Still, it is the perfect place to blame for any kind of outbreak because it has happened before. And, even if the animals are not being slaughtered there, these rarer species are often used in Chinese medicine. But the main reason it works so well is that the rest of the world does not understand that these places are a way of life in China. They are places for families to walk around and talk and try before they buy.

'Wildlife market' sounds different enough, but the shadow government's plan is to refer to them as 'wet markets'. They're not the same thing, but it works. And it makes it sound dirtier, somehow. And people need a place to point the finger at.

China will point at Dr Ikeda, and the rest of the world will point at the Wuxi wet market.

Death is so final. So the man in the perfectly pressed suit will continue to listen and watch until he is certain that he is pointing in the right direction.

SOMETHING TO DO WITH CIVETS

It's been two weeks. There haven't been any men in black suits bursting into Ikeda's office. Nobody has 'accidentally' released the hot steam over his work in the lab. Bauer hasn't been bugging him for more answers, he's not digging for information.

Maybe he can be trusted.

'You have to play this very carefully,' Kimiko tells him in her stern but delightful way. She is more cautious than her husband. She swears that the last two times she has used the telephone, there has been a clicking sound before anybody speaks.

'I've always liked him.'

'You're too trusting, Haruto.'

'But I'm right about Bauer. He is going through the same thing that I did. He's wondering what the point is, whether it's worth it. He's young enough and smart enough to do something else, you know? He has choices.'

She can see that her husband is fond of his colleague. Haruto Ikeda does not feel entirely understood at work – such is the problem with genius – but it seems he has found somebody he sees himself in. And he empathises with him. He feels awful that Bauer was infected at the lab and that infection killed his own father.

'Finish your eggs and clean up. Don't rush into it. If it happens, it happens. You will know.' Kimiko kisses the top of her husband's head and takes herself off to the shower.

Haruto Ikeda does as he is told. He eats the rest of his eggs and he drinks a cup of black coffee. He and his wife have a rule that they do not view technology while at the table. No distractions from reality, but he hears the shower running and takes a brief look at his mobile phone.

They're all still alive.

No mice have died for three days.

He is going to have to tell somebody that the vaccine seems to be working and that it now requires some robust testing. This is Ikeda's way of hiding in plain sight, making it seem as though he is fulfilling his obligation. The powers that be should be distracted enough not to notice anything else he is working on.

Ikeda sent an email to his superiors late last night saying that he will be more certain in a week. The good news was passed on to the investors. He is not built for subterfuge, but he is on a mission for humanity.

Ikeda washes his plate in the sink and places it on the rack to dry, then he goes into the bedroom where his shirt and trousers are hanging in the wardrobe, perfectly ironed. Kimiko is out of the shower and rubbing one of her skincare products into her legs. She is listening to the radio.

'Did you hear that?' she says.

'Hear what?'

'Looks like we won't be going to the market this Saturday.'

'What's happened?'

'It's shut for two days. Something to do with civets.' She shrugs.

Haruto Ikeda knows two things about civets. The first is that they are responsible for the most expensive coffee in the world. Kopi Luwak. The civets eat the coffee cherries, partially digest them and then defecate. The fruit ferments in the stomach of the civet and alters its composition. It sounds like a gimmick, but the beans sell for a lot. It's big business. But the consensus is that the coffee taken from the civet faeces does, in fact, taste like shit.

The other thing he knows is that SARS, which originated in bats, was not spread by bats. It was the civets that had eaten the bats that ended up circulating the virus.

'Well, I'm sure they have a good reason. Maybe we should go out to lunch on Saturday instead.'

Kimiko smiles and nods at the suggestion.

They both get ready, like they always do, like nothing important happened today.

But it did. They just didn't notice.

Kimiko is a little put out that the market is shut – it messes with her weekly routine – but the idea of eating out instead has distracted her. And Haruto is innocent. He's not a spy or a traitor. He thinks that people always find a way. He feels that humanity is fundamentally good. So he would never link his late-night progress email to the closing of the market because those two things seem incongruous.

But they are not.

Ikeda is working to the schedule set out by the secret Western cabal. The one he was not supposed to see. But the release of the Tau virus is only one part of the plan.

It is starting.

Events have been set in motion.

KEEP THEM SCARED, KEEP THEM IN LINE

'Harris, we have some poll results in. It seems that sixty-four percent of people are worried about corruption in our government due to … recent incidents that call into question the party's standards in public life.'

What he means is Harris Jackson's standards in his *private* life. That they are tarnishing the reputation of the Conservative Party.

Geoff Delaney is the prime minister's chief advisor. He's also an old friend from their time at Eton College and somebody he likes to go cycling with, although they do this less frequently than they used to.

'God, Geoff, don't beat about the bush, we have more important things to deal with than my indiscretions.'

'Quite. There is also concern that you are not living up to the promises that got you into power in the first place.'

'Is that not the same for every world leader throughout the history of man?'

'Of course, but we have to, at least, show a little initiative. Things are looking worse on the back of the indiscretion, that's all.' Delaney doesn't use his fingers to air quote the word 'indiscretion', but his voice changes enough that it has the same effect.

Jackson gives him a playful look.

'You said that you would increase the number of jobs in the NHS, and there are several environmental issues that are yet to be addressed. Almost eighty percent feel that you don't even care about the environment.'

'I don't.'

'Jesus, Harris, you—'

'I don't. Nobody does. We'll be long gone by the time it's up in flames. It's more likely that Russia drops a bomb on everyone before we're all living under water or choking on poisonous gases. Let's get something out about net zero. Nobody knows what the hell that is. Let's whack a date on that for the next government to deal with.'

Jackson has other advisors but none that he can speak with so candidly. They drink coffee and talk about the best way to spin things. Focus on the pledges that *have* been ticked off. Don't talk about the fact that the number of homes Jackson promised to build is falling way below expectations and go with something smaller, like the cycling-proficiency rollout for primary-school children.

His government has put tens of millions into public transport infrastructure. They're not on track with the recruitment of new police officers but they should catch up with the promised figure within the next year. The national-insurance decrease didn't happen. The rollout of full-fibre broadband to every home has been abandoned.

'The opposition are going to push you on the whole "Global Britain" thing in parliament, it seems, so you are going to want to be prepared for that. We are drafting something now.'

'What do I need?'

'A decent distraction. A statement of intent on one of these pledges would help. Other than that, a terrorist incident is always good for galvanising the masses against a common enemy who's not you.'

'I quite agree, Geoff. Keep them scared, keep them in line.' He winks and points a finger at his aide.

'Perhaps the slogan when it comes to election time?'

'Ha. You scoff, but we will see. There's a reason – what was it? – sixty-four percent of people think we are corrupt. It's because there's always something going on. Newspapers are all about scandal now. If they did their job properly, real journalism, then maybe more people would actually care about the environment.'

'So, you're not worried?' Delaney can't understand how Jackson always stays so calm. Perhaps that's the reason he holds the higher office. Nerves of steel.

'Something always rears its ugly head. There's an affair, or someone has been claiming something they shouldn't as expenses. Terrorists are trying to attack us all the bloody time. Give it a month and there will be some kind of crisis.' He says it almost optimistically. But he knows. He is ready to ride the wave for four weeks until the new virus is reported.

'I did hear that Warren was pulled over late last night and breathalysed.' It could have been a throwaway comment, but Delaney knows Jackson and he knows exactly what he is saying. If he had led with this, then nothing else would get done. Everything is some kind of spin. Somebody in Harris Jackson's government was driving under the influence.

It triggers the usually laid-back Jackson.

'He was drunk and driving home?'

'I believe, so, yes.'

'Was anyone hurt?'

'Warren's pride, I'm sure.'

'I'm going to hurt more than his pride, Geoff. Get him in here. We'll give the voters their distraction when I sack the goddamned chancellor.'

Geoffrey Delaney is responsible for spinning information for the benefit of the party. He went in to speak with the prime minister not to alert him to polling or push him on the environment, that was bluster. Foreplay for his true intention. He spun things to get someone fired and the media focus shifted.

And he lied about the percentage of people who thought politicians were corrupt.

It was much higher.

The people are right.

And they can never know.

THE DAMAGE IS DONE

They call it a presumptive positive. But not out loud. The result would be catastrophic.

Economically, there would be a trickle-down effect that would decimate industries.

If this happened in the UK or US, if there was a presumptive positive for a disease found in beef, millions of cattle would have to be slaughtered. Ranchers and farmers would struggle to survive the livestock cull.

There would also be an effect on all of the cows that have already been slaughtered. Supermarkets would have to take beef off the shelves. Restaurants and fast-food chains would suffer hugely.

Then there are the knock-on effects to the bean and grain industries, which provide the feed that allow the cattle to grow quicker and have tastier flesh. Not to mention all the antibiotics that get pumped into the animals because they get sick while being forced to grow, or are administered as a preventative measure. Almost three quarters of antimicrobials sold each year are to treat animals that are used for human consumption.

In an age of instant information and disinformation, it is imprudent to alert the public to a presumptive positive, because it causes hysteria.

It's fear. But it's not the good fear.

It's not the fear that allows a government to control its population.

It's the fear that destroys agriculture and hospitality and puts a huge dent in pharmaceuticals.

You can upset the little farmer but don't you dare piss off big pharma.

It takes seventy-two hours to do the appropriate testing. Three days to try and keep things under wraps without the media distorting it and causing chaos and panic. The Chinese are skilled in that area. They are better at controlling the information. Nobody will even utter the words 'presumptive positive'. The testing will be done at the Wuxi Institute of Virology, of course.

And even before the seventy-two hours have passed, Dr Haruto Ikeda, the foremost authority, already busy testing a vaccine, already busy developing a virus, will give the all-clear. It was a false alarm. Reopen the market.

There will be no fear and panic.

But the damage is done. The seed has been sown in the West. Harris Jackson wants it fresh in the memory that there was a possible outbreak in that wildlife market, so it can be brought up when the virus goes live. And he wants Dr Ikeda to be the face of the failure.

So he thought up a minor incident. One involving an animal that would not have as much impact as diseased cows in America or fish in Japan. Something that would only cause a small amount of worry in China but be mostly forgotten by the rest of the world. The civet.

Harris Jackson does this off his own bat, without first running it by the group. The fact he is not severely reprimanded for his actions calls into question what the US and Russian presidents are also doing off script.

The world media will be able to circle back to the initial scare around disease-ridden civets. Even though there was nothing wrong with them. Jackson chose them because he sees them as unashamedly Chinese.

And that will lead him to the reason that he will so delicately state in a couple of weeks, 'They eat dogs.'

THE CHARADE OF TESTING

Ikeda is hesitant.

And now he has to deal with all of this civet nonsense.

The doctor has become more cynical. He saw his wife's reaction to the market closure. It was rational. She was a little disappointed that they wouldn't get to go for their weekly walk around the stalls selling food, and herbs and spices, and traditional medicines, but she dealt with it for what it was and now they get to go for a walk and a lunch at a restaurant somewhere. Perhaps a glass of wine in the middle of the day.

But there will be conspiracy theories online as to why there is a sudden closure and there will be talk of government involvement – in the West, at least; China will control the information on their side. Some idiot will say that they are testing for anthrax, others will suggest aliens. There will be an anti-race/gender/animal cruelty angle somewhere.

It will be a mess.

But not with his generation. It's everyone younger than Ikeda.

Because he lives in an age of spin. Of agenda. Of open and unabashed self-interest. This is his worry. Information travels instantly. And because everyone now seems to know about everything, straight away, they care about nothing all the time.

Are there more school shootings in America now or is it just that everybody knows about them?

When the SAS abseiled from the roof of the Iranian embassy after it was seized in the 1980s and twenty-six people were held hostage, it was a major news event. A one-off. People looked on and reacted. They discussed it with friends and family and work colleagues. Their thoughts did not travel outside of their immediate circle.

Now it is every day.

And, worse than that, it has become *everyday*.

Just another hostage crisis in Iraq.

Just another car bomb in Northern Ireland.

Just another stabbing in China.

Shooting in Norway, Italy, Afghanistan.

Suicide bomber in London, Pakistan, Morocco.

Ikeda doesn't think that killing off a large chunk of the population is the answer any more than the NRA think that background checks will cut down on mass shootings.

That's why he is doing what he is doing.

That's the reason that, after he has completed the charade of testing civets, he will inject himself with the CompX virus.

A QUESTION OF ETHICS

Dr Bauer is already at the institute when Ikeda arrives.

'They've had me set up a lab to test these things,' Bauer explains. He doesn't need to go into detail – he knows that Ikeda would have been emailed or called and briefed. He's trying to be more like his mentor. Shorter sentences with the right amount of information.

'Civets, huh?'

'Worried about SARS, I guess.'

'But nobody has been reported sick, yet.'

Bauer screws his face up as if confused. 'Then what are we doing?'

'Disproving to prevent panic.' This is where any other doctor would roll their eyes. But not Ikeda. He doesn't ever do that.

This is not an incident where a human appears to have been infected. It seems to be a preventative measure. If a child is bitten by a skunk with rabies, doctors can retroactively treat the patient. This is different.

Virus testing in domestic animals is a large enough undertaking with two hundred species that can pass diseases on to their humans. Taking zoo animals and more exotic species into account can raise that number to a thousand. Veterinary clinics often specialise in particular animals. Few laboratories can handle such cases but the Wuxi Institute is one of them. It can take care of the need for electron microscopy and cytopathology in cultured cells. It has enough scientists for neutralisation and monoclonal antibody serology. But above all, there is the one person who can get this quashed in seventy-two hours, and he happens to also be the one guy they can pin everything on when something heads south.

Bauer explains that they have blood and nasal swabs. Tissue. Faeces. And cell lines from the kidney. 'We're not sitting around on this.'

'Sounds like you've got things running efficiently. You don't need me this morning.'

'They're going to want you on this.' Bauer is concerned.

'I'll be there. I have to go to my labs first. Make some checks.' Ikeda starts to walk down the corridor, his pre-packaged sandwich in one hand, a briefcase in the other.

Bauer steps across to block him. It's not threatening, he just wants to get in closer so that he doesn't have to speak so loudly.

'You said the vaccine we've been working on is done, right? You've tested it yourself? So what are you working on that's more important than this. I mean, orders have come from on high.'

Ikeda hears the American affectation in Bauer's German accent. He picked it up at Stanford.

'Get things moving. We can talk later.'

Bauer moves out of the way, and Ikeda goes to do exactly what he said he would do. First, he checks on the mice. They're all alive. They are sharing the food and water. There seems to be no more demarcation of territory.

He could smile here. But Ikeda doesn't do that. Not at work. He doesn't show any real part of himself in this building. He makes himself a coffee and goes to his office, where he sits for twenty minutes, waiting for his drink to cool, and he thinks. He contemplates the magnitude of possible future events.

There is a question of ethics that is upsetting Dr Ikeda.

He doesn't know what to do.

Is he right? Or is he just as bad as the people who want to spread disease? Sure, Ikeda's approach means that nobody dies, and they may even have the opportunity to go on and live in a better, kinder world.

Damn. Even now, in his head, it sounds ridiculous. Like he is going to save the world. He is going to cure humanity of the cancer of greed and apathy towards others. He, Haruto Ikeda, Japanese doctor working in a prestigious scientific institute in China, is going to somehow take on a secret shadow government programme to release a contagion, to prey on the weak and vulnerable, to blame it on a country who had no involvement, to place fear in the population and control them. To write their own history.

It's ridiculous.

Who does he think he is?

Ikeda tests his coffee. It's still too hot.

He hasn't thought ahead enough. He has had months to try to mutate the Tau virus into CompX, but the other plan to release Tau has been meticulously schemed for over a year. Longer, perhaps. He is one man against many. Ikeda has no idea who they are but he knows that the many have power, influence, money. They are the ones in need of Ikeda's virus more than anybody. They are most in need of some compassion.

And now his wife, Kimiko, is involved. He has read enough books and seen enough movies to know that her knowledge of what he plans to do is his weakness. She could be targeted. Where will they go? How can they hide?

He's sweating.

Ikeda takes a sip from his coffee and burns his mouth. It drips on the chair between his legs as he jerks the cup away.

He thinks.

It doesn't matter that his intentions are honourable. It doesn't matter that his goal is to save lives. The people will still be unaware of what they are taking into their bodies. It won't be consensual. It's deception.

He could write a paper explaining his findings. He could have something manufactured. But it would not be beneficial financially to have people consider one another. To not want cruelty of any kind to any species. The costs could be catastrophic for many industries – even if the spiritual gain far outweighs the use of fossil fuels or the barbaric nature of the dairy industry.

And most people probably already think that they are nice.

He tries the coffee again.

Perfect.

Ikeda takes a large gulp, places the cup on his desk and leans back in his chair. He looks around the room. It's a mess of paperwork and books and medical journals and hidden Post-it notes that he thinks nobody will read because they don't read anything that's not written on a computer. The packaging from his lunch, yesterday, is still in the bin next to his desk. Nobody has come in to clean overnight. They probably think that there is no need; the place is a mess.

The doctor is still wavering. But what he is doing is considering his options, which is more than Jackson and Co. did. They went straight in with death and destruction and what they could gain from the situation for each of the countries they represented. People are numbers and barcodes and a series of ones and zeroes.

He runs a hand down his face. Exasperated.

How can it be unethical to make people nice?

He wonders what would happen if he told the world of his discovery. Would he have to go into hiding? Would he just end up dead? Would they make it look like an accident? Ikeda does not trust the group mentality of people in this time. Somehow, a rumour would spread that you end up with cancer or blindness or your teeth fall out, and enough people would believe it and spread it further, and it would split the population on another important issue.

Everything is so black and white, now.

Decisions are fifty-fifty.

Important policies can swing on the strength of a social-media campaign.

There's so much to consider. And he's not even sure if his creation works the way he wants it to. The mice are sharing and they're not dying, and the males are not seeing who can piss highest up the wall anymore. But that's not enough.

The temperature of Ikeda's coffee is just right. He gulps the rest down like it is water after a marathon. Then he goes over to his office door, shuts it, locks it, and returns to his desk. He rolls up his sleeve and injects himself in the top of the arm. He places the needle into a packet and pushes it to the bottom of his office bin, filled with apple cores and sandwich packaging.

Ikeda tapes a wad of cotton wool over the spot he injected, to catch any blood, and rolls his sleeve back down. He picks up his briefcase, places it on his desk with his lunch on top, and he unlocks his office. Then he's walking down the hallway to the level-three labs and Dr Bauer.

They have seventy-two hours to show that there is no threat of contagion from the civets found at the Wuxi market. In this kind of situation, there is often a round of false positives that have to be retested, but Ikeda is confident that three days will be more than enough to lay this stunt to rest. If the injection works, that's about the same length of time the doctor has before the virus starts attacking his respiratory system.

THE CARING HERO

The chancellor resigns.

It's all over the front pages.

In the United Kingdom, the Wuxi market story is buried somewhere in the middle of the newspaper. But it's there. Poisonous. The resignation dwarfs all other stories, though. The chancellor is sorry. He says that he feels his personal conduct does not reflect well on the party and that he has no other option than to leave his position as it is one of great authority and his driving ban for being three times over the legal limit does not demonstrate the responsibility required for such a duty.

He holds himself accountable. The apology is quiet and genuine. There is an element of class that is not often seen in a Tory minister.

And Jackson throws it all away with his usual bluster and lack of care.

He is asked directly, during a press conference, how he feels about the chancellor's resignation. And he laughs.

'Resignation,' he says under his breath. 'I guess when I found that my cleaner had been stealing jewellery from my wife, she also handed in her resignation.' He laughs more heartily. 'Look, I don't want to stop somebody having a pint at lunchtime on a Friday and then driving home after work, but I don't want drunks on the road putting other people at risk. I'm firm on this. And that's why Warren had to go.' At this point, there is usually a raft of questions from various news outlets, but they understand where this is coming from and, while it is slightly disrespectful, they let it go, much like they always do with Jackson.

He paints himself as the caring hero.

Nobody asks him about his wife.

Nobody mentions his ex-lover showing up on daytime talk shows.

Nobody questions the deal that the former chancellor has allegedly signed to publish his personal diaries.

And nobody is wondering about the possibility of a widespread epidemic caused by SARS in a civet community being sold for meat at a market in China. But it's there to be called on at a later date.

It all is.

'I already have a list of candidates qualified to take over the position who do not try to speed home before the six gins have absorbed into their bloodstream.' And with that he turns to leave.

The questions come flooding in behind him. A mumble of voices, scrambling to be heard over the person next to them.

Jackson shouts back, 'Nobody is irreplaceable.' Then he disappears behind the door of number ten. Pleased with himself that he won an argument with a person who wasn't even present. The man in the perfectly pressed suit watches, the rest of China does not.

Harris Jackson is blissfully unaware of the irony that he wants to clamp down on drinking and driving to help prevent the 280 related deaths each year in his country but is happy to unleash a disease that will kill hundreds of thousands, most of them elderly, who are his core voting demographic.

The drinking and driving is all about his parents, and the forthcoming pandemic is about his power. Neither are about his country or the people who elected him. It's self-interest, of course. Harris Jackson's circle of care does not extend much beyond his belt buckle.

He thinks he has four weeks to weather any shit that people want to throw at him and then he will become the people's saviour. He will lock down. He will protect. He will make sure there is a vaccine. He thinks he has it all under control.

He's wrong.

IT'S NOT SERIOUS

He was sweating in the night but he felt cold. And that cough. Like a bark. Right on cue, Ikeda is feeling awful. He can't keep any food down. His already slender frame diminishing after a day in bed sleeping or vomiting.

'Is this how you expected it to go?' Kimiko asks her husband as she brings him some miso broth. Something simple that hopefully won't come back up again.

Haruto sits up in bed. 'This is how it has to be. It has to look as though the intended virus has spread. That way we can mask the true intention.' He places the bowl on his lap. And he coughs, covering his mouth so that his wife doesn't get infected.

She doesn't need to.

Her world extends to every corner of the globe and beyond. Kimiko thinks of others before herself. She wants to help. She wishes to enjoy her own existence but not at the cost of others'. She believes in the power of words and of passion and creativity and focus. She does not believe in God but she admires those who devote their lives to faith.

She is good.

Kimiko Ikeda is good. The very best of us. Already.

Haruto is not lying when he says that she is smarter than he is, that she is better. This is not some grandiose compliment to score points. He believes it because it is the truth.

'Can I get you anything else?'

'No. Thank you. Just leave me. My body has to fight this thing. It is not deadly.' He says it out loud and tells himself, *The mice did not die.*

'Would you like a book or something? Perhaps the television?'

'Kimiko, do not fuss,' he places a hand on hers, 'I will be fine in a few days. I am going to eat the soup you prepared and go back to sleep.' He smiles at her. This is not something he does often, so she understands that he means it. She leaves him.

While making herself a pot of tea, the doorbell rings.

It's Dr Bauer.

'Good day. I'm sorry to intrude,' he says. Kimiko only opens the door slightly. 'My name is Stefan Bauer. Dr Bauer. I work at the institute with your husband, Dr Ikeda.'

Kimiko knows who he is. Her husband has spoken about him. He was exposed to a virus that he passed on to his father who died. Haruto is very fond of the young German scientist. He feels that he can be trusted but wants to be absolutely certain before divulging anything.

'How can I help you, Dr Bauer?' She is not cold but she is straight. A little guarded. Protective, maybe.

'It is my lunch break. I raced over here on the train. I don't have very long but I wanted to check that he is doing okay.'

'He is resting.'

'That's good. And you are feeling well?'

'You hopped on the train to get here and ask me that? You could have called.'

'I'm sorry. I don't know. I guess I'm just worried. My father passed away very suddenly, and your husband is something of a mentor to me at work. I just ... I don't know. I want to make sure that he is coming back to the labs.'

Kimiko softens.

Bauer seems to care.

'He is exhibiting flu-like symptoms. It's not serious. He will be back.'

'It's just that there are a lot of talks of deadlines...'

'He cannot think about that, right now. People are entitled to not work when they are sick.'

'Yes. Of course, I just ... I ... He told me that he's already ... actually, it is fine. Of course. I should leave you alone. Please pass on my regards.' He nods and turns to leave.

'I will. Thank you.'

Then, from behind Kimiko, 'Dr Bauer.' Haruto Ikeda stands in the hall, pale and thin, his weight leaning more to his left side. 'Please come in. We have much to discuss.'

VIP LANE

A global epidemic will wreak havoc on the economies of even the most stable of countries. But it's also big business for those with a corrupt or exploitative nature.

Jackson can certainly help his friends make a few extra bucks from the crisis.

Personal protective equipment like face masks and sterile gowns are going to be vital for the National Health Service, whose stockpiles are currently far too low to deal with the incoming demand of patients exposed to the Tau virus.

The government will offer out contracts to supply the PPE equipment, but, in a time of great need, they can dispense with the requirement for these contracts to be competitively tendered. This gives way to the 'VIP Lane', which allows companies that have been recommended by MPs and peers to be prioritised.

Cue Lord Benedict and his recommendation of PPE Mediplus, which he sends to the personal email address of the procurement minister and the minister for the cabinet office. The company is yet to be incorporated in the UK, but it is quite obviously a subsidiary of his wife's company Quietfire, which, among other things, deals in financial services for the über rich, offering wealth management and off-shore accounts out of its offices on the Isle of Man.

They will be offered a contract worth two hundred million pounds. The same day, a company called PPE Mediplus will be set up on the Isle of Man. This works perfectly because ownership of companies there can be kept secret and no corporation tax is charged on profits.

The profits can be passed through several other accounts and companies before landing in a trust owned by Lord Benedict and his children. And they can use those profits to upgrade their yacht and private jet and purchase a few more properties in prestigious areas around London and Glasgow.

And they can do this while people are dying and the health service buckles under the weight of disease. And they can sip their cocktails on the white sands of Mauritius or in their Monaco crash pad. And they will smile at having prospered while millions perish and thousands witness the toll on human life from behind one of the masks PPE Mediplus supplied.

Of course, there is always the chance that Lord Benedict and family will be infected themselves. That they will become sick for a while. That they will get the headaches. And maybe they won't really understand why, but they will take their vast fortune and use it for something good.

NO MORE DOUBT. NO MORE FEAR.

When Kimiko Ikeda shakes her head, almost imperceptibly, Haruto knows not to go on. Even though he considers himself to be an excellent judge of character. Even though he has worked with Bauer for a few years now and considers him a close colleague with a bright future. Even though he is running a temperature and feels tired and nauseous, the one person he would never question is his wife.

He starts to sway a little. He talks a little gibberish.

'We are so far but also so near.' He is closing his eyes and wiping sweat from his forehead. 'The answer is so simple. Only love will set us free.'

It looks as though he is hallucinating. He's on something. Some freewheeling hippie.

Before that, he's completely lucid. Telling Bauer that the institute has wonderful facilities for research but that not everything is as ethical as it should be. Bauer pushes but Ikeda gives nothing away.

That's when Kimiko shook her head.

Ten minutes before that, they are drinking tea and Haruto is hypothesising with his protégé about a coronavirus pandemic. He asks how Bauer would act if something leaked from their facility and started to kill hundreds, then thousands and more.

Bauer says, 'What do you know? Is this about the vaccine they have us working on?'

Ikeda pushes, 'What would you do?'

Bauer says all the right things. First a curfew. Educate the public about how these things spread. He thinks that major cities would have to lock down entirely. He sounds naïve. Ikeda knows it would have to be entire countries. The world would move inside their homes. They would not be able to see their extended families. Hospitals would be overrun.

'The civet thing felt like a hoax, did it not?' Ikeda asks.

'I don't know. You think it was some kind of warm-up? Like a drill? We are surely more ready than most other places to deal with something like that, if there was anything to worry about.' She is trying to stay calm and reasonable but she is also paranoid. She knows that her phone was clicking before conversations but as soon as she mentioned it, it stopped.

Haruto Ikeda nods. The three of them drink tea. Kimiko is on edge. She doesn't trust Dr Bauer. Not because of anything he has done but because she doesn't know who to trust anymore.

And she hates that.

Because she is a positive person. She always has been. She believes that knowledge is power and that people are the answer. That the tonic to the inhumanity of the world is compassion and understanding.

Kimiko watches her husband feel his way around, poking and prodding Bauer to see what he knows and where his allegiances are and how much the death of his father affected him. That was an accident. It wasn't a precursor to the release of the actual virus; these things can just happen. Bad luck. Shitty timing. The labs are sterile. The doors and the airflow mean that a virus stays inside. But that is also where the technicians are and occasionally they will pick things up.

It seems to her that Bauer feels responsible for his father's death. He's grieving still. He is sad but there is also an anger there. And even if it is aimed at the right people or it's at his own stupidity, anger leads to mistakes. She doesn't want Haruto to make one and trust too soon.

So they talk. They drink tea. Her husband looks dishevelled, but his mind is still working. Kimiko watches. She is alert. She allows her husband his hypothetical questions. She listens to Bauer's answers. And, when the time comes, she shakes her head for her husband to desist.

When Haruto starts repeating, 'No more doubt. No more fear,' Kimiko takes it as her cue to get Bauer out.

'He's feverish,' she tells him. 'Was like this in the night.' She lies. She stands up, and Bauer follows her lead. She holds out a hand as though guiding the doctor out of the lounge and towards the door. 'Thank you for coming to visit. That was very kind. He just needs a couple of days' rest. I'll get him to message you when he feels a little more up to it.'

Bauer is perfectly courteous, like carbon monoxide – you can't see it or smell it but you know it's not good. He thanks Kimiko for the tea and bids her a fond farewell. She goes back into the lounge, expecting to see her husband rocking back and forth, repeating the same expression over and over, but he is perfectly calm and is pouring another cup of tea.

'What are you doing?' she asks.

'Having tea. Would you like one?'

'I was concerned.'

'I'm fine.'

'You were talking gibberish.'

'You gave me a look.'

'A look?'

'You shook your head.'

'He seems very nice, Haruto. I'm just not sure we have to divulge everything. I know you feel that you need help, but you are still not sure that you will go through with it. No sense in causing yourself trouble, you know? I worry about you. Who knows who is listening?'

He tells her that he feels better. That he has managed to keep the soup down. But that he's not quite ready to go back to work.

'If this goes how I expect it to, I'm a couple of days away from the headache. Then everything changes.'

Because the key to unlocking kindness is to first experience pain.

THE BULLET

The former chancellor is found dead in a hotel room. Fresh from celebrating a lucrative tell-all book deal, Warren drank enough champagne to wobble a rhino before throwing a handful of powder up his nose and heading back to his suite for a quick release before returning to the bar.

He got himself into a bit of trouble. When a staff member was sent in to look for him, they found the bathroom door was heavy to move. Warren was on the other side, hanging with a leather belt around his neck and his dick in his hand.

'That kind of thing really requires a chaperone,' Jackson says when he finds out. And he laughs. He refers to it as a 'stroke and choke'.

The disgraced Warren humiliated himself even further. Drink-driving to autoerotic asphyxiation in the space of a week. But the book will still come out, now with a hefty comical footnote, and his family will at least benefit financially from his sexual deviancy.

It's a problem within the current government. This peculiar perversion. This idea that they can't be touched. That they can get away with anything. That they will keep pushing and pushing until they find where things break.

Drink-driving. Infidelity. Sexual fetishes. Offshore accounts. Second homes. Millions in capital gains. Pennies in tax. Suspicious expenses claims. If you were writing a fictional story about their exploits, it would come across as unrealistically ludicrous. Yet here they are in all their tarnished glory, parading their indiscretions like a badge of honour, waiting to be chastised but instead being forgiven.

Except, it isn't really forgiveness.

And that is the problem.

The worst thing is that the public don't even bat an eyelid. They elected these playboys and they should hold them accountable for the reprehensible things that they do. They don't hear about a man fired from a prominent position, going on a binge and accidentally strangling himself while aiming for heightened sexual gratification as a sad incident. They don't feel it is concerning. They don't want to know whether something triggered this behaviour.

It's not their problem. It's not their issue.

The idiot died from a stroke and choke.

There's no compassion.

There does not seem to be a vaccine for the epidemic of apathy.

It could take something catastrophic to teach these men a lesson.

In the late 1800s, Allen Bresling of Livingston, New Jersey broke things off with his girlfriend. She was so affected by the decision, so devastated, that she ended up taking her own life. Her brother, in a fit of rage, loaded a gun and went looking for Allen in order to exact some revenge.

When he found Allen, he shot at him but missed; the bullet lodged itself into a tree near Allen's head. And the brother turned himself in to the police before he did something he would end up regretting forever.

Allen moved on with his life and, twenty years later, wanted to take down a tree near his house. The very same tree that had saved him all those years ago. It was proving too difficult with a saw so he used a small stick of dynamite to fell the thing.

The pressure from the explosion dislodged the bullet, which shot out of the tree and went straight through Allen Bresling's skull.

The bullet that was shot at him two decades before eventually killed Allen Bresling.

The current government took power eleven years ago, and they helped to appoint Haruto Ikeda to the Wuxi Institute of Virology six years later.

He is the bullet.

All that's needed now is the dynamite.

OVERCOME WITH EMPATHY

It was only three days but Haruto Ikeda is six pounds lighter. He is eating again, though, and keeping it down. And his temperature has levelled off. He's no longer sweating through the nights, but the cough does remain. He covers his mouth at home but he won't on the streets or the train into work.

Everything is going to plan, so far. He didn't die. But he is still wavering over the ethical dilemma of releasing his grown-in-a-laboratory virus.

Until he gets the headache.

This is the next phase after the sickness.

The unbearable, crippling migraine.

It happens in his office when he arrives at the institute. His brain begins to throb inside his skull. Then his vision blurs. He can see a crack of light with all the colours of the spectrum as the sensation of his skull splitting in two begins to manifest. He thinks he might throw up. He's been sick enough over the last few days so chooses to drink from his bottle of water and shut his eyes.

It doesn't help.

He's been sitting in the dark for forty minutes.

'Are you sure you should be back already?' Bauer arrives, right on time, at Ikeda's office door. It's as though he always knows where Ikeda will be.

Ikeda doesn't answer.

'Dr Ikeda, are you okay? Do you need anything?'

'Leave the lights off, please,' he calls out.

Bauer does as he is asked.

'I could get you some sumatriptan.' Bauer recognises the symptoms of a migraine.

'No, no. It's fine. It's not that. It will pass.'

Ikeda is confident because he designed the virus in this way. Sumatriptan narrows the blood vessels in the brain. It does not work in the same way as painkillers like paracetamol, which a person would use for a regular headache. And that is the plan. The virus mimics the symptoms of a migraine, but it is not a migraine. So Sumatriptan would be useless.

It would do nothing but allow the virus to take hold. And the virus has to take hold for the person has to experience the necessary pain.

Then, what follows, is the uncontrollable emotion of feeling the pain of others.

Absolute compassion.

That's what Ikeda is waiting for. That is why he is enduring this.

He waits.

And Bauer watches.

Like Ikeda said, it eventually passes. At first, there is a sense of relief. He asks Dr Bauer to flip the switch on his desk lamp. When he sees the concern on the young doctor's face, Ikeda is overcome with empathy. Ikeda feels opened up. More aware. He understands that Bauer has recently lost his father, that he probably blames himself and that he probably looks at Ikeda as some kind of paternal substitute. And that he may have been overly worried that Ikeda, too, would fall too sick to recover, that he would also be lost.

Ikeda comforts the young doctor. He reassures him that he feels fine. That he is more than ready to go to work. That he is not going anywhere. And then Ikeda searches the deepest recesses of his mind to look for a reason not to encourage the world to feel the same as he does, right now. And he concludes that it would, in fact, be ethically remiss of him not to infect as much of this planet as humanly possible.

A SIDE ORDER OF CHARITABLE DONATIONS

Dr Ikeda works late on Friday. He wants to be the last one in the labs.

He has two tasks. First, he has to kill Tau: the virulent strain of coronavirus found in the bats that was discovered in that mine – the one they expect to be released, whoever *they* are. This requires high-pressure steaming for thirty minutes to decontaminate glassware and utensils used in examining and developing the deadly virus. Luckily, the bats were destroyed once cell samples had been taken. It would be difficult for Ikeda to dispose of the animals with the levels of compassion he is currently experiencing.

His second task is to leak his own virus.

The one that will save the world.

It has to escape the Wuxi Institute. The building is only twenty minutes from the market. The civet incident may have been a political stunt of some kind, but Haruto and Kimiko Ikeda plan to use it to their advantage. They will take their weekly jaunt for food and medication, and their virus will spread around octopus tanks and livestock pens, water and ice and blood.

Pet myna birds and vipers will come with a dash of future kindness.

Fancy a snack on hedgehog? You may be volunteering at a homeless shelter by the end of the week.

Freshly slaughtered marmot? Delicious. And will go well with a side order of charitable donations.

It's going to work. He knows it. Ikeda feels buoyant as he exits the building. It's the perfect plan. The Western world will blame the 'wet markets' and they will undoubtedly pin it on overspill from bats or pangolins because they know it has happened before.

Misinformation will spread faster than the virus. Somebody will blame the Wuxi Institute. They will bring up the civets incident. They will drag Dr Ikeda's name into it. And they will look like conspiracy-theory nuts.

But they will end up discarding themselves from any debate because a leak from the institute is not outrageous enough to attract attention.

When your own government acts in such ridiculous ways and gets away with it, a conspiracy theory has to be even more outrageous to attract any attention. Suggesting a leak from the institute is almost too plausible to be a consideration.

Ikeda isn't worried about that.

He can play along. He can be the face of whatever name some political marketing guru creates for the virus. He can get on television and advise the best course of action. People will get ill. And then they will get nice.

He can fuel some fires. Talk about some of the diseases that are being studied at the Wuxi Institute. African swine fever, bovine ephemeral fever, rinderpest virus, rift valley fever. He can baffle people with long words to stop them paying attention.

Porcine polioencephalomyelitis.

Vesicular exanthema.

He can suggest the migraine medication that will have zero impact but will allow people to let the pain wash over them and spark their kindness.

He can sit back and watch the effects, and never have to tell anybody that it was him who saved the world.

It's perfect.

How could anybody be against kindness?

A CHEMICAL INCIDENT

In 1995, millions of commuters bundled onto trains in Tokyo, unaware that the Aum Shinrikyo cult had placed five bags of sarin – a Nazi-developed nerve agent – on certain carriages. Commuters knew nothing of the attack until they started choking, vomiting, or were blinded or paralysed.

The cult was something to do with truth and doomsday, and whatever else their leader could concoct. It was an atrocity, but it is also a good model for Haruto Ikeda to heed.

Ikeda does not have the luxury of hundreds of disciples who are willing to commit crimes for him or follow him into the abyss of creating a chemical incident, so he has to do it himself. Two carriages per day for a week.

Many people in Wuxi wear face masks on public transport, so he does not look out of place. He cannot leave a scientific canister on a train carriage, because it would lead back to the institute, so he has had to procure his own plastic containers that he can then open and leave on the carriages.

The beauty of the CompX virus is that there are no sudden side-effects to its exposure. Nobody collapses on the trains, or the two he leaves on buses. And nobody went blind or vomited at the wildlife market where Dr Haruto Ikeda employed the only person he can trust to release the airborne virus while he contaminated the waters where the fish were being kept and sold.

It doesn't feel like a lot. It's not like having an explosion at the institute with poisonous gases being released into the atmosphere. And it's not like he found a way to taint the city's main water supply, because that would be too ferocious. Too loud. And the Ikedas are both quiet. Thoughtful. Precise. Kind.

This is the perfect way for them to disrupt the entire world.

THEY EAT DOGS

'They eat dogs.'
Seven of the most powerful leaders and influential political minds in the Western world are, once again, sitting in a room together, this time in Maryland. This is not a publicised event. It's not a summit. Nobody knows about it.

They can't.

Millions of people are going to die, but that is not their concern – the vaccine has been developed alongside the contagion. That's how it's done. That's the best way to make money, to control the people. The companies that create sicknesses are the same ones who sell the cures. Sure, there will be deaths but there are clear benefits for the countries represented around the room.

The world is overpopulated, anyway.

Pile them up in the streets.

Give us our contracts, our wars, your votes.

It is an intricate balance of policy and purposely-leaked-to-the-mainstream-media misinformation and theatre and misdirection. And the buffoon pontificating in the centre of the room thinks he has a genius idea of how to cover up the early leak from the research facility and, essentially, blame China for the outbreak.

He is the UK prime minister. And he wouldn't know a genius idea if it stuck a dry thumb up his arse.

'What do we know about the Chinese?'

Samsung TV screens. Apple phones. Google phones. Each of the middle-aged white men comes up with three or four tech companies who have giant factories in the East. They say words like Zhejiang, Jiangsu and Shandong. They understand business.

'Not us. Not what do *we* know. The people. The plebs. What do they know?'

These statesmen fight not to roll their eyes as Harris Jackson attempts to tease them to breaking point with what he considers to be probing questions.

They talk of communism and Mao and that little red book. One mentions the size of the population. Another brings up Buddhism. It's not what Jackson is poking at. Eventually, he just has to say it. He has a reputation for 'just saying things' as they come to him, veering off message with no apparent forethought. There is no valve that can shut off the poison that drips from his idiotic brain to his blathering mouth.

'They eat dogs.'

The Russian laughs. The others do not.

Jackson doesn't react. He's unaware of anything outside of his own ego. He's a perfect politician. Besides, he's about to dazzle them all with his brilliance.

'Don't you see? If they eat dogs, they'll eat anything. Snakes. Horses...'

Here it comes.

'... Bats.' He smiles triumphantly.

It's a stupid idea, as so many of Jackson's are, but, faced with the unknown, and in a time of desperate panic, the people will swallow up a stupid idea and let it run.

And half of them will run alongside it.

So they form a plan of action. Report the virus. They will say that it sprung from a 'wet market' in China. Most likely from a bat – at least one part of the story has to be true. Warn of an escalation in the local area: people getting sick, trouble with breathing, that kind of thing. There may be some disruption to air travel in order to contain the spread.

Planning to this point has been meticulous. Research has gone well. Testing has scored highly. There was the issue with one strain that would have proved too violent and difficult to contain. The plan is not eradication. The plan is fear, control and the preservation of self-interest.

There will be casualties. Cannon fodder. Collateral damage. And this has to be at a level to scare the general public into cooperation.

People will get sick and recover.

Some will get sick and die.

It has all been plotted out.

But it has come two weeks early. And nobody in that room is asking why. Instead, they talk about how the Chinese will eat anything that moves. And Jackson is secretly relieved because his favour has been waning since his party's last big lie. At least this will take the heat off. The people will soon forget.

And the Russian is thinking about his next war, who he can bomb, how he could gas an entire country. And the American is thinking about the next election. And they all agree to go with the stupid bat-meat story because they think the electorate are idiots with a twelve-second attention span and believe it's science fiction that they are being listened to on their phones. Some of them still even believe in God.

And these people would rather be outraged than thankful. They revel in conspiracy over facts. It's more difficult to be kind than malicious. It's the reason that tragedy is more unifying than good fortune. Each country will come together for a time, a chunk will die off, and the remainder will split in half, once more.

That's the plan. At least, it was the plan for two weeks' time. But these powerful men toast their success prematurely and slap one-another on the back, and not one of them asks why such diligent preparation would result in early contamination. They are too focussed on how to spin what looks like a mistake. It's a fault of those in positions of power; they think they have complete control over everything in their domain.

But this is not an error.

And it's not their virus.

THE
SECOND
SCOURGE

WE KNEW IT WAS COMING

Amurder of crows.
A parliament of owls.

And, it seems, a 'cluster' of patients.

The news reported that a 'cluster of patients in the Jiangsu region of China, in the city of Wuxi, has been admitted to hospital with pneumonia-like symptoms – fever and shortness of breath. The response to standard treatments has not been promising. So far, the causes are unknown'.

The incident is being closely monitored.

Three days later, there are around forty cases. Many of which seem to be connected to Wuxi's wildlife market: 'There are fears in China of another SARS-type outbreak like the one experienced in the early part of the new century.'

This is only how it is reported in the West.

It is the week before Christmas and a Cabinet Office Briefing Room meeting is called. (Affectionately known as a COBRA meeting.) A special committee meets to discuss how overseas events such as a large-scale epidemic may have implications for the UK.

The prime minister does not attend.

He doesn't, actually, have to. It is a misconception that he has to personally oversee these discussions. But, today, he couldn't go, even if he wanted to, because he is currently in a more secret location, explaining to a select group of leaders that, in China, 'they eat dogs'.

The other men in the room are annoyed that Jackson went at things alone and planted the civet story, but it seems to have worked out for them because the virus has leaked two weeks before schedule and they need to act immediately to spin this in the right way.

And they can't be that mad because each of them has their own secrets. Each has a side hustle. Each member has their own self-interest as well as that of the group.

'Look, it's out. We knew it was coming. We're prepared. We didn't want people dying before Christmas but that's just the way it is. Let's go and enjoy the rest of the year because the next one is going to be a clusterfuck.'

A cluster of patients.

A clusterfuck of world leaders.

Jackson thinks he knows what is coming. That there will be a couple of weeks of grace while the world catches up to what is happening in Wuxi. Most of the West will have never even heard of the place. They will think it is spelled 'Wushi' until they see it written down somewhere. European countries won't understand the impact until cases start occurring in Milan and Stockholm and Berlin. It will take another week to realise that the airports need to be shut down, and by then it will be too late.

And Jackson thinks they are so ahead of the curve because they have developed the vaccine already. And it'll be another month before he starts to twig that things aren't quite right, that more people should have died. That the air is cleaner and wildlife is thriving and something different is going on. That saying the Chinese eat dogs and going at it alone with the civet story will seal his fate. That the epidemic will be the least of his problems.

But, for now, he finishes his meeting and heads back to the residence where he will be briefed on the COBRA meeting. In the car, he gives his old friend, Lord Benedict, a call and asks him how he feels about earning a shedload of money.

NOBODY HAS DIED

At home, it works. Haruto Ikeda can talk freely with his wife about what is happening in the country they currently call home. They have lived all over, from their native Japan to Rome and Hamburg. They've always had each other. And it works. At home.

But Haruto Ikeda has to go into work every day and act.

And Bauer can tell that something isn't right.

'Are you worried about the things they are saying on the news?' he asks Ikeda.

'The respiratory thing?'

'Nobody is calling it that, but yes.'

'I am keeping up to date, cautiously.'

'It's only a matter of time before they say it's some kind of overspill from here.'

'What?' Ikeda looks shocked.

'Come on, we are one of the largest virology institutes in the world. We are funded largely by the US, The West are going to say this thing came from the market, and the Chinese are going to say that it's from here and it is America's fault.'

Ikeda usually appreciates Bauer's German efficiency, but that explanation feels cold.

'Nobody has died. It could be a freak incident.'

'You know that's not the case.'

Ikeda pauses. He is wiping the work surfaces with a 10% concentration of hypochlorite – a bleach that eliminates most bacteria, fungi and destroys viruses. Bauer is immersing some of the implements used in sodium hypochlorite. It's everyday for these scientists. They understand the protocols and they follow them stringently.

But Ikeda is struggling on his own. He believes that he can trust Bauer but knows that he has to be sure before divulging anything incriminating. He assumes that Bauer is inquisitive because he is a doctor and worried because of his father's recent passing. He's a good man, he shouldn't be kept in the dark.

Ikeda, however, has an increased level of compassion and is finding it more difficult to lie.

'I know what I can see,' he says, in his usual cryptic, almost monosyllabic, manner.

'You think it could have come from animals at the wildlife market?'

'I do.'

Bauer did not think that would be Ikeda's response after the civet debacle.

'But ... I mean ... we both know what came out of that mine. That was not easy to find. Nobody is going down there for bat meat. I know ... apex predators or whatever, but...' He's not so much discussing with Ikeda as with himself. 'You think it's more likely that this thing came from a food market rather than here at the institute?'

'Why can it not be both?'

FULU HUANG IS DEAD

The virus that wasn't supposed to kill anybody, kills somebody. One of the mice has died.

Haruto Ikeda is middle-aged but he's healthy. He works for most of the day on his feet. He walks a lot. The bus travels fairly close to his home, but he always gets off a few stops before so that he can decompress and get a few extra steps into his day. He eats well. Mostly vegetarian but one of those vegetarians who also happens to eat fish. One of those people who switches themselves off from the fact that eating a piece of cod is the same as eating a chicken breast.

He doesn't eat any meat, now. Since infecting himself, he cannot abide the suffering of a single living thing. Fish. Chicken. Cow. Duck. Dog. It's going to make testing on mice an issue, but he can cross that bridge when he comes to it.

Right now, he is utterly distraught because he caused harm to a human being.

Fulu Huang was almost seventy. She was mobile but by no means sprightly. She liked sweet things. Almond pudding. Steamed pears with rock sugar. Pumpkin pancakes. And she loved her granddaughter, Ling.

They were close.

But Fulu Huang is dead. The doctors think it looks like pneumonia. She was overweight. Diabetic. Her calves were constantly swollen and her asthma was getting worse with every passing day.

People saw her as a strong, old woman because, despite her physical ailments, she wheeled her trolley around so that she could be independent, although slow. She would ride the bus. She would go to the market. But her insides betrayed her plucky exterior.

The virus wasn't designed to kill her. But kill her, it did.

For a person of average health, the virus will feel like you have a mild case of the flu. For some people, there may not be particularly dire symptoms and for others it will feel more severe. But nobody is supposed to die.

Everybody is different. And in a country like China there is the widest spread of body types. The tallest people in the world. The shortest people in the world. The US doesn't seem to want to let go of the heaviest people in the world.

Make America Healthy Again.

So, it makes sense that there will be some fallout. A high population means the possibility of more people with underlying health conditions. Respiratory difficulties. Heart problems. A quarter of the country smokes cigarettes. That could lead to complications.

Ikeda has never done anything like this before. He got into this area of study because he was good at it, it came naturally. And he could help people.

Now he's a murderer.

If he had released the virus *they* wanted him to release, he would have been a mass murderer by now. But no amount of 'collateral damage' talk or rationalisation can justify what has happened, especially when you are feeling more compassion than you ever have.

Ikeda cries and Kimiko comforts him.

IT HAS TO TRAVEL

Wen Tsou feels awful. She's not the sickly type. She doesn't earn a lot of money working at the airport lounge, so she can't really afford to have the day off. She has already had a two-day break to visit her parents in Wuxi.

Her mother cooked for her. She thinks Wen is too skinny. That she is running around on her feet all day and needs more calories. They went to the market to stock up. Wen's mother buys her fish and her herbs from Wuxi market, along with her gingko because her memory is not as good as it once was.

Wen's parents are fine. They're not showing any signs of illness. But Wen lies in her bed in her tiny apartment in Beijing, sweating and coughing. She doesn't feel hungry. She just feels exhausted.

'I'm sick.'

'Partying too hard, more like.'

'With my mother? Yeah, she's non-stop.' Wen is too tired to laugh at herself.

'I can't believe you are leaving me on my own, today, Wen.'

'I promise you, I'd be there if I could get out of bed.'

'Okay, okay. I can cover. But you owe me a real night out next week.' Wen's friend knows that she is not a liar. If anything, she has always found Wen to be too nice. She's too thoughtful. Too considerate. Too conscientious. If that's a thing.

'You're on.' Wen hangs up. She's thirsty, but the kitchen area seems so far away even though her place is so small the kitchen is almost a part of the bedroom.

Wen will be fine after a few days of rest. She won't be another statistic on the news. She won't be a part of the cluster. She is young and healthy. Her mother is right, she is thin, but it's genetic. It's not because she doesn't eat enough. She won't die from this virus.

But she will return to work before she should. And the virus will still be present in her system and communicable with all the people she comes into contact with, who will be flying to different areas of the world, transporting Ikeda's contagion and allowing it to spread widely.

And that's the point.

If a local epidemic is to become a global pandemic, it has to travel. The people who wandered around the Wuxi market, touching things, squeezing fruit, they have to go home and hug their families. They have to travel on public transport. They have to go into their schools and jobs and not know that they have been infected. And they need to get on planes and take that virus to Italy, Spain and the United Kingdom.

The only way Dr Ikeda can forgive himself about the inevitable collateral damage is if his reach extends further than Wuxi, if he can genuinely make the *world* a better place.

FREE TO DEVELOP WHATEVER THEY WANT

There is an easier way.

While most people are worried about robots that can build cars or deliver food in a restaurant, taking jobs from real people, or AI completing tasks in moments, tasks that human intelligence would complete in days or weeks or months, such as writing essays and making art, they should have, actually, been thinking smaller.

Much smaller.

As small as it can possibly get.

Nanotechnology. The manipulation of matter at a near-atomic level. It can create materials of new sizes, shapes and physical properties that will advance medicine and energy and manufacturing.

It's too small to comprehend. But Ikeda gets it. And he is not afraid of it. There is so much potential. So many ways that it can be used to advance humanity in the right way.

Many widespread food-borne diseases will come from meat, dairy or poultry. This is what Ikeda deals with on a daily basis. Nanotechnology can be used to tackle food pathogens that multiply from salmonella and campylobacter infections. Nano-based disinfectants, biocides, clothing, water filters and packaging can be used in preventative applications.

Nanotechnology can help to improve the shelf-life of fruit and vegetables and help the environment. It is already used in the construction industry, where nanoparticles are used to help bind cement and steel coatings. The word 'sustainability' is thrown around to make companies seem like they have ethical considerations but, in this case, it is true.

Machines will be able to repair themselves. Computers will be miniaturised to fit on the head of a pin. Nano-scale devices can be used in medicine to create modifications in the human body that aid diagnosis. Nanoparticles can bond with current drugs and medications to target specific organs within the body that are affected by cancer. Like all technology, it seems so far away but it's also moving so fast.

And Ikeda knows that any kind of emerging technology that can be used for good, that can help the sick or have a positive impact on the environment, can also be developed into a weapon.

It's exciting and it's frightening.

The Wuxi Institute of Virology is largely funded by the United States. They put billions into it. The billions the institute receives is more than enough to cover their work. Some of that money travels east towards Nantong, where most of the world's cutting-edge nanotechnology development takes place.

The paper trail is clean because there is a lot of collaboration and testing between the two sites. Most of the research in Nantong is focussed on manufacturing, because China houses so many of the factories for large tech and clothing companies. But they are free to develop whatever they want. Ikeda has an old college friend that works in Nantong who he regularly trades ideas with.

If they were creating something that could be used to defend their nation from attack, nobody would know. If they were working on nanotechnology that could be used to attack somebody else, that country would not know how to defend itself. It probably wouldn't even understand what was being set upon them.

If China developed something and used it to attack, it would have been funded by the US, which is no shock because they have been supplying weapons and training to their enemies for decades – Saudi Arabia, Egypt, Nigeria and the Philippines have taken weaponry and then acted in ways that undermine US interest and entangle them in unnecessary conflict. Afghanistan alone was supplied with nine billion dollars of arms between 2017 and 2021.

If Ikeda's plan to make the world care was supported by the Chinese government, he could have collaborated with those nanotech geniuses, and nobody would have seen it coming.

Instead, he has to sit on his own hands and wait.

Saving the world is a lonely business.

WAITING FOR THE HEADACHES

Another cluster at the hospital in Wuxi.

Five people are admitted with similar symptoms.

Lack of energy.

Nausea.

Hacking cough.

Shortness of breath.

Wei is forty-four. He works for Wuxi Biologics. They call themselves a 'global solutions provider'. A contract research, development and manufacturing organisation.

They make drugs.

Wei's work is precise and cerebral, but he is lean and healthy and fit. He cycles to and from work every day. And when he's not at work, he is cycling. On the road. In his garage, hooked up to his turbo machine.

He vomited in the night and kept his wife awake for an hour while he was having a coughing fit. When he tried to get up for work in the morning and collapsed on the floor, his wife took him straight to the hospital.

He will be fine.

He's just waiting for the headaches.

Ying is different. She is older. In her sixties. She works with the elderly and infirm. She loves her job. She hasn't had a day off sick in years. She is constantly on her feet, walking around all day. Picking things up off the floor, delivering meals, helping people to stand up or sit down safely.

But there has been a rasping with her breathing over the past few days. And that cough. It's not right for this time of year. She will be okay. But she won't be able to return to work for a week. Because all the people around her are vulnerable. Ying will be fine, but she can't risk passing something on.

Li Wei is obese. Both of his parents are gone. Heart failure. It hurts him that they didn't look after themselves and it's going to hurt him even more that he has followed them. He has tried every diet he can find. Low carb, low fat, Atkins, five:two, Cambridge, Slim Fast, Intermittent Fasting. They work for a few weeks and then the weight comes piling back on, often with a little more than there was before.

He's diabetic. His knees ache. His hips hurt. He thinks he is mobile because he works on his feet. He's a chef. He always says, 'Never trust a thin chef.' He was at Wuxi market over the weekend buying some of the more exotic meats for recipe ideas.

In a couple of days, he'll be a dead chef.

The fourth patient, Hao, is a kid. Asthmatic. This virus is no good for anybody with underlying breathing difficulties. Dr Ikeda would never forgive himself if he knew that his virus hurt a child. But he is lucky on this occasion, the kid will be fine. Some discomfort. A dose of steroids. And an inhaler in his pocket, just in case.

The fifth guy is also young. Yi Quianxi. Late twenties. An entrepreneur. And a real asshole. He's got money. He eats the right food. He takes care of his body. He parties. Drinks a little. Takes drugs. Fucks anything that moves. He thinks you have to be a prick in order to be successful in business.

He is not a good person. It's almost a shame that he is one that gets to live, but contracting Ikeda's mutated virus means that he, at least, has the opportunity to change.

Quianxi designed a yearly planner that could be customised week by week on a home computer to keep tasks streamlined and efficient. He did this at sixteen and sold it on Etsy for $15. He sold the same product over fifty thousand times that year. So he changed a couple of things and did it again the year after. And the year after that. By the time he went to college, he'd already earned his first couple of million.

Then he developed an app.

Now he is using AI to enhance things even further and is investing in hardware to create a device that will act as a companion to a mobile phone. A concierge of sorts. And he will tread on anyone who tries to get in his way.

But he's in hospital. He wasn't feeling great. That has subsided, but he has a skull-shattering migraine, and the medication that the nurses have given him does not seem to be touching the pain.

It hurts.

He feels awful.

When the pain in his head finally dissipates, Yi cries. He can't remember the last time he did that. He saw it as a weakness. He felt that he had to condition himself to be a certain way if he was going to be successful in business. He had to become somebody that he wasn't.

Emotionless and driven. He would betray anyone to get ahead. It was about his success. It was about self-gain. He didn't want to create a product that would make the world a better place, he created something that would make *his* world a better place.

Materially rich.

Morally bankrupt.

Yi feels guilty. He feels everything. He swore at his nurse when his head was pounding, when the drugs didn't work. Who the hell is he to do that? He doesn't know how he can repay her. The only thing he has is money. So, he looks up how much a nurse might earn a year in China and, when she comes back, he uses Alipay to give her 260,000 yuan to say sorry.

It's not good enough, though. He knows that. But he is new to this. He doesn't know what it is to care about somebody else. It is going to wash over him in an overwhelming way.

For now, he sits in his hospital bed like a terminally ill patient who runs through the list of their life's regrets before the end, only he has the benefit of youth. He has the opportunity to make good on those regrets. It may be a slow process but it begins now.

Yi Quianxi, the millennial maestro. There is a compulsion for benevolence building within him. He wants to help. He wants to pay it forward. Not to make up for the things that he has done. Not because the act of kindness will make him feel good. Because it is right. Because, for some reason, he now believes that it is how the world should work.

He hasn't been himself for a long time.

Now he can be a better version of the Yi he didn't even know he had lost.

Ikeda didn't have the luxury of time to test his virus. He knows it works in theory but he cannot fathom the impact. Perhaps, the worse a person is, the more it hurts, and the more compassionate they will become.

The only certainty in Ikeda's mind is that, from this moment, the world can only become kinder.

MAYBE EVEN BECOME FRIENDS

Henry Dunning is a bully. He picks on kids that are smaller than he is, which means he can pick on just about anybody. But he doesn't. He likes to be sure that he can overpower them. He likes it to be easy.

He doesn't want to make too much effort. Not with his studies, and certainly not with his lifetime of terrorising those he considers to be weak.

He's had his comeuppance several times. Josh Hinckley had enough of Dunning ruffling his hair every morning and putting him in a headlock, and the kid just starting swinging. It was luck more than judgement, but he caught Dunning sweet on the side of the chin a couple of times and dropped the big guy. The kicks to the ribs when Dunning hit the floor didn't really hurt that much, and Josh Hinckley was probably lucky that a teacher came along in time.

Dunning simply moved on after that. He found someone else that was smaller and scared of him. And he pushed him around all through junior high but Danny Aiken wasn't the type to blow up. He wasn't the kind of kid who lost his temper and lashed out. He even tried to talk it out, knowing that bullies often feel more insecure than the person they are victimising. In the back of his mind, Danny thought that his persecutor might even have a thing for him and he just didn't know how to deal with it.

But even the most mild-mannered kid in Cooper, Texas, has his breaking point.

He's had three days of freedom this week, though, because Henry Dunning has been off sick with some kind of virus. In fact, he's at home right now crying like a little baby to his mother about all the shit he has dished out over the years to other kids. He's apologising for putting her and his father through visits to the school on the back of his bad behaviour.

Dunning wants to get in contact with Josh Hinckley to apologise. Damn it, he's a big guy, there are other bullies in the school, he could be a protector rather than a tormentor. He's had it wrong all this time.

The truth is, Dunning doesn't even really know why he does it. Boredom, maybe. He's not that bright. It could be that. He's not in the closet. He doesn't have a tiny dick. It must have come from somewhere but it would require some professional unpacking to discover.

He's wrestling with it. The kid is nearly fifteen and he is trying to examine his life and his purpose. He is overcome with compassion. He doesn't feel sick anymore. He could have gone into school today but, mentally, he is struggling. He just wants to make things right. He wants to do some good. He wants to see Danny Aiken and not take his lunch money or push in front of him in the queue or nudge him into his locker.

He wants to apologise. He wants to do more than apologise. He wants to be kind. Maybe even become friends. There's an opportunity to not only make things right, but make things better.

Danny Aiken also wants an end to this, of course. And he should have enjoyed his week at school with Henry Dunning at home. He should have felt more free, more relaxed, but he has been on edge for three days. Because last Friday, Danny finally snapped. And all week, he has been carrying his father's pistol into school so that he can end this cycle of suffering.

Kindness can be enough.

But it can also come too late.

IT'S SPREADING

Grapeshot. That's what it's called. A few iron balls fired from a cannon at the same time. One might hit the target but the rest are scattered around the area in an undetermined pattern. It can be seen with crop circles. One large circle or fractal design within a field of oilseed rape and three smaller circles on the outside, seemingly sporadic and random.

That's what happens with the virus.

Wuxi is the epicentre.

Ground zero.

Suddenly, clusters of cases start to appear in neighbouring regions. On the news, they show a map of eastern China, then they zoom in on the Jiangsu province. Wuxi is a mass of red, and there are smaller orange blotches dotted around the region.

Grapeshot.

It's spreading.

It's only been a week.

The social-media machine in the West is in full swing, too. People are worried about SARS. Reports suggest that this as yet unidentified virus may have originated at the Wuxi Wildlife Market. But they are not calling it that. Someone referred to it as a 'wet market'. It got hash-tagged.

#WuxiWetMarket.

One source mentioned bats. Another harked back to the situation with civets from a few weeks before. A parody account speculated that it came from meerkats just so they could get #WuxiWetMeerkat trending.

It's another few days before a comment appears about the Wuxi Institute of Virology, but very few people take notice. It's not sensational enough. Where's the story in that?

In the UK, the country is so divided, the best way to pull people together is through fear and tragedy. Failing that, it's always good practice to find a common enemy. So they go to town on the 'wet' market.

Raw meat. Wet.

Live fish. Wet.

Exotic flesh. Wet.

Wet wet wet.

The tabloids use the word so much, it conjures an idea of dirtiness. Of weird animals used in soups and stews. They find pictures of dog meat and deep-fried chicken feet and they relentlessly plug the idea of a wet market.

It's all a part of the plan. So that when this disease finally reaches the UK shores, it is greeted with all the vitriol that is usually saved for asylum seekers.

The prime minister has seen that cases are showing up across Europe but that Valencia has been hit the worst. He knows it is only a matter of time before it arrives on his island. Until that moment, he wants to continue the smear campaign against China. He can galvanise his people by having somebody to blame.

Harris Jackson, actually, thinks his plan is working. And why wouldn't he? The virus may have leaked a couple of weeks earlier than expected but it is still doing exactly what was anticipated. Perhaps at a slower rate, but he's not worried.

Soon enough, there will be an onslaught on the National Health Service and Jackson will come to the country's rescue, and people will forget all his bad decisions and infidelities and broken promises.

That's the plan.

Jackson is powerful and he knows it. He runs the sixth-largest economy in the world, which is backed up by the largest. He's charmed. Privileged. And, as such, he has been getting away with things his entire life. He has coasted along with entitlement and abandon, and it has made him feel invincible. He is so filled to the brim with self-importance that it doesn't even cross his mind that the Chinese will do anything other than sit back and allow him to hurl fault to the east. He thinks that he can say whatever he wants, and whoever is in his way will just lie down and take it.

There are lines within his marriage that Harris has stepped over, but he has somehow come back from crossing them. And there are lines he has crossed with the people who voted him in to power, and for some reason, he has, again, been forgiven. But there is a line that runs through Greenwich. It's a line that separates the west from the east. It's a different kind of line.

Harris Jackson is powerful, that part is true, but he also has to be careful where he steps. He probably thinks he could get away with murder, but he'll never get away with sixty million.

DEAF EARS

He only goes by one name. Leon. Like Prince.

Or Bono.

Or Liberace.

He calls one of his girls in. She is scared. Ready for the usual, 'Where's my fucking money?' that he usually throws her way. But not today.

Leon doesn't want to exploit these women anymore. He doesn't want to profit from them selling their bodies and compartmentalising their souls.

There's no sick pay when you're a self-employed pimp, so Leon has been collecting money and standing out on cold street corners while trying to look tough as he blows his nose or sniffs or coughs. He has felt like shit for days.

And then he didn't. It was just the headache.

And then he felt shit again, but not in the same way. He decided that he just couldn't do this anymore. He couldn't beat people. He couldn't exploit women. If anything, he had to find a way to protect them.

He's not stupid. He knows that people are always going to pay for sex, whether they want to be held or choked. Whether they want somebody to do all the work and make them feel special, needed, wanted, or they want it rough because they need to feel like they are taking control of one part of their life. Whether they want to be tickled with a feather or rubbed with a cheese grater, or paraded around the room like a dog while getting peed on. It's going to happen.

He can't stop that.

But he can help the women that he has been pimping by no longer taking his cut. He can allow them to still use his name so that nobody else tries to pinch them and take their twenty-five percent. He can't get them all out of the game. Some of them don't even want to leave.

Sure, he can encourage, he can point them in the right direction, he can try to inspire them with the story of how he is finally following his dream and training to become a pastry chef. But it would fall on deaf ears. And, even though he wants to do the right thing, there is only so far his new-found compassion can take him.

Not everybody can take their kindness and use it to find a cure for malaria or find homes for the homeless. For some, kindness has to be small but that does not mean it is inconsequential. Every act of compassion has the power and opportunity to be paid forward, to be harnessed as an energy, a catalyst for change.

The virus is spreading, indiscriminately. Eventually it will hit the rich and influential, there is no way around that. And they have the reach and the resources to make instant and significant impact. One person could affect millions. But a million Leons, altering their ways and becoming a force for good has its place, too. It has its purpose.

Everyone who chooses kindness counts.

It will build.

WE SUGGEST SUMATRIPTAN

The Chinese government are not at a point where they feel they need to encourage curfews or lock down certain areas. It has only been a week. It has to be the right message; not the same as the West.

At this point, the minister of the national health commission is content with stemming the flow of the contagion by instructing people to wear a face mask on public transport, as this seems the most likely cause of dispersion. Many people already do this.

It is not necessary to close airports or train stations or shut off the buses. They need to examine the numbers and they need to reassure citizens that this is not another SARS outbreak. And, for that, the health commission needs Dr Haruto Ikeda.

The citizens need an expert to tell them not to worry.

Unlike the UK, where anyone with a vague grasp of Google is, apparently, an expert on any subject, Ikeda's opinion is something to respect in his adopted home.

'A press conference? I've seen preliminary data. Isn't it a little early to go out with something? It could create panic. There's nothing to suggest that it's deadly.' His heart aches for all those who have already lost their lives to his crusade. 'It seems to be those with an underlying condition that are most at risk of more severe symptoms.'

'And that's exactly what you need to say. Nobody is asking you to lie or protect the work of this institute. Be honest.'

Ikeda has never seen this man before, but he is dressed smartly and has an institute ID clipped to his suit jacket. He looks official. He's talking as though he is important. And he's not trying to make Ikeda say anything that he doesn't want to.

'People need to be reassured, and you are the best person to do that.' He smiles at Ikeda.

'I don't love being on camera. Could I write a statement instead?'

'The message needs to get out there and people are more visual now. This is how they consume their information. You can keep it short. Stick to the facts, what we know. Stay away from mentioning anything to do with the market. Just say it how you said it to me, okay?'

Ikeda agrees, even though he wants the virus to spread. So, he decides to keep things non-specific. He mentions face masks – many people wear them in the larger cities due to air pollution, anyway – but he doesn't mention any of the deaths, only that those with underlying respiratory conditions should be extra vigilant.

He stays on script.

Until the end.

'Symptoms include a dry cough, nausea and lack of energy. We recommend rest and plenty of fluid. Please do not take this into your workplace or your school. In most cases, the presence of a headache signifies the end of the illness and infection period. We suggest sumatriptan, a migraine medication, which will have a better impact than paracetamol.'

Ikeda is testing himself. It seems that he can still lie despite his increased compassion if the result of that compassion outweighs the detriment of his lie.

As long as it is for the greater good.

That's what he tells himself.

There is a power in that. The kind of power a lesser man could easily get drunk on.

Bauer has been watching in the conference room along with several others from the institute. He follows Ikeda when he leaves and catches up with him in a corridor.

'What the hell was that?' Bauer calls out.

Ikeda turns around. 'What do you mean?'

'That part at the end about migraines? How do you know any of that? Someone is going to come down on you about it, you know that, right?'

'I know people at the hospital. I want to keep up to date with this thing, whatever it is.' He hates lying to Bauer. He is recently orphaned.

'Excuse me for what I'm about to say, but bullshit. You know something.'

Ikeda looks at him and doesn't say a word.

'Oh, my God, you know something about this virus.'

Again, nothing.

'You are the great Haruto Ikeda, of course you know. You're the best. Where did this thing come from, Doctor? What the hell is it?'

Haruto Ikeda doesn't want to draw any attention to their conversation. He's just given a press conference and the parasitic journalists didn't just walk away when he left the lectern. The mics aren't even switched off, yet. He takes Bauer by the arm and leads him to the side.

'I am heading home now, I have to speak with my wife. Come over for dinner. I'll tell you what I know and perhaps we can theorise over the things I don't know, at this point.'

Bauer doesn't even have time to respond before his mentor walks off in the opposite direction.

HOW TO SOUND MORE ASSERTIVE

Remy Durand doesn't lose. If you screw your secretary and your wife finds out, if she wants to take you for every penny you've got, Remy Durand is the man you want. If a prostitute falls through your glass coffee table and stops breathing, better call Remy.

He's smart. He's young. He's good-looking. And he's earned a reputation as the shrewdest, most formidable trial lawyer in Marseille, perhaps even the whole of France.

Lawyers don't have a good name, and successful lawyers are even worse. They're bulldogs. They're arrogant. They're aggressive. They only care about the case and not the person they represent. They have no morals, no sense of humour and too much ego. The stereotypes may apply to many people in that profession.

But not Remy Durand.

He's not like that.

He just doesn't lose.

Sure, he's tenacious, but he's not representing gangsters from *Le Milieu* or getting people off a murder charge, knowing that they are guilty. He just does his job well. He's disciplined. He's up every day at six so that he can run or lift weights. He eats a varied and healthy diet. He works for twelve hours and, at night, he reads or watches old black-and-white movies. Occasionally gets laid but he doesn't have the focus for a relationship.

He's a great lawyer, but that does not make him a bad person.

It doesn't mean that he cannot be better, though. His days are filled, but he could do more. He could have more compassion.

Remy Durand has contracted Ikeda's virus. He hasn't had a day off work in years and, suddenly, he was bedridden, weak and vomiting. And then that headache. What Remy imagined was a skull-splitting migraine. But he was too sick to go out and get medication, so he just rode it out.

Now he feels better.

But he also feels guilty.

Because he realises that he should do more. He works hard for his clients but he could help others. And so, like many other young, good-looking people, he records a video of himself to upload to the internet.

It's not a fitness video with his top off, though he has the body for it. It's not a book review or a recipe or a statement about his faith, though he does believe in God. He does what he is good at. He uses what he has learned.

Remy Durand has worked hundreds of cases where one side of a relationship is living with abuse of some kind, often without realising it until something awful happens. In fact, he has become something of a relationship expert. He knows how to talk to people, how to not escalate an argument.

He puts on his best suit, rests his phone against some books on his shelf, stands near his lounge window, the curtains half closed, the giant abstract painting he fell in love with a few years back that cost more than most of his furniture deliberately in shot, and he hits record.

Remy Durand introduces himself. He says things like, 'What do you say to someone who is grieving? How should you react when somebody calls you crazy? You want to define your boundaries? You want to stop people-pleasing? How do you know if you are being gaslighted and how do you respond to that?' He tells his audience of zero people that he has years of valuable experience working with people in toxic relationships, that he knows what it is to be on trial, to argue a point and know when to concede, and he looks professional and concerned and genuine.

Because he is.

Durand presses stop. He reviews the video and trims the ends to tidy it up before releasing it to the world. A world that doesn't know who he is or why he is famous in a Marseille courtroom setting. And hundreds, if not thousands, of people are uploading similar advice videos to their social-media platforms only to reach a few members of their family and random people whose algorithm points them towards such subjects.

But this is Remy Durand.

And he does not lose.

He spends the next twelve hours – a full working day – devising and recording videos.

How To Sound More Assertive.

What To Do when Somebody Is Talking over You.

How To React if Somebody Is Shouting at You.

He makes thirty videos in total and then he lets the world do its thing. He showers and eats chicken and quinoa while watching *Le Jour Se Leve.* Then he goes to bed. When he wakes up in the morning, he has 249,000 followers watching and commenting on his videos. Over the next year, this number will grow closer to six million.

Remy did not start off bad, he just got better, more compassionate.

Haruto Ikeda is not concerned with converting bad people into good people. It's about all people. It's about action. It's about making kindness real rather than a motivational poster that people quickly forget. And it looks like it might be working.

THIS IS LONDON AND THIS IS NOW

Outside Shepherd's Bush Station in West London, a couple with their ten-year-old daughter are waiting at the side of the road for the light to turn green to signify that it is safe to cross. A double-decker bus pulls out of its stop and halts halfway across the pedestrian crossing.

The mother rolls her eyes.

The father grips his daughter's hand tighter so that she doesn't try to cross without him.

The sound of a horn.

Somebody shouting.

An engine revs.

Suddenly, a short but muscular man on a moped arrives at the bus driver's window, shouting something in Polish. Then he switches to English.

'You saw me coming and you pulled out.'

The bus driver doesn't enter into it. He has long nails on his right hand that have been painted white. He tries to wave the angry courier away. This angers him even more. He gets more aggressive. Shouting. Switching between languages. Eventually, he punches the bus three times and drives off, his masculinity undermined somewhat by the moped's lack of power. The bus follows.

The little girl is scared. Her father tells her not to worry. 'It's called road rage,' he tells her, then reassures her that she is safe with him.

They cross the road and see the moped driver stomping towards a restaurant with the large box from his bike. He delivers food. The father thinks, 'No wonder he's in a shitty mood.'

And that's what passes for empathy in the English capital.

More central, in Charing Cross tube station, a woman plays the guitar and sings her heart out. She's good, too. There's talent there. Her gig bag is filling with coins as commuters and tourists pass her, enjoying her sound, dropping whatever they have into the guitar case. It's a good day for her. She doesn't necessarily do it for the money. She wants people to hear her, but the money sure helps. And it's validation, a way of measuring how much enjoyment she has provided.

But this is London and this is now.

How dare she have talent and ambition and the strength of conviction to follow her dream? Some entitled little shit should really try to ruin that for her. For a laugh. For something to do because they are bored and need constant stimulation.

The busker is partway through a haunting version of 'Fields of Gold' when a twenty-something woman walks up with a five-pound note to drop into the case. The singer nods a thank-you before closing her eyes to hit a higher note. That's when the other woman grabs the guitar bag of money and runs.

People watch.

They watch as the busker takes her guitar off her shoulder and rests it against the subway wall before giving chase.

They watch as she disappears into the crowd and heads up the escalator.

And they watch as she returns empty-handed and forlorn, only to find that, as one person ran in one direction with her money, another ran in the other with her beloved guitar.

She has nothing.

Why would somebody try to crush her dream?

This is London and this is now. Young people are not thinking of anyone else. They do not know nor understand the meaning of consequence. The disenfranchised youth are bored because there's too much that they can do, now. Too much choice. Instant gratification. Porn on tap. McDonald's deliveries. Home workouts. Movies that appear on their televisions at the same time they are released in the cinemas.

When you are told you can be whatever you want to be or can do anything that you want to do, you end up doing nothing. Becoming nothing.

There's been another teenage stabbing in Islington, a right-wing march near Westminster, and there are always bystanders. People watching. Doing nothing. Somebody there, not stepping in because they are capturing it on a mobile phone so they can upload it later, hoping to overdose on dopamine as the likes come pouring in.

And, tucked away on Downing Street, a road with steel gates and armed guards, the prime minister slaps the arse of the woman who brings him coffee to say thanks. And she doesn't know what to do because he is a powerful man and she needs the job and who would believe her, anyway? So she lets it happen.

Because this is London.

This is now.

This is just how it is.

The virus has made its way here and it could change all of that. But maybe it's too late. Maybe humanity has passed its empathetic tipping point. Maybe what it really needs is a plague, an act of God or a final warning from Mother Nature. To make way for a new beginning.

IT'S GETTING BETTER

Ikeda walks the streets.
This is Wuxi.
This is now.
And it's different.

At the bus stop, a young man in his twenties stifles a cough into a bent arm. He takes a face mask from his jacket pocket, places it over his mouth and helps an elderly lady lift her trolley onto the vehicle. It's not heavy and she's not that old. She could manage, probably. But he helps, anyway.

Ikeda is hungry. He has been busy today, and the press conference threw his routine out. The same sandwich he has every day for lunch is still sitting on his desk, so he takes a detour through the supermarket.

There are two people ahead of him in the queue. The man in front of him is buying a newspaper, banana, lychees, pomelos and beansprouts. An odd combination. Ikeda only has a sandwich and a bottle of water. The man ahead notices and gestures to let Ikeda through. Ikeda politely declines, saying, 'That's very kind but I am in no rush.'

He wants to watch.
And somebody wants to watch him watching.

In front of him is a mother with a toddler and what looks to be her weekly shopping. The child is bored or hungry and is agitated in the trolley, crying, shouting, lifting its arms up for its mother to help get out of the seat.

She talks softly to the child as she frantically packs the shopping in her bags.

'It's okay. Mummy won't be long.'

She drops a dragon fruit on the floor and the cashier rolls her eyes, flicking the button to stop the conveyor belt, ruining the flow. The man in front of Ikeda looks back at him and screws up his face. He's not annoyed like the woman behind the till, he feels for the mother, on her own, juggling everything and clearly struggling.

The kid cries louder, reaching down for its mother as she scrambles on her knees for the dropped fruit.

She emerges and the conveyor kicks back into gear.

The kid screams.

The mother starts throwing some of the heavier items on top of the lighter ones just to get everything in the bags as quickly as possible.

The child screams louder.

The conveyor belt stops.

'Cash or card?'

'Er, card,' she responds. Then, to her child, 'Nearly there, sweetie. Hold on.' She opens her purse and a handful of coins spills out onto the floor. She sighs and disappears again. Ikeda can feel her frustration. He understands how tired she is.

The man in front of Ikeda reaches a hand into his pocket, pulls out a credit card of some kind and taps it on the pay machine. It's so quick that the cashier doesn't even notice at first. It takes her a moment to realise what has happened when she sees that the receipt has started to print. She looks at the man as if to say, *Why would you do that?*

The mother stands up again and tips the coins back into her purse. She takes out her card.

'It's all paid for.'

'I'm sorry?'

The child cries.

'Your shopping has been paid for. Have a nice day.' She glances towards the man.

'Why did you pay for my shopping? You can't do that.'

Ikeda winces. He has seen benevolence backfire before. Pregnant women or elderly people seemingly insulted that another person has offered their seat on public transport. The world has become so unkind that people no longer know how to accept kindness when it is given to them.

The man speaks gently. 'Things add up. Little things pile on top of each other and become bigger things. I thought that maybe I could help and take something off the pile.' He smiles.

'But ... that is a lot of money. It's ... it's too much.'

The baby cries for attention.

'It's really not about the money. Honestly, it's fine. Please.'

There's a moment of silence. They just look at one another. After a few seconds, he nods at her, reiterating that everything is okay and that she probably should attend to her child. She thanks him again and wheels the still-crying kid outside with her trolley of free food.

'That was very nice of you,' Ikeda says. 'You do this kind of thing a lot?'

'Never in my life. I don't know, I could just feel her struggle and I wanted her to not feel that way. Maybe it helped her, maybe it didn't. But nobody was hurt from trying, right?'

Ikeda nods and smiles, and the man pays for his own shopping. He wants to ask the man if he has been ill recently. If he suffered with a migraine. If this sudden change of heart happened after his illness. But he doesn't. He can't let on what he knows, what he has done. And, deep down, he wants to believe that there were already some kind people before he infected the world.

Outside, Dr Ikeda continues to walk, eating his favourite sandwich along the way. Cars stop when they don't have to in order to allow him to cross the street. People look up from their phone screens to bid him a good day.

It's working, he thinks.

This is Wuxi.

This is now.

And it's changing.

It's getting better.

Slowly, the world is getting better.

Small acts of kindness to begin with, but that could build. Acorns, all across the world, sprouting into oak trees. Larger incidents of true compassion. A shift in humanity. Suddenly it seems possible. Ikeda doesn't know what comes next, but he's hopeful.

Political change.

Environmental impact.

Mental wellbeing.

This could be the beginning of something beautiful.

Now, he has to actively search for these changes, but it is only a matter of time before others begin to notice.

In a few short months, this same street will be shown on UK, US, Russian and German television as the people of Wuxi are ravaged by a plague. Locusts. Pestilence. A gas that melts the skin and the eyes. A scourge that will herald the end of the world.

THESE THINGS CAN SNOWBALL

It starts with something small.

Scott Russell has been home for a couple of weeks. A trip to Beijing that could have been a phone call or video meeting, but he combined it with some sightseeing with his wife, whom he adores.

Then they both got sick.

A couple of days back in Canada and she was throwing up in one bathroom while he hacked his lungs up in the spare room.

'We shouldn't have had that snake soup, Scott. It's the snake soup, I know it.'

It was nothing to do with the snake soup.

It was Ikeda's virus.

It was CompX.

The media haven't deployed their spin doctors and marketing gurus yet. They haven't given the thing a catchy name that people will remember, that they can hashtag on social media. Their focus is still on pushing the idea of the *wet market*. And it is clearly working because Scott Russell's wife immediately attributes her illness to the ingestion of an exotic animal. She forgets that it is only exotic to her. That snake soup is something of a delicacy that has been around for centuries. That she was just as likely to have picked up something from the chicken she ate as from the shark-fin steak with grated puffin penis.

'Babe, it's a sickness bug. We just need to rest for a couple of days. I've got the rest of the week off, anyway,' he said.

A couple of days later and they saw it on the news. People in China were dying of a virus.

'My God, Scott. That sounds like the thing we had.'

'So probably not the snake soup, then.'

'We don't know where they got that meat from.'

And the headaches came.

And the headaches went.

And Mrs Russell found herself at a restaurant in town, waiting to have lunch with a friend who she could tell all about her trip to the East. On her way back to her car, she passed a homeless man resting between two buildings, and cried all the way back to the house.

'Scott, we have to fix Lethbridge.'

Technically, Lethbridge is a city. When people think of Canada, they probably think of Toronto or Calgary or Edmonton, not Lethbridge. It's not really famous for anything. Maybe the Nikka Yuko Japanese Garden, which is beautiful. The viaduct is an impressive sight, but it's not worth catching a flight for. There's always Fort Whoop-Up, a replica of an old fur-trading fort from the 1800s. They celebrate things like Heritage Day and Indigenous People Day.

It's a city and it is huge, because everywhere in Canada is huge, but it feels like a small town. And the homeless problem isn't really a 'problem'.

Mrs Russell doesn't agree; it is an issue. And her husband concurs.

Because they're different now.

It isn't even that they were awful people before. They're Canadian, so they are naturally nicer than most. They don't play hockey or live on poutine or speak French, but you could bump into them on the street and they would apologise to you.

The Russells already cared but now they care with a vengeance.

Scott finds a copy of a recent Point-in-Time homeless count. It was performed in cooperation with the Streets Alive mission and found that, in the city of Lethbridge, on a certain day and a certain time, there were found to be 234 homeless people.

A couple of hundred people living on the streets in a city of over one hundred thousand.

Not even half of one percent. But that is too much for the Russells.

There are programmes within the area that offer transitional housing for those getting back on their feet. They have not been included in that figure. The youths in emergency shelters and those who have suffered domestic violence also haven't been counted. Couch surfers. Correctional facilities. That's a larger number to be added on to the two hundred or so that are perched in shop doorways, bus shelters and public parks.

Scott Russell is a titan of industry and an influencer of local government. And his wife is a steamroller when an idea takes hold. They want to use their money to build a shelter that would house half of that number. Until then, the Russells will rent a space in which to feed and speak with the less fortunate. They will pitch an initiative to their councillors to eradicate the problem of homelessness. And they are going to succeed.

It seems like a small issue in a small city, but it's a start. These things can snowball. If it catches on, it could diminish the tent cities in Toronto, Hamilton and Niagara Falls. Luckily, there were more flights out of Beijing to these places.

More people infected.

More who will want to do good.

A DOWNSIDE TO KINDNESS

Haruto Ikeda opens the door to his home, walks into the kitchen and kisses his wife.

'Kimiko, it's working.'

She holds his face in her hands and smiles back at him. 'Why would you even doubt that it would not, Haruto?'

'I see it spreading. Kindness. Gratitude. Thought for others above ourselves. Empathy. It's all there.' He goes on to tell his wife what happened in the supermarket.

'Haruto, you haven't even taken off your shoes. Go. Sort yourself. I'll make tea and then you can tell me everything.'

Ikeda does as he is told. He is like an excited child. Kimiko is pouring tea when her husband returns and sits at the table in the kitchen.

'I'm sorry for talking at you. It's ... it's just so unbelievable. Please, tell me about your day.'

She hands him a cup. 'Nothing as exciting as yours, I am sure. I had a patient with such chronic anxiety that they haven't been able to perform their work for almost seven months. But their boss has no idea. The patient emails his boss and lies about everything he's been doing, and his boss just takes him at his word. He doesn't know how much longer he can keep it up, and knowing that he will be found out at some point is making him even more anxious.'

Haruto is listening but he also wants to talk.

He doesn't have much time.

'He is definitely going to get found out.'

'He is. He's in too deep now.'

'What did you tell him?'

'That he needs to resign.'

'Will he?'

'I doubt it.'

Haruto Ikeda is confused. He wants to help the world, and he knows that his wife feels the same way. But that doesn't seem like help. She is giving advice, but what is the point if her patients do not act on it?

His new-found empathy is causing him trouble. Perhaps there is a downside to kindness that he has not considered.

'Can we set an extra place for dinner?'

'Haruto, what is going on?' She gives him one of her looks.

He tells her, quickly, about the press conference that he was made to deliver.

'Oh, Haruto, what did you do?'

'Nothing. I swear. I toed the company line. I added a little something about the headaches, the migraines. That's all. Nothing suspicious.'

'And what does that have to do with me setting an extra place for dinner?'

The doorbell rings. Haruto Ikeda stands up.

'It's Bauer. He's not stupid. He is a good man. He knows something is going on. He doesn't buy what the British and Americans are saying in the news.'

A knock at the door, this time.

'I told him to come over for dinner, so that we could discuss it.'

'Haruto, I think it's a mistake to bring anybody else in on this.' But it's too late, he is already walking out of the kitchen.

He pokes his head back around the doorway, 'Don't worry, Kimiko. I have a plan.'

A CIRCLE OF DEATH

James Ritchie is a dick. Restaurants all over the world, Michelin stars, and host of *Can't Take the Heat,* a cooking show where he whittles down a group of wannabe head chefs from twenty to one and gives them a job in whatever new venture he has boiling away.

Ritchie seemingly loves the sound of his own voice, especially when he is shouting profanities at the incompetence of some of the cooks. He comes across as an arsehole. But not as much as he does when he talks about vegetarians and vegans.

He hates them, it appears.

There is always a vegetarian option on his menus – he's not stupid – but they are the butt of his jokes on many an occasion.

He loves bacon.

He loves butter.

He thinks that we were born to consume flesh.

The winner of the last season of *Can't Take the Heat* now lives in Shanghai. Because that is where Ritchie just opened a new restaurant. It has become something of a culinary hot spot, but it is also a breeding ground for Ikeda's kindness virus.

And, right now, Ritchie is on CNN saying that he is taking meat off the menu. He can no longer contribute to the cruelty in the world. He has woken up and had an epiphany. The newscaster doesn't understand the turnaround.

And then begins the tirade.

'We have flat teeth at the backs of our mouths. That's because they are used to grind down nuts, seeds and plants. A carnivorous animal has sharp teeth and a jaw that does not move side to side to grind its food – it moves up and down to tear apart flesh.' He speaks with such conviction.

'Which is why a lion can eat a gazelle.'

'Yes. Because it is a carnivore. But we cannot take one aspect of another species and apply it to humankind just because we like the taste of bacon. Go and bite a pig now and see how that turns out. We're not built for it.'

'But isn't it just the circle of life?'

'For a lion, yes. For us, it is a circle of death. A circle of torture and death. And I want no part in it.'

The newscaster is flabbergasted.

'This is quite the U-turn for you, James. You have been vocal in the past about the absolute opposite stance.'

'A person can't realise they were wrong about something and change their mind?'

'Of course. It just seems so ... sudden. What happened?'

James Richie goes on to explain. He had been ill. 'I've seen the thing on the news. Similar symptoms to what is being reported. I wasn't too bad, just very low on energy.'

It cleared.

He got a splitting migraine. He took some medicine. Once the pain subsided, he felt overcome with grief. He is responsible for the death of so many animals just so that people can overpay for a piece of meat.

'I spent an hour scrolling through videos of pigs jumping from trucks they knew were taking them to slaughter, cows being hung up by one foot and having their throats slit open. I watched animals skinned alive and dropped into hot water, screaming. I saw cows being born and then ripped away from their mothers so that we can get the milk to make cream and butter and cheese. And I wept.'

This is a vulnerable side to the highly decorated chef that few people have ever witnessed.

And it's obvious that he means every word of it.

This is not a publicity stunt.

'I'm taking meat off the menu in all of my restaurants. While farmers and so-called ethical suppliers are out in the world killing millions of animals each day for food, we have no right to refer to ourselves as human*kind*.'

Taking a radical step like this elicits several kinds of response.

Some mock the stupidity.

Others are inspired to follow suit.

And somewhere in between, there are those who believe it is a way to divert the public's attention away from something more important that is happening. These are the kinds of people who are mistrusting of their governments, who are labelled as crazy or conspiracy theorists.

Some of them are crazy.

Many of them are wrong. They don't realise they are sheep.

Then there are the kinds of people who like to ask questions before they follow the majority.

The same sorts of people who would refuse to take a dignity pill even when there appears to be proof of a devastating chemical weapon heading for their country. And just because you make them more kind, it doesn't always mean that you can make them trust.

And just because you make them more kind, doesn't mean that you make them less stupid.

VIRUS-INDUCED HUMANITY

'Come in, Dr Bauer. I'm so glad that you could make it.'

Bauer wipes his shoes on the mat outside, takes them off and steps into the Ikeda residence. He has been here before, when he visited Haruto during his sickness. It's the only reason Kimiko is allowing this to play out. She takes her husband's word that his associate is genuine and worthy of their trust, but she is also wary. Haruto is an idealist. He sees the world differently from most people. It is a better place in his mind.

If there is one person who does not need a virus that makes them more kind and compassionate, it is Haruto Ikeda.

'Thank you for inviting me,' Bauer responds. He seems genuine.

'Come through. My wife is just making the dinner. Would you like something to drink?'

'Yes, thank you. I'll have whatever you are having.'

'Did you drive? We are having red wine.'

'No, I took the train.'

'Perfect. Follow me.'

The colleagues walk down the hall and into the living area. Kimiko has laid three places at the small dining table. There is a slight tension. Bauer is there to enjoy the hospitality but he is also there to hear what Haruto has to say, why he spoke about the headaches at the press conference, where he is getting his information from regarding patients who are showing symptoms of the rapidly spreading virus.

Haruto tells Bauer to take a seat and that he will be right out with drinks.

In the kitchen, his wife has already opened a bottle of Beaujolais, because it is light and sits well with Chinese food.

'What are you doing?' she asks, stirring something in a pan.

Haruto is emptying a powder into one of the wine glasses.

'Would it sit better with you if I said it was crushed magnesium?'

She gives him another one of her looks.

The ethics of kindness is a particularly grey area, it seems. The virus can be considered a success if a world-class chef suddenly takes meat off his menu in order not to be a contributor to animal cruelty. It's also a success when the miserly, wealthy entrepreneur decides to donate his money to a worthy cause. It's a success on a more grass-roots level when somebody holds a door open for another person, or aids the elderly across a busy road, or carries shopping for a single parent or reaches for something off a high shelf in the supermarket for someone.

But what if someone believes that they are doing a kind deed but there are minor negative side effects? Is collateral damage an acceptable part of success? What if the person is certain the world will be a better place if the population is given a boost of artificial compassion, some virus-induced humanity?

What if Dr Haruto Ikeda truly believes that it is best if his colleague is mildly sedated before he drops his potentially world-altering plan on him? What if the good doctor feels it is an act of kindness in itself to have Bauer in a state of ease before he confesses to releasing a contagion on purpose?

What if the bad guys truly believe that they are doing good?

Does Lex Luthor believe the world would be a better place without Superman?

Did the Nazis think they were doing the right thing?

Do the Eagles really think we need another *Greatest Hits* album?

'I would have picked something with a fuller body had I known that we would be drugging our guest,' Kimiko says, under her breath. 'Not that I knew we were expecting company.' She looks away as she mutters.

Haruto stirs the unidentified powder into one of the glasses with his finger before swirling the wine in the glass to dissolve the final particles. Then he exits the kitchen.

'Here you go.' He hands the glass to Bauer. 'My wife tells me she is cooking Chinese food this evening, and that this pairs excellently. I know not to argue.' He smiles.

Bauer smiles back.

Haruto drinks.

Bauer drinks.

'It's very light,' Haruto says, hoping his German friend will be polite and agree.

'Are we going to be able to speak openly with your wife present or should we perhaps go somewhere after the meal?'

'I have no secrets from Kimiko. I wouldn't be able to. She is smarter than I will ever be and understands psychology better than anyone I have met. Drink. Relax. Eat. We can speak openly.' He prompts his guest to take another swig by doing so himself.

Bauer obliges. It shows that he has empathy.

Kimiko emerges from the kitchen with three plates. Both men stand up.

'It smells amazing, Mrs Ikeda.'

'Chilli paneer,' she responds. No *call me Kimiko*. No *get it while it's hot*.

'This really is something,' Haruto jumps in.

They all sit. Blocks of deep-fried paneer, coated in a chilli batter and sticky sauce with spring onions and green chillis scattered across the top, steaming on the table. The Ikedas use chopsticks. They have provided Bauer with both chopsticks and cutlery, but he has lived here long enough to have picked up the necessary skills to eat out.

Bauer starts to tease out the information.

'Did you know that your husband was on the television today, Mrs Ikeda?'

'Yes. I saw. Always saying more than he needs to. Quite the fan of the spotlight, it seems.' She smiles at her quip.

'Ha! Hardly,' says her husband. 'I doubt anybody was watching, anyway.'

'There's always somebody watching,' Bauer adds. 'What was all that stuff about the migraines and the medication? We haven't looked into that at the lab.' He drinks to punctuate his sentence. Making him more drowsy. More malleable.

'I have friends and associates at many of the hospitals in southern Jiangsu. I worked closely with them on a number of incidents during the SARS outbreak.'

'And they keep you abreast of ... situations?'

'Situations that involve unknown viruses, of course. Possible epidemics.'

'You think this thing is going to be another epidemic?'

'I'm hoping it will be a pandemic.'

'Hoping?'

'It has to be global.'

'Has to? What are you talking about? This killed my father, Haruto.'

'It was not this virus that killed your father, Dr Bauer.'

'And how can you be so sure of that? Because some nurse at the hospital sent you an email?'

'Because your father was already dead when I released this one.'

PAY IT FORWARD

It is working. All across the globe kindness is spreading. The larger gestures from prominent figures look like moments of madness. The world's most famous chef suddenly turning vegan seems to be a publicity stunt.

That's how it stays hidden.

Moments of madness.

Compassion and psychopathy, ironically, going hand in hand.

This is how Ikeda stays off the radar – of the secret cabal, at least.

Jackson and his cronies believe that it is their virus. That it is Tau. It's just not acting as quickly as it should. Not enough people are dying. Enough fear has been generated, though, to start pushing whichever agenda each leader feels will benefit them the most. The last thing they would want is an outpouring of warmth or generosity.

But they don't see it.

Because it happens little by little.

To the little people.

The ones they pretend to serve.

Nikki Griffin, in Wootten Bassett, Wiltshire, woke up one day and just stopped being a bitch. It sounds like nothing. But it's not. She was a gossip and a liar. She masqueraded as the perfect mother but the truth was that she couldn't handle her kids. She didn't know how to hold in her temper. And she felt so goddamned worthless because their father had cheated on her with her best friend, and the woman at number ninety-six, and the guy who delivers the UPS parcels with the nice legs.

She took that insecurity and she turned it into spite, into venom. And God help anyone who got in her way, because she was relentless in her victimisation.

But no more.

The abused would no longer be the abuser.

She is starting again. She wants to put out into the universe the things that she wants to get back. She is going to attract the people that will make her life more fulfilling, and she will help to fulfil them.

It's not a cure for malaria but it does stop another ten women from walking on eggshells, from living with caution, and they can take that new-found positive energy and pay it forward. That is how an epidemic spreads.

Martin Travis of Fort Warren, Wyoming, rules the football team with an iron fist because he thinks that's how it should be done. A coach should be a drill sergeant. It doesn't get the best out of his players. It doesn't make them respect him. The team is not that good. Even on their best day. But they're also kids. And they want to play sport and have some fun with it.

Being the coach gives Travis an identity. He is known and respected in the community. He's hard but fair, they say.

Today he is going to quit. He doesn't want to do something that he's no good at. He doesn't want to do something that makes him unhappy, that makes those kids unhappy. It doesn't sound like he is doing the world a great kindness, but he is. He's being kind to himself. In turn, that is being kind to at least five players on that team. And they can pass that on.

Marcus Butcher has stopped trolling politicians online.

Janice Dunsmore has started a food-delivery service for the elderly.

Myfanwy Freeman is using her family's wealth to start a charity in South Africa that helps impoverished communities by promoting green areas and food security.

A pop star posts, 'If you can't say something kind then don't say anything at all,' and thousands of people hit like. But that is it. There is no action.

Ikeda's virus is different.

People aren't talking about kindness or giving it a thumbs-up, they are *doing*. They are *being*. They are making a difference. But perhaps Ikeda's problem is the same as Harris Jackson's problem: it's all happening too slowly.

Too slowly to stop the gas.

THE MEASURE OF A MAN

Prime Minister Jackson calls him 'Benny'. That's his short and rather disrespectful way of addressing Lord Benedict.

'Benny,' he says loudly into the phone, 'have you seen the news in China?'

'Harris, I'm a busy man, you're going to have to be a little more specific.'

Harris Jackson bites his tongue. *Busy? I'm the goddamned prime minister of the greatest country on this planet.*

Take a breath.

'The virus. The outbreak.'

'Oh, God, yes. Is it that serious? What do you want from me?'

'It's not what I want from you. We've got a guy, Dr Ikeda, out in China. Virus expert. He's gone out to the press saying that people need to wear face masks to help prevent the spread of the disease. I mean, the horse has already bolted, but if he is suggesting it, the Chinese will do it.'

'And what does that have to do with me?'

Harris rolls his eyes. His old Etonian classmate is making it hard to earn some easy money.

'There are already indications that this will be a global situation. There are cases here. We are going to follow suit with that suggestion when the time arises.'

'And...'

More proof, if it were needed, that you don't have to be the smartest person in the room to be the wealthiest.

'We are going to need a company to supply the Personal Protective Equipment. PPE. We are going to blast those letters everywhere. PPE this and PPE that. I reckon it could be a contract worth around two hundred million.'

'Bloody hell, Harris.' Suddenly, Lord Benedict clicks. This is a language he understands. Cold, hard figures. For Benedict, the measure of a man is not the family he raises or the company he keeps, but the yacht he owns or the money in his bank account. It's how well he is treated when he walks into Coutts.

Harris doesn't say anything explicitly. 'That company may not even exist yet or it may be part of a larger organisation. I'll leave that with you, Benny. And, when the time comes, you can make your recommendation to Procurement.'

'Understood.' He doesn't say thank you.

'So how are the family?'

'Yes, yes, all good.' He doesn't want to do the small-talk thing.

'Excellent, well, maybe we should meet for a drink when this all blows over.'

'Sure, sure, Harris. On me, of course.' That's as close to thanks as Lord Benedict will stretch.

Of course.

'Ungrateful little cunt,' Harris mouths after hanging up.

'Sanctimonious prick,' says Lord Benedict.

Benedict opens a notepad and starts scribbling. *PPE. PPE. Medical Equipment. More than Medical Equipment. PPE Plus. PPE Medical.*

He scratches his head like a cartoon. He's a caricature of a foppish aristocrat.

Then he writes *PPE Mediplus.*

Perfect.

'Janice,' he calls out to his assistant. 'Get my wife on the phone, would you.'

TRYING TO SAVE THE WORLD

'**Y**ou released a virus?' Bauer is, understandably, shocked. He holds up a hand and then downs the rest of his wine. He leaves his empty hand up, as if telling them, *Don't say anything, yet*, then lifts his glass and shakes it.

Ikeda gives his wife a look, and she retreats to the kitchen for a moment before returning with the wine.

She pours.

He drinks again.

His head already feels a little light after one glass. He should not have taken it down so quickly, but he didn't know what else to do.

They sit in silence for a few seconds.

'You...' Bauer starts.

'...Released a virus,' Haruto Ikeda finishes his sentence.

Bauer looks at Kimiko, 'And you...'

'...Knew about it. Of course.'

'You're goddamned sociopaths.'

Kimiko has to bite her lip. She hates it when people assume psychopaths, sociopaths and narcissists are all the same thing. There are subtleties. It's like saying that everyone with ADHD is autistic. Or that all stand-up comedians are depressed.

Bauer stands up but feels unsteady. He wants to leave. But he can't.

'Please, Dr Bauer, sit down. I will explain. It is not a virus that is built to harm people.' Haruto holds back from saying that they are trying to save the world. It sounds so grandiose. So braggy.

Bauer sits. He drinks more wine. He doesn't know what else to do with his hands.

'We do good work at the institute. It is valuable work. We are scientists. We work with some of the smallest things on the planet, but they can have the biggest effect. But make no mistake, wherever there is good to be done, there is exploitation. And the majority of our work is leading us to create a weapon. An invisible missile that can disperse and eradicate life on a grand scale.'

Bauer listens. He doesn't take his eyes off Haruto. Kimiko finishes her paneer.

'We develop the vaccines but we are also responsible for the viruses. It is dangerous. It is thorough. You understand this, yes?'

'Of course. We have to study the disease if we are to find the cure.'

'Yes, but there are powers who would like to harness these diseases to control the population. To lead through fear. The vaccine for Tau has been scheduled. Which means that Tau has been scheduled. I don't know who is behind it and I don't care. I couldn't sit by and watch people die just so that the governments who ordered the release of a contagion could come across as saviours for dishing out a vaccine that you and I and the team developed before anybody even became sick.'

'It sounds like a wild conspiracy theory, Haruto.'

Kimiko intervenes. 'We are not talking about the moon landings or 9/11. Haruto has clearance. He has access. The vaccine is scheduled but the virus is still contained within the institute. This is pre-school mathematics. One add one is two.'

'Jesus.' Bauer stands up again, his wine in his left hand, his right hand against his head. 'This is a lot to take in. I ... I just don't understand what you have done.' He wants to leave. He needs to get out and tell somebody.

The Ikedas explain, bouncing off one another like a well-rehearsed bit. The virus acts in a similar way to what they believe was intended for the scheduled virus. This is to halt any suspicions and give their kindness virus a chance to take hold. People will get sick, but not too sick. They will get a headache, and that pain is what stimulates their uncontrollable compassion.

Bauer can't believe that Ikeda got this to work.

'I tested it on myself.'

'You what? You tested it on yourself?'

'We were on a time constraint. I saw the schedule. The Tau virus, the deadly Tau virus, was imminent.'

'I need a moment to digest this.' Bauer has so many questions. What about the people who have died as a result of this compassion contagion? How long does it last? What is the end game? What will Ikeda do when he gets found out? Has he even thought further than tomorrow?

But Bauer can't get the questions out. He's drowsy. He feels his eyelids closing. He looks at his glass of wine and can't believe that he has been duped by a couple of old Japanese scholars.

Bauer knows he is going to fall asleep. He downs the remainder of his glass of wine and lets it wash over him. He almost smiles.

'Haruto, what on Earth did you put in that man's wine?'

'It wasn't magnesium.'

'When he wakes up and realises that you drugged him, he may not keep this quiet. I'm still not sure that we have done the right thing.'

'When he wakes up, he may just think that he is not feeling very well.'

'Why would he think that?'

Dr Haruto Ikeda doesn't answer straight away, he's tending to his guest. Kimiko watches as her husband tampers with Bauer's shirt sleeve. Eventually, he turns around and she can see the needle in his right hand.

'Don't worry about Dr Bauer, Kimiko, he will be fine. He will be kind.'

IT'S A DIFFERENT MENTALITY OVER THERE

Red tourism. This is something separate from domestic or international tourism, where visitors are specifically looking to visit a location that bears some kind of significance to its communist past. It is prevalent in countries like China and Russia. Great for infection because these people live in close communities, but the reach is 'grapeshot' at best.

To make a real impact, you don't want to be hitting small villages – though that is needed – you want to hit a city like Bonn and a country like Germany.

Luckily, a quarter of a million Germans visit Beijing alone, each year. They are the number-one European visitors. Perhaps it is the Forbidden City: once off limits to the masses, it is now open to all. Or the Summer Palace. Or the Temple of Heaven. Maybe they want to compare the Bird's Nest Stadium to their own Olympic venue in Munich. Whatever the reason for their Sinophilia, the Germans are feeling the effects of Ikeda's virus on a scale that makes the world sit up and listen.

Cologne Bonn Airport shuts down. The German chancellor orders a lockdown of both Bonn – the former capital – and Berlin after thousands of people are taken ill with what appears to be a 'SARS-like virus', according to the news channel Deutsche Welle.

The rest of the country is advised to stay home and only leave for necessary activity – work, school or grocery shopping, but a face mask must be worn at all times.

The German media does not mention a wet market. They do mention Haruto Ikeda. They do reference the Wuxi Institute of Virology and the similar cases in China.

Harris Jackson is thrilled.

'Couldn't happen to a nicer bunch,' he scoffs.

Many of those around him want to say that the people who live in Germany now are not the same as those living under the Third Reich. They want to list the country's achievements since Hitler & Co. bit the bullet. They want to remind the prime minister that he is driven around in a bulletproof Mercedes when he's not in the BMW. But they don't want to say these things more than they want to keep their job or their seat at the table. So they continue to let the moronic buffoon get away with this behaviour. Some even encourage it.

'Look at their efficiency, though. The Chinese are still running around and spreading it among themselves. The Germans are almost locked down. Can you imagine if I told the country to stay in? What would they do? Riot? It's a different mentality over there.'

A few nods around the room at his casual racism.

Though Jackson rarely engages the filter between his brain and his mouth, he doesn't say everything out loud. He stops himself from mentioning two world wars and one world-cup win. And he certainly doesn't comment on his admiration for the German leader.

Instead, he throws out some predictable quip about their trains running on time and his underlings laugh along.

Keeping themselves in the room.

Retaining their power.

Ensuring that they die.

GREY IS NOT THE KINDEST COLOUR

Bauer doesn't wake up.

'This is awkward, now, Haruto.'

'He's still breathing.' Haruto finishes his wine. 'You know, this really is a quaffable grape.'

Kimiko wants to be annoyed with her husband for going behind her back with this decision. She maintains that Bauer should not be trusted, but her husband seems slightly intoxicated. She is not used to him being out of control in any way and she finds herself laughing. For anyone watching this play out from across the street, it would be difficult to understand what is going on.

'Perhaps a coffee before our guest wakes up.' She walks towards the kitchen, taking two empty plates on her way.

Haruto Ikeda sits on the single-seater and stares at his sleeping colleague. Perhaps this was not the best way to go about things. But, Haruto tells himself, if he is acting with more compassion now, then what he is doing cannot be bad.

This comforts him.

It shouldn't.

When protestors are trying to make a statement about the corruption of the oil business or the environmental impact the drilling has on our planet and they decide to don masks in the Louvre and spray paint over the *Mona Lisa*, they believe that what they are doing is right. It is just. They are giving a voice to our planet. They are fighting dishonesty and misconduct.

But they are not conducting themselves in the best way.

What does Da Vinci have to do with the production of plastics or chlorofluorocarbons?

If somebody is infected with Ikeda's kindness virus and believes, with compassion, that the elderly and infirm should not be made to suffer by prolonging their lives, is it kind of them to switch off all the life-support machines?

Grey is not the kindest colour.

Bauer stirs.

Haruto smiles. He believes he is helping.

He feels compassion towards the man on his sofa who recently lost his father. Haruto understands this because his own father has also passed. He can empathise. He sees the younger scientist as something of a protégé. He likes him. He trusts him. He doesn't want Bauer to waste his life making diseases for governments when he could be curing them for the less fortunate.

Haruto's mobile phone vibrates in his pocket. He takes it out. A text from a colleague he hasn't spoken to in some time. He doesn't work on viruses in Wuxi but further north in Nantong at a separate research facility.

Friend, it starts. *It has been a while since we last spoke, but your name keeps coming up. And not only on the news. I hope things are well with you. Let's talk?*

Haruto Ikeda does not know how to respond. What could his friend mean?

He wants to write back but feels himself falling sideways as Bauer wakes up and tips the chair that his superior is sitting in onto its side.

Kimiko comes into the lounge area from the kitchen to see Bauer standing over her husband, his shoulders raising and dropping with heavy breaths.

'Oh yes,' she says, 'that's very kind.'

IRONMAN

Haruto Ikeda's friend in Nantong is Xiang Lao. Something of a maverick in the world of nanotechnology. He is abreast of the vaccine situation because Ikeda contacted him a few months back to discuss how the use of nano carriers made up of lipid nanoparticles could aid in the success of vaccine development.

Hypothetically, of course.

Nanotechnology sounds sexy. Like it's the future. Everybody will have a suit like Ironman, one day. But it's not always that interesting.

Lao headed a team that worked on nano materials that helped with water filtration; nanotechnology can support chemical reactions to help with purification. It's cheaper and less laborious than conventional methods. Not only can this have an environmental impact but a social impact in areas where clean water is not readily available.

It's not as fun to talk about as a bulletproof suit that helps you to fly, but it is worth column inches in any newspaper.

Lao also flew to the California Institute of Technology to help test a fire-retardant aerogel that could be used in building materials – it creates a web to hold out oxygen while not releasing toxins produced through combustion. Surely everyone would love to know that their house could never burn down, but they would rather have an arc reactor and vibranium nanoparticles powering their heart than think about cellulose nano fibres and metallic molybdenum disulphide being a lightweight and durable material that can prevent fire spreading.

But Xiang Lao loves it all.

Everything is interesting to him.

That's why he gets on so well with Ikeda.

They are scientific idealists.

Two years ago, Waylon Taggart – oil magnate, steel magnate, property guru and tech venture capitalist – enquired about placing solar panels in the Sahara. He figured out how much space he would need and how many panels would be required so that he could provide the entire world with electricity.

People thought it was a nice idea but joked that he was crazy. That it wasn't serious. A stunt. Maybe some kind of tax dodge. But it wasn't. He thought it, so he said it. But it was doubtful the oil and gas companies would tolerate free power for all – and might even put a hit out on the man providing it. So nobody took him seriously.

Nobody but Xiang Lao.

He told Taggart to wait. That technology was developing so quickly that almost fifty million transistors could now fit onto something the size of a fingernail. He told Taggart that incorporating nanotechnology into solar panels could reduce the manufacturing cost but also enable them to capture sunlight and convert it to electrical energy in a more efficient and powerful way.

But not yet.

Taggart was in Nantong a few weeks ago for a meeting about the batteries used in his fledgling electric vehicle brand (he wants them smaller). He stayed one night in a hotel near the airport and, one week ago, became sick at home. Coughing. Headaches. Lack of energy. A few days later, he dropped into Lao's inbox and said he wanted to talk about the Sahara solar panel idea again.

He wants to do some good.

He wants to give something back.

No stunts.

Xiang Lao wants to help. Of course. They should talk soon. He can only imagine the furore around such a bold task. But, in a couple of days, he will be called into a meeting that would make Ironman shit the bed.

IN DEVELOPMENT

It was July 26th, 1953, and Alan Turnbull was desperate to make it in show business. He didn't care what it was, he just wanted to be a part of Tinsel Town. He'd be a show runner or he could host a gameshow. Maybe he could act – how hard could that be? But he finally broke through when he wrote the song 'Fall into My Arms'.

The song was released to great acclaim and commercial success, and, in the winter of that same year, Turnbull's pregnant wife skidded on an icy road and hit a tree, dying instantly.

In the book he released later in his life, he details the rise of his fame and fortune, stating that, after he lost everything that he held dear, he was approached and recruited by the CIA to carry out assassinations. Apparently, he fit the profile.

So, by day, he was a mild-mannered music producer who eventually remarried, but had a side gig of taking out threats to national security or people who were simply getting in the way of America's success and global dominance.

The CIA refuted these claims when the book was published, of course, but Turnbull held strong, and the book was optioned to be made into a movie but sat 'in development' until his death in 1982.

People believed Turnbull. That would be less likely today; there's too much information out there. It wasn't as accessible back then. And false information was even less accessible. He spoke with conviction and that was enough.

Things have changed.

The CIA are even more cautious and protective and secretive, but they still use the same profiling techniques when searching for possible informants or sleeper agents, or people that they can call on at a moment's notice to perform a task that may not appear on any highly redacted documentation.

Ikeda does not have the profile of JFK or Martin Luther King. There won't be a shot heard around the world. But, if he continues, if he becomes more of a threat, whichever version of Alan Turnbull is sent, they will come quietly.

No gun.

No conscience.

No dignity.

THIS IS A TRIAL

Bauer towers over Haruto Ikeda. He's 6ft 3" and German. Ikeda is 5ft 5". But it looks even more out of balance with Ikeda sitting on the floor. Ikeda does not look scared. He's more resigned. He doesn't believe that Bauer will hurt him, despite being drugged and injected.

And he's right.

The German feels disoriented. He woke up in a room that was not his own, and then something came back to him that flipped a switch. He didn't punch Ikeda, he pushed him. Not even that hard but it caused the older man to fall backward.

'You put something in my drink.'

'A light sedative.'

'What the hell were you thinking?' Bauer turns away, rubbing his face with his hand. He's angry, but Ikeda's wife is watching and she looks even smaller than her husband. Bauer understands that he will seem like an imposing presence, and, though part of him wants to throttle his boss, he doesn't want to intimidate a woman.

Bauer walks back over to Haruto and holds out a hand to help his boss back to his feet.

'You've got some explaining to do.'

'I'll make some tea,' Kimiko adds.

The men sit back at the dining table, and Haruto Ikeda explains everything to Bauer. How he found the files with the schedule for the rollout of a vaccine against a virus that was contained within the institute. How he realised what was happening because he was being pressured to have it completed by a certain date and that had not happened since the SARS outbreak.

He knew that millions would die. He didn't know why this was being sanctioned and he doesn't think it has anything to do with the Chinese government.

Ikeda knew that his priority was to get the vaccine ready. But if a virus was somehow leaked he would not sit on that information, either.

'Why would any government want to kill off millions of people?' Bauer sounds so naïve.

'I don't know. I assume for all the reasons they do anything. Money and power. Control.'

Haruto says his wife gave him an idea when she spoke to him about pain and empathy so he experimented on mice to see whether he could replicate a part of the virus but alter it so that it induced compassion within the host.

'And you got that to work?'

'In the crudest of terms, yes. A little more time and I could have come up with something better, but I had to get it out there before the awful thing they found in that cave.'

'And nobody has any idea?'

'Not yet. It replicates the symptoms of the original virus, at first.'

'Damn, Haruto, you really are the best at what you do.' Bauer wants to be mad but he can't help being impressed.

Haruto smiles, as does his wife, who has returned with tea.

'Why are you telling me all this?' Bauer asks.

'Only myself and Kimiko know anything about this. It will get out, though. Have you seen the chef who took meat off his menu because it was too cruel?' Bauer nods. 'That's the virus. There will be more. We are hoping that it will make the world a better place. More caring. More benevolent. More thoughtful. But I am paranoid, and not as much as my wife. This will upset people. I cannot affect everybody. I feel that we may have to leave Wuxi. We may have to return to Japan or even go somewhere else entirely to enjoy the rest of our days. And I don't want this information to stay with us, to die with us. I fear even a global epidemic of compassion will not be enough to reverse the corruption and apathy of this age. I need somebody that I can trust to keep this information. Perhaps even work to enhance the virus for next time. Which means I also require somebody with the necessary skills and education.'

Now Bauer understands. And, finally, so does Kimiko.

This is a trial.

Bauer has been chosen to continue the Ikedas' work.

'Wow, Haruto. That is a lot of responsibility to put on somebody's shoulders.'

'I understand. That's another reason why I drugged you.' Haruto smiles.

Bauer does not.

THE ALGORITHM IS 'OFF'

Waylon Taggart is a billionaire. He's got the yacht. He owns a football team. One of his homes is so large that it has an underground river system: he can take a boat from one wing to another without ever being seen. He's used it twice.

His latest toy is a social-media platform that he has turned into a porn-infested, bot-driven haven of hatred and filth-peddling. When he first took it over, he changed things and people left in their droves. Of course, they came back. And they moaned about it being a cesspit now. And that indignation only contributed to the cesspit feel they say they don't want.

But, recently, it has been less like that.

It has felt like old times.

People are connecting, talking about movies and books and music. There are just as many pictures of cute dogs as cute women with their tits out. People are scrolling past the videos of fights and shootings and road rage.

The algorithm is 'off'.

People are not reacting to vitriol, they are reacting to kindness.

And they are reacting *with* kindness.

A three-star chef in South Korea follows James Ritchie's example and takes fish off his menus. He says that people often choose fish over other meats because they think it is better for them or it is better for the environment or something. He tells KBS World that it's worse. That fish farming is fundamentally cruel.

Iceland's top chef does the same thing, as do two more in Brazil.

No French chef has got sick enough just yet.

Three Hollywood actors come out as Canadian and scream their support for the homelessness project pioneered in Lethbridge. They want it rolled out to other tent cities and the governor of California calls for funding to clean up LA. He says that the sight of such poverty has taken the shine off Hollywood Boulevard and is affecting tourism.

The biggest giveaway are the UK tabloid newspapers. They're not clean. The front pages are still packed with lurid puns, but inside, some of the stories actually appear to matter. It's not just celebrity affairs or break-ups or bust-ups. It's those stories that are usually saved for the end of the news, the ones that are a little twee or saccharin. They get the column inches.

There's a feeling that news doesn't just have to be bad news. Luckily, Harris Jackson only cares about the reports that are focussed on his antics or policies, so the slight shift in tack goes largely unnoticed.

If he finally does figure it out, it'll be an easy spin.

Caring is bad for your health.

Compassion makes you tired.

Sympathy gives you cancer.

All of the effort and risk that Ikeda has gone through to try to make the world a better place, and it can be gutted in moments with a thoughtless smear campaign like this.

Hate is easy.

Hate is too powerful.

It beats kindness.

But it doesn't beat hope.

A BREATH OF FRESH AIR

The Chinese, though hit first by the wave of hospital patients exhibiting symptoms of the virus, do not lock down until after the Germans.

Large cities were glowing red with high concentrations of cases. The death toll was not as high as with the SARS epidemic, but the number of people infected seemed to be larger. This was a highly communicable virus. Easily transmitted. People had to stay at home unless it was absolutely necessary to go out.

It didn't take long to notice changes to the planet once other countries jumped on board with the idea of curfews and lockdowns and grounding flights and face masks.

Firstly, the dense orb of fog that seems stuck to the atmosphere around Beijing lifts. It disappears. There is sky behind those buildings. And it is blue. It is not that pink/brown haze that hangs over the city every other day of the year.

People aren't outside in their vehicles. No planes are in the air. A skeleton rail service is operating. Keeping people at home is cleaning up the pollution. It is having an environmental impact. It is a breath of fresh air rather than the toxicity that is usually sucked into the lungs.

The same happens in Delhi.

And São Paulo.

Bangkok.

Bogota.

Exhaust fumes are non-existent. The only problem is that people cannot enjoy the fact that there are more fish in the rivers or birds signing in the trees or wildflowers in the fields because, in some countries, they are only allowed outside for food or medicine or short bursts of exercise.

This was not something that Haruto Ikeda had envisioned. He just wanted people to be nicer to one another. But this is a welcome ancillary benefit. The world has been at an environmental tipping point – maybe there is hope.

Ikeda was primarily concerned with the social tipping point, the mental tipping point, he didn't have time to consider the physical ramifications. Perhaps this will help with the hurt he feels for the deaths that have occurred.

Thousands across the world.

Too many for a man who wants to do good.

Not enough for Harris Jackson.

'What the hell is going on? This was supposed to be deadly. I was expecting ten times the level of fatalities. AT A MINIMUM.'

The Russian rolls his eyes and gives the Brazilian a look.

'It's creeping up,' says the American with his usual quiet confidence.

'Creeping up?' Jackson is agitated. 'Creeping up? Who is going to be scared by "creeping up"?' Inside, he was wondering who was going to be distracted enough by such low figures to forget that he had fucked his secretary, and an advisor, and some social climber planted by a tabloid newspaper at a party.

'Just lie,' the Russian chimes in. Smiling. Knowing.

'We don't have to lie about our figures,' the Brazilian offers, but Harris blows over it.

'What?'

'Lie. How do you say it? *Fudge* the figures. Harris, you seem to be able to say anything you want to your country, no matter how...' he wants to say *stupid*, '...testing. Tell them that five thousand people are dead. Tell them there are not enough beds. Not enough doctors and nurses.'

Harris Jackson comes across as a buffoon. A dolt who can't help but get in his own way. He says things before thinking about them. He parades around, doing what he wants, led by his libido and his position. And it's true, the only time he is the smartest person in the room is first thing in the morning when he evacuates his bowels.

But damn, that man, like all the best narcissists, can manipulate.

'It's always good to spitball ideas.' He smiles. 'But I have something better in mind.'

Harris has no issue with lying, he's made a career out of it, but figures – that kind of thing is easy to expose. If he says he's going to give half a billion more to the NHS each week, someone will know, pretty quickly, if he doesn't do that. It's simple maths. It's one column. If it doesn't add up, he's screwed.

So, he could say that ten thousand people have died and everyone needs to stay at home, but it will come out eventually that the number was wrong. And he can be forgiven for finger-banging the au pair or getting a lap dance from the home secretary or getting a blow job from a woman whose Adam's apple he didn't notice in time. But he can't lie about British people dying.

There are limits.

Hopefully.

Harris decides that he is going to tell the country that he has been infected. In fact, he won't do it – one of his staff will make a statement. They'll say that Harris Jackson has been infected and is in a critical condition but being cared for by our hardworking National Health Service.

Give them a boost.

Give them a clap.

The deputy prime minister will take control while Harris recovers. Harris can return and be the knowledgeable superhero who survived the deadly virus. He will have experience. Listen to Harris Jackson, he understands.

Harris Jackson survived.

Harris Jackson knows.

Do exactly as Harris Jackson says.

It's back on plan.

The Russian leader is starting to wish there was an easier way to terrify an entire country.

THIS IS A MOMENT

A month after the first reported death, the world has, indeed, changed.

Environmentally, the results have been greater than Ikeda could ever have imagined.

Clean air.

Cleaner water with thriving life.

And, as a result of the most well-known and accomplished chef on the planet going vegan, there has been a dramatic reduction in the consumption of meat, as several online campaigns about the benefits of cruelty-free eating have gone viral.

The difference is, where they would once show videos of animal cruelty to shock viewers, before preaching about the horrors of the dairy industry, the message is, instead, one of hope. Of positivity. And those affected by the virus pay that message forward.

There are still trolls. Small-minded individuals who don't even know why they are in opposition other than to dial into their daily outrage quota. But it's not as many. In fact, their negativity is far outweighed by optimism.

Social media has changed its face to something more naïve, something a little more pure. The way things were when it was new. When people thought it was just a way to keep in contact with old friends who had fallen out of their lives.

Bragging is down.

Humble bragging is down even further.

Talking to dead relatives and wishing them a happy birthday is still rife.

Scepticism still exists, of course. People are showing more kindness but they retain the ability to question. There are already talks of a vaccination, and many are swearing that they will not accept it. That the virus is not that deadly. That the people in power have an agenda.

It's healthy to present an opposing argument when it can be backed up with data or science or examples. Ikeda can't fix everything.

There has been a handful of porn stars who have openly quit the industry to follow their passion for teaching, woodwork or other entrepreneurial endeavours that can be funded by the money earned from having sex on screen. But pornography still exists and is still consumed.

Masturbation is kindness, it would seem.

Nobody can get close enough to the pope to infect him. It would be interesting to see what the virus would do to the man closest to God.

Right now, this is a moment. The kindness needs to spread more to become a movement. To effect real change. To be worthwhile. The Ikedas will have to disappear at some point, and it can't be for nothing.

But change is happening.

And it is everywhere.

People just don't realise where the shift came from, yet.

The education secretary returns from a bout of flu – he thinks – and tells the prime minister that they should find a way to revert to student grants rather than student loans, because nobody spending four years to obtain a degree should enter the real world with that much debt.

'How will we get them to buy their first house?'

'How will they be able to afford to start their own family?'

Harris Jackson tells the education secretary that he is out of his goddamned mind and that his illness has clearly had an effect on his brain.

It has.

Harris Jackson dismisses his now-much-kinder colleague and buzzes through to his secretary, saying that he is not feeling well and will be retreating to the residence for the rest of the day.

BEAVER FEVER

Harris Jackson has been admitted to hospital after exhibiting symptoms including fever and breathlessness. This does call into doubt his ability to handle the pandemic effectively, though sources close to the prime minister assure that the admission is merely precautionary.

A spokesperson for the Conservative Party says that Jackson has been taken to an unnamed hospital for testing and that the deputy PM will take charge for the duration of the visit, which has not been designated as an emergency.

The *Guardian* relays the facts as they have been given while also managing to question Jackson's qualification to handle the dangers of the pandemic. It then goes on to say that the pound fell against both the dollar and the euro as exchange markets become panicked at the thought of the PM being out of action.

The broadsheet also hints that sources close to the government have suggested that Jackson's condition is, actually, far more serious than is being conveyed, but Downing Street vehemently denies such claims. This all works in Jackson's favour, of course. Division is healthy for business.

One tabloid goes with the headline 'Beaver Fever', after Jackson's former secretary sells a story that the prime minister films his office rendezvouses. They say he may have gone into hiding to avoid the shame rather than actually exhibiting signs of the virus.

Meanwhile, another red top suggests that the epidemic is Labour's fault for allowing so many migrants to cross the country's borders.

Harris Jackson bids farewell to his wife and children. He is wearing a face mask and stands over two metres away from them – to keep them safe.

'It's only for a few days. Some tests, that's all. Don't believe the bloody papers, you know what they're like. You can see that I'm still standing.'

'I also know how fond you are of a camera in the bedroom.' His wife speaks under her breath and side-eyes him.

Jackson ignores her remark. 'A few days, that's all.'

The prime minister is escorted from Downing Street in a blacked-out BMW and driven south. Photographers hold their cameras up to the window, knowing that they won't get an image of anything, but they all still do it for some reason.

The vehicle is followed for a while, but those cars get lost on the motorway, and Harris Jackson ends up at some kind of safe house that only a handful of people know about. It has wine but no wifi. No phone signal either.

He will have a few days to sit and think and plot and plan, and watch the videos saved on his phone. He can sleep. Eat cheese. Drink Merlot. And, when he re-emerges, he can thank the doctors and nurses, and receive a hero's welcome back to the fray.

The man who will lead his country back to health and fortune.

PROGRESS REQUIRES SACRIFICE

Bauer knocks on Ikeda's office door, where Haruto is having his usual sandwich lunch.

'Are you busy?' Bauer asks, knowing the answer.

Ikeda has a mouthful of bread. He shakes his head and beckons his colleague inside.

'Have you seen the news today?'

Ikeda shakes his head.

'The British prime minister has been taken to hospital for testing. Imagine what could happen if he has been infected. Somehow, there are more people in England with the virus than there are in Germany.'

'They won't do as they are told,' Ikeda finally speaks. 'Have you seen them? They won't stay at home. They won't stop hugging. They are having parties.'

'I think they learn from their leader.'

Both men laugh, feeling slightly superior about the way their home countries conduct themselves.

Bauer is stuck. He has all the information that Ikeda gave him swilling about in his mind. He's reading the newspapers and going online and finding out everything he can about how the virus is performing, how it is affecting people, how it is changing the world. Do the benefits really outweigh the costs? Will it all go wrong? Should anybody be unknowingly infected, even if the outcome is something positive? But sometimes progress requires sacrifice.

It's an ethical minefield. And the Ikedas, for all their intelligence and thoughtfulness, really did not plan this assault on humanity well at all.

Bauer never asked for this responsibility. He wasn't a part of the organisation or the execution, he has just been picked to be the legacy. His father was killed by one of these viruses. There have been deaths across the world. There is no consolation for someone dying of a virus that was intended to do good.

It does not make the pill any easier to swallow.

Bauer wants to know what is supposed to happen next. He has seen some of the impacts on the environment. Politically, there are also rumblings about policy changes and despotic leaders stepping aside. The Ugandan leader took his own life after admitting ballot rigging and now his country is in the hands of a beloved pop star.

Is that part of the world really kinder now?

Bauer wants to know what they are supposed to be working on. The vaccine was developed for the virus that they found in the cave. It won't work on Ikeda's virus. If it is rolled out, someone is going to make a lot of money off an ineffective vaccine.

There's so much to consider.

So much to discuss.

But that is not why Bauer is here.

'I don't feel great. Do you mind if I take the rest of the day off?'

Ikeda told Bauer about the sedative he used to spike his wine, but he didn't mention the fact that he also injected his colleague with the virus.

Details are out in the open now.

Both men were looking for trust.

Both are still lying.

UNPLUG EARTH, THEN PLUG IT BACK IN AGAIN.

The prime minister is in a critical condition.

That's the statement.

And it works in much the same way as the virus and the vaccine were supposed to. The story of his 'critical condition' originates from the very same office that flat-out denies such a concept.

Fake news at its very best. (And worst.)

Whoever came up with the notion that *love conquers all* had clearly never encountered hate. Or misinformation. Or social media. Or stupidity. Because each of those things has the ability to crush love and compassion into dust.

One free-thinker, sitting at home in a tin-foil hat so the aliens can't read their thoughts, posts that a vaccination programme is simply a way for the government to keep tabs on us.

They could be putting anything into our bodies.

Human beings latch on to this kind of thing. Whether they are kind, poor, gay, Venezuelan, it doesn't matter, it is somehow easier to believe something that is highly improbable than something that is almost certainly possible.

People can be made to be kind, but there is nothing to say that somebody cannot be kind and stupid.

Kind and promiscuous.

Kind and drunk.

Kind and impetuous.

Kind and gullible.

Whatever the government are putting out into the media, the majority of British people believe that their prime minister, whether they like him or not, has contracted a potentially fatal disease.

And now they are scared.

If this thing can get to the man at the top of government, a protected man, then it can get to them.

There's a rush at the supermarkets.

People 'kindly' buying up more hand sanitiser than they will ever need, and packets of face masks that were 'kindly' supplied by PPE Mediplus, as the supermarkets 'kindly' raise the prices on all of these essential items.

Can a person be kind and selfish?

The problem is that kindness doesn't solve things. The human race is too far gone. As abhorrent as Jackson and his cronies' plan may have been, perhaps the best bet is to start again. To erase as much as possible and give it another go.

Unplug Earth, then plug it back in again.

Because even compassion can be spun into something negative.

In Lethbridge, Canada, the Russells have been hard at task to eradicate homelessness. They have been working tirelessly for a month. And that means they have also been caring tirelessly for a month.

Mrs Russell gives an interview after cutting the ribbon on the new homeless shelter that she and her husband have opened near the centre of the city. She talks about why they felt such a need to do what they have done, why they care so much about homelessness. The interviewer asks how she is feeling now that the building is in operation.

'There have been some long days, and we have heard a lot of stories about how individuals end up on the streets.'

She says that it is overwhelming to have seen the project through and be able to help so many people who are struggling and need more understanding than they are often given. And this gets misquoted somewhere as Mrs Russell saying that the project was overwhelming. That the stories she heard were overwhelming. That she had burned herself out in order to get a few extra people off the street in a city where there wasn't even really a problem.

Then some bright spark hoping to make a name for themselves revives the idea of 'compassion fatigue'.

Apparently, it's just like burnout. But it's more specific. It's the physical, emotional and psychological impact that comes from helping others. Regular burnout comes from tiredness and dissatisfaction, but compassion fatigue occurs when you have to deal with other people who have experienced trauma.

You, feel this trauma vicariously. It's second-hand. You are part of it. So you absorb the stress of others. If you are a care-giver, you will be regularly subjected to the pain and problems of those around you. You soak up their struggles. And, because you empathise, you share that anguish, and it fatigues you.

Symptoms can include insomnia, headaches, digestive issues, mood swings and memory loss. You may begin to feel detached.

So, having the ability to empathise with the pain of another can cause you to lose your attachment to others.

Giving a shit can make you ill.

It can give you anxiety.

It can give you depression.

People will hear that and think, 'Great. Better not do too much of that, then.'

They will be told to make time for self-care as well as time for caring for others. Stay hydrated. Take time to eat well. Stay active. Get a massage. Whatever.

Perhaps they will find themselves caring so much that they require professional help. A counsellor or therapist. But they also know that professions like psychiatry are at a higher risk of compassion fatigue. So they don't want to impart too much of their trauma to a shrink because they know that they will be sharing their anguish. They are probably making their therapist sick by talking about their own problems.

It's all so contradictory.

There's too much information.

Haruto Ikeda just wants the world to be a little kinder. And now some schmuck says kindness is dangerous. It's bad for you.

When did it become so difficult to do something good?

A CERTAIN PROFILE

Bauer has nobody. His mother died before he moved to China, and his father was so useless without her that he brought the old man with him when the opportunity at the Wuxi Institute of Virology was presented to him.

He had been in a relationship before that.

She did not want to move to China. She had her own career to think about.

'They have banks in China,' he had said.

'They have laboratories in Düsseldorf,' she had responded.

'Not like this one. Not with the opportunity to work with Haruto Ikeda.'

Bauer and his partner were seemingly in love. Living together. Talking about marriage but not kids, neither was ready for that. His mother had always told him not to let anyone hold him back from what he wanted to do. If it was to better himself, a partner should want to be with him, because he was already the best that she would find. And he was only going to get better.

Anna didn't care. She kept the rented flat, and Bauer took his father to Wuxi to die.

Now he is alone. Solely focussed on work and bettering himself. Though, suddenly, he appears to have acquired a surrogate Japanese family. Parental-type figures. They are intelligent and well meaning and hardworking, all qualities that Bauer admires.

But it's not enough.

Bauer is an ambitious loner.

He's been trying to get information out of Ikeda since he came back to work after his father's death.

He fits a certain profile.

That's why he tells someone in the Chinese government what he knows.

Kimiko Ikeda was right.

She always is.

Bauer takes his laptop home with him. Haruto Ikeda suspects that the virus is kicking in and his colleague will have a couple of days of sweats and fatigue before returning to the lab with an increased empathy towards some cause he may not have even realised he cared about before.

But Bauer is not unwell. It is not long since he recovered from the virus that killed his father and, as such, his body seems to have rejected, or at least tolerated, whatever Ikeda injected. He is the child that was given cowpox that stopped him getting smallpox. He just needs a little time away.

The level of clearance that Bauer has within the institute is not as high as Ikeda's, but he navigates his way to the folder with the information about the vaccination rollout. He cannot open it, but he takes a screenshot of the file's location and attaches it to his email.

He explains it as it was told to him. That there is a schedule that appears to include the release date of a deadly virus. That the West will blame China for the outbreak. He says that he is confident that the Chinese have nothing to do with it, of course.

Bauer goes into detail about the virus itself. He says that he does not know who is behind it, that is not for him to find out, but that he thought somebody within the Chinese government should be aware.

He does not mention Haruto Ikeda.

He doesn't even hint at the kindness virus.

Because there is no benefit – for Bauer – in that.

A DOWNSIDE TO COMPASSION

Somebody realises the world is getting kinder. And it couldn't be anyone worse.

Freya Hely-Hutchinson.

Her father made his fortune in steel, which means that Freya doesn't have to work a day in her life. But she does. As an unqualified mental-health advocate and influencer around the subject. She has struggled her entire life with anxiety and low self-esteem, apparently.

Freya's schtick divides viewers. Many find her insipid. She says she has a low opinion of herself but posts videos drinking cocktails on yachts in her skimpiest swimsuit.

But she does speak passionately about mental health and she does allow herself to appear vulnerable and fragile at times. And she acts as a voice for the younger generation, who see her as an advocate. A friend, even. There are enough people in the world, for now, that four million haters doesn't seem like a lot when you have six million followers who hang on your every prerehearsed word.

'Has anyone noticed what's been going on?' she says into the camera, her thick, blonde hair seemingly messy but she spent a while making it look that way, as though this thought occurred to her when she woke up. 'There is an abundance of kindness in the world right now.' She lists some of the stories that she has found from across the globe.

Then she says, 'It worries me.' And she follows it up by talking about something she read recently. 'It's called compassion fatigue.'

Kimiko Ikeda finds the video after one of her patients suggests that she might be suffering from it.

'And what makes you think you have compassion fatigue?' Kimiko had asked.

'A saw a video online and everything she said just made sense to me.'

'Who said?'

'A mental-health expert.'

Kimiko Ikeda found the video when her patient left. Freya Hely-Hutchinson is an expert in spending family money, she thought to herself.

'This is what we are up against, dear,' Haruto Ikeda says to his wife when she shows him the video. 'She is going to tell kids that it is dangerous to be kind. She may not be saying those exact words but some of them will take it that way. Already, we are fighting.'

He sighs and slumps into his favourite chair.

'I did not see this coming, Kimiko. I did not consider that there would be a downside to compassion.' He feels distraught.

'Haruto, it is one video. It doesn't make sense. She doesn't understand compassion fatigue. It's not something you get from being too kind.'

'But people will think that. They only watch half a video. They only read quarter of an article. All the work. All the risk. It could be undone so easily.'

'I think you underestimate the impact you are having. Kind people will not believe this woman. Let me make you some tea.'

Kimiko is right, but something like this video can spark debate.

It doesn't take long for something to become a movement. With the right spin, words, even false words, can be weaponised. And it is because the Ikedas are inherently kind that they did not see this coming. And it is because people like Freya Hely-Hutchinson are so fame-hungry and desperate for attention that they cannot foresee how ruinous their thoughtlessness can be.

FIT TO RETURN

Three days later, the prime minister returns to Downing Street and spins the hell out of his alleged illness.

'I understand that there was a great deal of speculation,' he begins his video. 'I was, indeed, admitted for testing, at first, but my condition deteriorated quite drastically.' He looks down for a moment as if in deep contemplation. It's all part of the performance. 'I could not breathe. I needed help. And, luckily for me – for all of us, in fact – we have the greatest health service in the world.'

He pauses and imagines people at home, watching this statement on the news, pumping their fists in the air with patriotism.

'I will always be grateful to the entire staff at the hospital.' He does not mention at which hospital he was a patient. 'Everyone. The doctors, nurses, cleaners, anaesthetists, management, pharmacy.' And then he mentions a couple of nurses, in particular. He says their first names and their nationalities – Brazilian and Romanian – hoping that it goes some way to fix the many faux pas he has made over the years with regard to Muslims and Travellers and West Indian cricketers. His insincerity is transparent to any cynic, but many viewers are too caught up in the story of his fight for survival.

'We are a country of great heritage, we have pride in our royal family. For me, like many of you, my faith in God keeps me strong of mind. But our health service is the physical heart of our nation. And that is why I know that with our history, our minds and our hearts, we will defeat this virus.'

He makes a fist with his right hand to indicate that this is the rousing part of his address.

'My heart goes out to anyone who has experienced this terrible illness or whose family has been affected by it. I feel incredibly lucky to be here right now and am in eternal debt to the staff who have got me on the road to recovery. And mark my words, I will not rest until this country is safe from this wicked, wicked disease.'

Then the news anchor announces that the prime minister will retire to Chequers for a few days to rest and recover. His deputy will continue to run things until he is fit to return.

The next day, it is announced that there will be a further four weeks of lockdown. This time, there is very little outrage across social-media channels, the public seemingly galvanised by the almost-tragedy of Harris Jackson.

He travels to Chequers, feeling triumphant, ready to usher in a new dawn of prosperity.

Soon, the virus will be the least of his worries.

THE
THIRD
SCOURGE

ANYTHING WORTH DOING TAKES EFFORT

Sometimes, it takes a devastation to find hope.
To remember that there is still good in people.

Hope is harder than cynicism or outrage or apathy or selfishness. And it is lonely.

In four weeks, Harris Jackson will announce that the number of deaths in the UK has stalled and that people are almost allowed to be released from their quarantine.

Still, millions of people have been infected with Ikeda's compassion virus.

Millions of people experiencing more empathy than they ever have.

Millions of people acting more kindly.

Millions of people with hope.

Millions who now feel alone.

What they need, to bring them all together, is some good old-fashioned devastation. And it can't be an exploding train carriage or a plane flying into a skyscraper or some kid with a short attention span and the keys to his father's arsenal. No nail bombs in the post or school shootings. It has to be bigger than that. It has to be plague-of-locusts big.

It has to be Biblical in proportion.

It has to be water turning to blood. Lice. Boils. Hail. And darkness.

The video will show a yellow fog enveloping buildings and cities in China. It will swallow busy pedestrian walkways. The sound will be screaming. Agony as skin melts and hair falls out. As Chinese people roll on the floor before their eyes turn to liquid and they choke on the air that was cleaner than it ever had been only a month before.

The image is of indiscriminate disaster. Children, pensioners, women and men, writhing and panting. Death on a scale to parallel Sodom and Gomorrah or the great flood. As if God Herself has decreed an end to times.

That's how to give people hope.

Haruto Ikeda wanted to make the world a better place, but he sits alone in his office, wondering whether he made a mistake. Perhaps things were too far gone. Fighting evil with good seems so futile. It's not strong enough.

Caring isn't as contagious as he had hoped. Ridicule and fury are more likely to go viral. He hypothesises that it is due to our laziest generation. The entitled ones. Treading the path of least resistance. They don't understand that anything worth doing takes effort.

Ikeda is at a similar crossroads to the one he found himself at a few years back. Where he is more interested in the human mind and human nature than he is in studying viruses. He spends more time at his desk philosophising about existence. Alone.

Bauer has been off sick for a couple of days, and Ikeda doesn't know what to do. Studying viruses seems pointless, now. He eats his sandwich and reads an article on his laptop.

From the corner of his right eye, he swears that he sees the cursor move. Just a slight wobble to the right. Then it arcs carefully to the bottom left corner and brings up a menu. Instinctively, Ikeda grabs his mouse and takes the cursor away from the corner.

Perhaps he is not as alone as he thought he was.

The office phone rings and startles Ikeda. He places a hand on his chest then answers.

There's a clicking sound.

'Dr Ikeda,' he says, feeling his heart pound.

'Good day, Doctor. This is Chen in Tech. I am running a diagnostic on everyone's computer in the institute. It's not just physical leaks we have to worry about, these days, it's information leaking out, too. So I'm running a patch to shore up security.'

'Okay.' Ikeda has a scientific mind but not a technological one. 'Do you need me to do anything?'

'If you could leave your mouse alone, that would be great.'

'That was you?'

'I just need to run the script. You can watch on your screen now, if you like.'

Ikeda does that. He holds the phone with one hand and the sandwich in the other. The cursor moves to the left and brings up the menu. It clicks on something called *terminal* that Ikeda has never used before. It looks like computer screens once looked in the nineties. Black background. White text. At the top, it says, *The default interactive shell is now zsh. To update your account to use zsh, please run 'chsh -s /bin/zsh'.*

Ikeda has no idea what that means.

More gobbledygook springs up on the terminal screen as Chen types something in remotely. Then it disappears and a box blinks in the centre of the screen saying the update will take forty minutes.

'So, I cannot use my laptop?' Ikeda asks.

'I know it says forty minutes but it will probably only take twenty. I thought that I would update everybody's computer during the lunch period so as not to disturb their work.'

All Ikeda wanted to do was scan the news for more stories of goodwill and benevolence. The virus was far from perfect, but there were reports, every day, of compassion, both locally and globally, that showed he had had a positive influence.

An American baseball player had donated a fishing net to Africa for every base he stole in one season. And then he delivered them himself. He had no links to the specific fishing community he helped, he just wanted to do it.

On a smaller scale, some local teenagers got together to help deliver food to those with physical disabilities. It wasn't a school project. It wasn't extra-curricular activity. They just wanted to help another person, someone less fortunate than themselves.

Ikeda finds it helps his head to remind himself of these types of stories. It helps him remain on the path he has made for himself. But now he has at least twenty minutes to kill.

'Well, I am on my break, but you don't have to sit here with me on the phone and I don't need to watch a software update, so I'll take a walk and check back later, if that's okay?'

'Works either way for me, Doc. I've done all the hard work.'

Ikeda puts the phone down. He takes his sandwich and a book and leaves his office, closing the door on his way out. He leaves the building to walk through the trees for a while. He won't even read his book.

And as he walks, Chen – or whatever his name really is – will navigate the files on Ikeda's computer, using his access to search through the folders that Bauer could not open, and he will make a copy of all the information he needs.

It won't even take twenty minutes.

THE WATERS ARE RISING

Xiang Lao calls Ikeda while he is out for a walk.

'Haruto, where are you?'

This seems like an odd thing to ask, but Ikeda answers, anyway.

'I am outside on my lunch break. Taking a walk.' There is hardly anyone around. Not every job has been deemed crucial. Bars, restaurants and theatres are still in operation, for now, but with spacing guidelines meaning they are all functioning at half capacity. Shopkeepers and medical professionals are vital and are being told that they can still go out to work, whereas many others who can perform their work from home are being advised to do so. Even teachers are holding classes over a video network. The children's education will suffer. It's another negative reaction for Ikeda to wrap his brain around.

Ikeda is not suspicious of Lao. He hasn't seen him, socially, in almost a year, but they have spoken about scientific matters over the phone and on email.

'Ah, good. So you're not in the office.'

'What is this about?' Ikeda stops beneath a cherry tree.

'I have been called into a preliminary meeting and your name came up, again. Could we meet?'

'Are you nearby?'

'No. I'm in Nantong, but I can get to you later this evening.'

'Can you tell me what this is about?'

'Not over the phone, friend. It has been a long while since we sat down together. Let me take you for a drink this evening. I can get to you around nine. You remember where we met before?'

'Yes, at...' Ikeda stops himself. Lao has him feeling more paranoid. Why doesn't he want to mention anything over the phone? What could this be about? Does he know something about the virus? '...at nine.' He saves it.

If only Xiang Lao had called Ikeda half an hour before, perhaps Ikeda would have been more wary about 'Chen in tech' who had gained access to his computer for an alleged software update. Now they have his recent research notes, the results of testing a vaccine on humanised mice, his internet search history. There are spreadsheets and half-written papers. Ikeda has been looking at property prices in the town of Hakone, west of Tokyo.

None of this matters. That is not why Chen was snooping around.

He wanted one file that possibly details the scheduled rollout of a deadly vaccine in China, so that he could confirm the information that Bauer had relayed.

As a matter of policy, Ikeda's emails were also copied. They show recent correspondence with Xiang Lao, who works in the nanotech research facility in Nantong.

The waters are rising and nobody has noticed.

NOT THE RIGHT PERSON

The prime minister meets with his deputy at Strangers' Bar in the palace of Westminster. Pubs and restaurants around the UK have been closed for weeks, but this is a bar for MPs, peers, officers of the House or staff members of HEO grade or higher. And they don't seem to be able to follow their own rules.

'Well, bloody hell, Hen, you've done a marvellous job while I've been out of action.'

Henrietta Adamson. Forty-three. Smart. Sharp. No-nonsense. She has a legal mind and a passion to serve the country. Anything she puts her hand to she performs with professionalism and efficiency. She gets the job done. She could have been anything she wanted. A judge, a CEO, a spy. It has always mattered to her more that she do something where she feels she is making a difference.

And she just got to run the entire country for a week.

'Thank you, Harris. These are difficult times we find ourselves in. I take it you are feeling much better?'

She's out of the loop. Henrietta Adamson has no idea that Harris Jackson was holed up in some secret location, drinking red wine and fiddling with himself. She thinks it was the virus. That blasted virus that is causing fear across the country and costing billions in grants and bail-outs for companies and small businesses that have had to cease trading due to the lockdowns.

She has no idea that Jackson was planning to release something much worse but was beaten to the punch.

She is just doing her job and doing it well.

Adamson is out of the loop because she is too good and too clever. One day, she will be a brilliant leader.

'Much better, thanks. But I am still the prime minister and expect to be addressed as such.'

'Oh, gosh. Yes. Of course. I'm sorry, sir. Prime Minister, I mean.' She is flustered.

'A week in the job and suddenly I'm Harris.' He lifts an eyebrow disapprovingly.

'Sorry again, Prime Minister, I just ... I thought this was informal and...' Henrietta Adamson is rarely lost for words.

Jackson smiles. 'Relax, Hen. I'm joking. Of course it's informal. Bloody restrictions have made everyone lose their sense of humour.' He throws out a laugh. 'Now, what would you like to drink?'

The deputy PM takes a second to compose herself. She can't laugh it off. It wasn't a joke. It was mean. A power play. She understands the threat she poses to men in her line of work. 'I'm not sure we should really even be in here, should we?'

'There's nobody putting themselves at risk, Hen. It's just us. And I know how to pull a pint or open a wine bottle.' He smirks and walks behind the bar to pour himself a lager.

'A glass of red, then, I guess.' She answers like a real politician but she wants to say, 'Thanks, Harris'.

'A fine choice.'

Jackson tells his deputy that he is coming back to work tomorrow. That he, and the country, appreciate her stepping in the way that she did. He compliments her, as he should, and asks whether there is anything he should be aware of as she hands things back over.

She bores him with some figures and talk of how the grants will roll out to help small business owners. She says *it was the right thing to do.* Jackson nods even though he hates giving money away.

Jackson brings her glass of wine to the table and sits with her. No face masks. Close proximity. But there are no photographers around. They are safe.

'And how is the party? There has been some division, I know.'

This is where Adamson relays the news that three members were off sick and have decided not to return to their roles. 'Perhaps it is some kind of epiphany after been infected but they just don't feel that they can continue.'

'What a time to leave. When we are in the middle of a crisis.' He swigs his beer and Adamson looks at him intently. He doesn't seem jaded. He doesn't look to have lost any weight from his critical condition. She doesn't tell him what the three MPs said. That they would happily follow her into any fire, *but not that idiot, Jackson.*

They had come back from the illness as new people. It was an epiphany of sorts but it wasn't of their own doing. They were not bed-ridden and contemplative. They didn't come up with the idea on their own.

It was Ikeda.

They had a swelling of compassion and couldn't be a component of a party that was running the country into the ground.

People are going to be ruined. And Harris Jackson is not the right person to deal with such a delicate and unprecedented predicament.

A generation of students will be taught at home by their unqualified parents. They will suffer for that. They will struggle. There is a mental toll a lockdown will eventually take that has not been considered. More people with agoraphobia, more people with anxiety, depression. It will come. But Jackson's government focusses on the tangible: money and jobs.

It's bigger than that.

Of course, his staff couldn't help feeling worried for him during his alleged sickness but as soon as he completed his televised statement about recovering, they handed their resignations to Adamson with a less than glowing review of her superior.

She understands his ego, so she doesn't go into detail and, instead, moves on to the next issue.

Harris interrupts her when his mobile phone rings.

'Sorry about this, Hen, it's Lord Benedict, I have to take it. I won't be a moment.'

He answers. 'Benjy, how are things?'

'Honestly, Harris, they've been pretty bloody wretched. The wife has been as sick as a dog and then she passed the bloody thing on to me.'

'I'm sorry to hear that.'

'Well, you should know what it's like, you've been in hospital with the bastard thing.'

'Yes. Quite.'

'Anyway, we've had a bit of a discussion, and it does seem a little unfair that you recommended us for that contract when we didn't really know what the hell we were doing and we made a boatload of money.' It is definitely Benedict at the other end of the phone but it doesn't sound like him. He still has that brash tone and bravado, but they're somehow softer.

'That was the point,' Harris smiles and holds up a finger to Adamson to show that he'll only be a minute. She drinks her wine.

'It's just not right, though. We've been talking about it and don't think that we should buy a property in Milan or a boat or whatever.

We don't want to sit on it. We want to use it to ... er ... help or something, you know?'

'I'm afraid I'm not sure what you mean.' Harris screws up his face.

'We're not sure yet, either. Build a new wing on a hospital or a library for a university. That sort of thing. We don't want any of this money. We want to put it to some good. A school or something.'

'Sorry ... what...?' Harris shakes his head.

'Nothing you can do, old boy. Thanks for the tip, of course, but it wouldn't be right to buy another island, would it? I just wanted to say, don't worry about any future recommendations. We're good.' And then Benedict hangs up.

Jackson returns to the table, looking confused.

'Everything okay?' Adamson asks.

'Yes, yes. Everything is fine. Except for the fact that the entire world has gone bloody crazy.'

TOE THE COMPANY LINE

The train from Nantong to Wuxi takes almost three hours. The bus takes a little longer. The quickest way is, actually, by car. An hour and a quarter, and it's a fairly straightforward route. But Xiang Lao doesn't want to drive. He is going to dinner with an old friend. They will eat good food and drink even better wine. So Lao orders a taxi.

He could put it down as a business expense because he will be discussing 'work', but it's not that expensive and the main reason for the meeting is to warn his old friend.

Still, Lao is late. There is some traffic getting across the river. His driver was talkative at first but quietened down after about thirty minutes. Only really speaking one more time to say, 'That same car has been behind us for almost an hour. Maybe they have a booking at the same restaurant as you.' Then he laughed, and Lao thought nothing of it. He wasn't really listening.

He sees Ikeda, sitting alone, drinking something red. Ikeda is small but something about him always makes him look bright. Healthy. Approachable. His smile widens as Lao approaches.

'I'm so sorry, Haruto. The traffic, you know. It's great to see you.'

'It's great to see you, too.'

They both mean it.

'I took the liberty of ordering wine.'

Xiang pulls out the chair opposite his friend, turns over his glass and pours the wine. He sips, nods in appreciation and starts with small talk.

'How is Kimiko?'

'Why are we here, Xiang? It's nice of you to ask, but let's dispense with the pleasantries until we know what this is about.' It's not aggressive, Ikeda is not like that, but he doesn't like to waste words, and this meeting was unexpected after months of little correspondence. 'Should I be worried?'

'Worried? Have you done something wrong?'

It's awkward for a moment, neither man wanting to give anything away.

'I have not but, in this world, you do not always have to do something to have your name and reputation tarnished.'

'That is unfortunately true.' Xiang drinks. 'Look, there is nothing wrong as far as I can tell, but I have heard your name a lot over the last couple of weeks. It is not that crazy. There is a mysterious virus sweeping the planet and nobody knows more about that kind of thing than you, so I'd expect to hear you mentioned.'

'Then what is the problem?'

Xiang Lao pauses. He finishes the wine in his glass, pours himself another, offers Ikeda a top-up and begins.

'First it was the initial cases in Wuxi. Of course, there was concern, but the mention of your name was positive. That you would understand the virus. That you would be working on a vaccine. I said that we had spoken over the last year about the use of nano materials to aid with vaccination.' Ikeda nods and Lao continues. 'Then there were more cases. And your press conference.' Ikeda bows his head at this. 'Important people around the world started to become affected. There also seemed to be a swell in benevolent behaviour.'

'You think that the virus had something to do with that?' Ikeda thinks he is holding his nerve, double-bluffing, like the idea is preposterous.

'It was just something that was noted. Often tragedy can bring out the best in people.'

'It is a shame that it often has to be that way.'

'Please don't say things like that in front of anyone else, Haruto. This is what I am talking about. Things died down but then I am pulled into a meeting to discuss some classified tech I have been working on, and there is talk that the leaked virus was planned.'

Ikeda cannot hide his reaction. His eyes widen.

'Who said that?'

'It doesn't matter who said it. *Somebody* did. You didn't, right?'

'Didn't what? Deliberately release a virus that would kill thousands of people?' Ikeda doesn't raise his voice, it would be too much of a tell. He stays level. 'Xiang, you know me. My work is everything. Why would I deliberately kill people?'

'I don't believe it. But I just want you to say—'

'No. I didn't do that. I wouldn't.'

'Look, I believe you, I've taken a taxi here tonight to see you because I knew what you would say. To me, it seems like a catastrophic accident. But there are people in high places who are considering whether this was released on purpose. If they find that to be true, I can't imagine it will end well for the person responsible.'

Lao asks Ikeda to be more considered before he speaks on the television again. Or the radio. Or writes a paper. Mistrust is in the air and somebody is looking for a public hanging. He asks Ikeda to lie low and toe the company line until things are clearer.

'Now we've got that out of the way, perhaps we should order some food.' Ikeda tilts his head to one side.

'Indeed. Now, tell me, how *is* Kimiko?'

THAT'S NOT HOW YOU SAY GOODBYE

The infection rate in the United Kingdom is somewhere in the millions. Deaths are in the thousands. There is an even spread across demographics with regards to infection, though considerably fewer children are affected. Deaths seem to be concentrated on the elderly or those with underlying respiratory conditions.

A few thousand deaths for a few million cases may not seem like a lot. But every life carries weight. Every person is linked to other lives.

They mean something.

Even if only to one other.

And they have been taken unfairly.

Jim Bardsley was considerably overweight. Morbidly obese. He was told that he had a weak heart. It would have been easy for him to sit around, afraid that he would die if he taxed his heart too much. His doctors seemed to hint that a more sedentary lifestyle might prevent stress on this vital organ. Of course, he would also have to eat much better.

But Jim Bardsley took a different initiative. He decided that, as the heart was technically a muscle, instead of leaving it to atrophy, he would make it stronger.

He did start to eat more healthily. And he started to move. Walking long distances at first but then more functional fitness, using only his considerable body weight. It was a journey. These things do not happen overnight. Jim had been working hard for almost two years. He started feeling strong – not lean, but certainly not heavy. It might take another year to get to the vision he had in mind, but he was determined.

Then he picked up some kind of virus and died.

Snuffed out on his way to greatness.

It is not just the bereavement that ruins lives. With the current restrictions, funeral services are limited to ten people. These are to be made up of people in the person's household and close family, who must ensure they have been tested for the virus and remain two metres apart. If there are no close family members or they are unable to attend, close friends will be allowed.

The funeral director, chapel attendant and other funeral staff will, obviously, be present, and a celebrant of choice is also permitted.

More people are allowed to attend the outside section of the ceremony as long as they adhere to the distancing policy.

Somebody may have died, but there will be no hugs or pats on the shoulder, no physical comforting of any kind.

The problem is that it is highly communicable. So if somebody in one household passes away, there is a high probability that the other people in that household will test positive.

Which means they will not be able to attend the funeral of somebody that they love.

They can tune in on a live-stream service.

Or watch a recording.

But that's not the same. That's not how you say goodbye. It is not how you celebrate the life of somebody that you love. But this is how Carol Bardsley had to watch her husband's final hour on Earth before he was incinerated. She will get his ashes delivered and she can try to make up for not being there, but the long-term psychological impact is ultimately destructive.

Luckily, for the hundreds of Mrs Bardsleys who won't get to send off their Jims, there will be no long-term psychological damage because everyone will be dead in a month.

WE DEAL IN CERTAINTIES

After the early snafu, Ikeda and Lao settled into their meal, and conversation flowed almost as well as the drinks. Lao had originally planned to get a taxi back to Nantong but decided he would stay in a hotel and get up early instead. Ikeda offered him a room, but Lao did not want Kimiko to see him in such a condition.

Though men of great scientific renown, they settled on an after-dinner coffee to sober themselves up, which did not work.

Lao let Ikeda take the first cab and he waited for a second.

He arrives at the Wuxi Marriot Lihu Lake hotel, which he managed to book on his phone while he ate dessert. It's one of the more expensive places to stay in the city, but he's been there a few times before and he knows what he's going to get.

He goes to the front desk, tells them his name, gives them a credit card and gets his key. The seventh floor. Two men in suits step into the lift after him. He presses the button for his floor and asks them which one they want. The men look at one another, then at the numbers on the wall.

'Seven,' one of them says.

The doors close. The lift moves. And nobody says a thing.

It stops on the fifth. There's a young couple waiting.

'Going down?' they ask.

'Sorry,' says Lao.

When they reach the seventh floor, Lao steps out into the hallway first. He looks at the number written on his key card then stares at the sign on the wall with an arrow. He doesn't look back but he knows the two men are walking behind him. They are not speaking.

He finds that fear is more sobering than an espresso and speeds up a little. He can see his door. He thinks about looking over his shoulder but doesn't. He fumbles with the key card, taking it out of the folded piece of hotel-branded card, ready to swipe the door. These stupid keys never work first time, he thinks to himself. But he paces towards his room with intent, drops the card into the slot and pulls it up. The light goes green and he turns the handle just as the two men from the lift pass right behind him.

Xiang Lao breathes a sigh of relief.

He opens the door to his room and steps inside, where another two men in suits are sitting in the bedroom beyond. He doesn't know whether to say something or run. Adrenaline surges, giving Lao two choices. Fight. Or flight. He turns to leave only to be confronted by the men from the lift, blocking his exit before pushing him inside and allowing the door to close behind them.

'What the hell is this? Who are you?'

'Nobody is here to hurt you, Mr Lao,' one of the elevator goons says.

'How do you know my name?'

'Please go on through and all will be explained.'

'Are you MSS? I haven't done anything wrong.'

'Please, Mr Lao.' He gestures towards the bedroom ahead.

They are not forceful. They don't get physical with him. But their presence is one of authority and they are letting him know that they are in charge without hurting him in any way.

The men are dressed similarly but it's clear who is in charge. The tall, slender, well-manicured Chinese man sitting on a chair by the dressing table exudes coolness. He doesn't get up when Lao enters the room. Everyone else stands. He has taken a bottle of water and small tin of nuts from the minibar and makes everyone wait while he finishes chewing and drinking.

'I'm sorry that my associates did not address you correctly, Dr Lao. You are an important man, yes?' It's not really a question, and Lao doesn't know how to answer, anyway. 'You are a leader in the world of nanotechnology and you are meeting with a leader in the world of virology. A meeting of world leaders.'

'I'm not sure I'd say that.'

'Do not be so modest, Doctor. We understand that great minds must get together. We see it all the time. Writers, philosophers and titans of industry.'

'You see it all the time?'

'Of course. It is a matter of national security, is it not? If a politician meets with a wealthy CEO, is it not in the interest of China to understand what such a meeting could entail? We understand that your meal tonight was an act of friendship rather than anything nefarious to do with your particular specialities.'

'You think we were planning something?' Lao is still standing his ground, but the man in the chair looks like he has lost the ability to sweat.

'No, I do not. Because we heard what you were saying. But we have to be careful. If we simply reacted to events, we would not be much use.'

'So why are you here?' It must be the wine giving Lao some courage.

The man in the chair stands up. His skin is so clear it is almost feminine. He is beautiful but there is a quiet menace to him. Lao senses that the man could flip a switch at any moment, and he doesn't want to see that happen.

'Courtesy, Dr Lao. Your good friend Dr Ikeda did not plan to release a virus. In fact, the information that we have so far gathered suggests that he may have already completed work on a vaccine.' So far, he only knows what has been taken from Ikeda's computer: Tau. Ypsilon. The Tau vaccine. Everything related to CompX is inside Ikeda's head or written on a piece of paper, the old-fashioned way, and stuffed between the pages of a random book in his office.

'Already?'

'And this is the problem we are facing. This is normal work at the institute. They discover new threats all the time and develop ways to combat them. Future-proofing. This vaccine appears to have been on some kind of schedule, which makes us believe that the virus itself may have been scheduled. Not by Dr Ikeda, I should add.'

'An attack on China? Who would do such a thing?'

'We deal in certainties. We are not even sure it was an attack. We simply wanted to inform you that Dr Ikeda appeared to be working in the best interests of his organisation. You also work with sensitive information, Dr Lao, so will understand that anything that has been discussed in this room goes no further than these walls. And you know that we will be listening to you.'

This last sentence is said with a coldness that isn't quite a threat, but everyone in the room knows that it is.

Nobody talks for a moment. Then the men in suits start to walk out, leaving Xiang Lao dumbfounded in his hotel suite. He is comforted to know for sure that his friend is not a traitor but also feels paranoid that his every waking moment is being watched and listened to. Surely not. There are more important things going on in the world. But this is China.

'Oh, yes, Dr Lao,' the leader turns back, 'I think the solar-panel project is possibly a moment of madness. Your focus should be on your current workload.' He closes the door.

Lao is alone.

And uncomfortable.

They know everything.

A VACCINE TO END HOPE

Bauer returns to work after a few days. He remembers everything that Ikeda told him about the virus, but he never really felt sick, and he certainly doesn't feel any more compassion today than he did three days ago when he informed somebody within the Chinese government that the virus may have been leaked on purpose.

'Stefan. How are you feeling?' Ikeda asks when he sees his colleague getting his first coffee of the day.

'You know, I feel okay. I don't think it was the virus, because I never got a headache and I haven't volunteered at the local soup kitchen or anything.'

Haruto Ikeda is confused. He knows it was the virus because he administered it himself. He can't say that, though. So he says, 'Well, that's good to hear. We can jump straight into work, then.' He lingers, stirring his coffee even though he doesn't take it with sugar.

'I'm looking forward to it,' Bauer tries.

Ikeda continues to stir and stare. 'So, you were at your apartment while you were off?'

'That's right. Resting.' Bauer feels the sweat gathering in the dip in his back.

'I'm sorry I didn't get a chance to visit. Did you have many visitors?'

'None.'

'You didn't talk to anyone?' Ikeda is as subtle as a sledgehammer to the sternum. Bauer and Kimiko Ikeda are the only people who know what happened and why it had to be done. For his old friend, Xiang, to come out of the woodwork with genuine concern, somebody must have said something. And he trusts his wife without question.

It's not coincidence, it's Occam's Razor. The simplest answer is usually the best. And the simplest answer is that Bauer talked. Kimiko Ikeda is smarter, and she is almost always right.

Then Bauer says that he doesn't feel comfortable knowing what he knows. That it could make him an accessory to the fact. That he doesn't think he would stand up well to interrogation. That the people who planned to release a deadly virus will eventually work out that Ikeda's kindness virus is the real cause of the pandemic. That the vaccine they paid him to develop will have no effect on people's compassion.

Ikeda hadn't even thought that far ahead. He had naively believed that the world would become a better place, and nobody would care what he did because they would all be thinking of others before themselves, helping their fellow man, loving their neighbour.

Why did he have to get involved?

Because he stopped millions of people from dying.

Because he wanted to save the world.

Because he just wanted people to care.

And now, in order to not get caught, he has to work with Bauer to create a vaccine that will work against CompX. A vaccine to end hope.

Cue the frogs. The lice. The flies. The pestilence.

FOLLOW THE RULES

Then Harris Jackson mentions Ikeda.

Another recorded video because press conferences require too many people in close proximity. It's filmed inside 10 Downing Street. A room clad in dark wood. Jackson sitting behind a large oak desk. Flag in the background. Expensive pen ready to sign some important document. Books on a shelf that he has probably never read.

He talks to the country, who have seemingly made a 180-degree turn in their opinions of their leader. Jackson's approval rating continues to soar as he deals with this unprecedented situation.

'We have the greatest minds in the field of virology working on this, including the Japanese scientist Haruto Ikeda, based at ground zero in Wuxi. And I am told that we are close to a vaccine. Tests are under way, and if effective, we will begin a rollout across the country and lift this blasted lockdown.' He pauses as though imagining his adoring fans cheering. 'But I urge you, until that time, to stay at home. Stay safe. And protect those around you. We will defeat this thing, and we are closer than ever to doing so.'

He has the country's hopes up.

Parents are exhausted from trying to work from their homes while their children are there, trying to learn by looking at a computer screen. They haven't been able to be with their friends for weeks, and this will undoubtedly have an effect on their social skills when they do emerge into the new normality.

Alcohol consumption has increased dramatically. Of course, the bars are not open, but it is becoming a habit, a coping mechanism. The NHS can only just handle the current level of virus cases. The next crisis could involve an influx of anxious alcoholics and suicidal adolescents.

This is a mess.

This may have come about because of Ikeda's unethical practices but it is not his fault. He came across some information he was never meant to see. This is the fault of Harris Jackson, his idea to infect the world, and the faction of Western leaders who thought it would be a good way to maintain their superiority.

The death of one person haunts Haruto Ikeda. But Jackson and his secret league were nonplussed by the potential dispatch of millions. And for what? Four more years in power? A distraction from personal depravities and calamitous policies? To rid their country of weakness?

Personal gain.

Absolute power.

Harris Jackson is buoyant after the filming. It is only himself and a cameraman in a face mask in his office. He takes a bottle of whisky and a glass from a cupboard beneath his desk.

'Thank you for that,' the prime minister says to the cameraman. 'I would pour you a glass but ... restrictions, you know?'

'Not a problem, sir. I need to be heading out. A wonderful message. I think the people at home will take great comfort in your words.'

'Well, that's mighty kind of you to say, and I hope you are right.' Jackson reaches back into the cupboard and takes out another glass and pours a small amount of whisky into it. 'Here. Just a short one. I'll stand back here.' Jackson steps back and perches himself on a cabinet a few feet away from the desk.

'Thank you, again, sir, but I'm not sure we should even bend the rules slightly.' The cameraman feels like he has overstepped the mark. 'Not that I don't want to, I just think that if we all follow the rules, we'll get out of this quicker.'

Jackson doesn't say anything and the man takes his camera and leaves.

When he is alone, Jackson goes back to his desk and adds the contents of one glass to the other and says, under his breath, 'I make the rules, son, they don't apply to people like me.' He downs his whisky. It burns his throat. He coughs and is glad that nobody is around to see it.

And to show that he is still the big man, the one in charge, he sends a group message to several high-ranking cabinet members inviting them to lunch the next day.

JUST ANOTHER FREAK ACCIDENT

The company line, Haruto.

An early-morning text from Xiang Lao to Ikeda, reminding him of their conversation a fortnight ago.

Ikeda worries, immediately. What has been said now?

It's still early and he doesn't want to wake his wife, so he creeps out of the bedroom and into the lounge, where he turns on the television. There is nothing on the news that should have him worried. Information from the West can get held back. He is not technically minded but he knows how to use a VPN so that his computer can look as though it is in a different country.

It's too much hassle. But Lao must know something to message that early.

Something I should know? Ikeda types.

Then he waits.

Lao texts back after a moment. He explains what he knows. That Harris Jackson is shouting his mouth off, saying that Ikeda has a vaccine.

'Shit,' Ikeda says out loud. He rarely curses. He's afraid that the truth will come out. Bauer knows that it has to. The Tau vaccine will not work against CompX. Months and months of work by Ikeda's team. But they have deniability. They were just doing their job. They're not in charge of which viruses take hold in the real world.

Bauer wasn't a part of it, though. He was dragged in by the Ikedas. But neither of them knows who is behind the original plan to release Tau into the world. Haruto Ikeda will deny until the end that he had anything to do with this global crisis. He has made a difference. Maybe not the one he wants but more than most people ever will.

Stefan Bauer has no such conviction. He is not a crusader. He is a scientist. It's all he has left. He knows that he can work with Ikeda to produce the vaccine for CompX if that is what they have to do. But they can take their time with that. Nobody will ever have to know.

Just another freak accident.

Wuxi Institute of Virology.

Wet markets.

Bats and civets.

If they play this right, Ikeda and Bauer could come out of this as heroes. They just need a lot of luck and a little more time.

They have neither.

TOP OF THE FOOD CHAIN

Two days later, everybody seems to know something that they shouldn't. Harris Jackson has an emergency meeting with the clandestine group.

'Thanks for meeting, gents. I've had word from Wuxi that the vaccine does not work.'

Incredulity rings out around the room.

'Yes, yes. Quite. The problem is not the product that was developed. It's the virus. It's not ours. It's not the one we planned. It didn't leak early. This is dumb bloody luck.'

'So it really was this wet market story?' the Russian asks, almost scoffing.

'No, we planted that idea. That was the plan all along. Create a scapegoat, it's more believable. It could have been some kind of overspill from the institute. We don't know yet.'

'Ain't that a kick in the nuts?' The American chimes in as if the death of *only* thousands of people across the world is a bit of an inconvenience.

'We abandon the plan? Move to plan B?' The Russian has turned serious again.

'Was there even a plan B?' America's turn at sarcasm.

'A bomb. A gas. A poison.' The Russian speaks as though this should have been the plan all along. 'They always seem to work.'

'It's a setback, that's all.' Jackson is calm. He does not address the Russian's response. 'This may, in fact, be something of an opportunity.' He tells them that they could emerge as heroes in each of their home nations. Leaders who battled a dreaded virus – that they knew was not as deadly as it could have been – and they won.

They have to develop a vaccine for this new virus and vaccinate everyone. Then they can release the lockdown situation. People will go outside. They will feel good. Like champions. Like Mother Nature tried her best to keep mankind as her servant but mankind prevailed.

Top of the food chain.

Instead of populations galvanised through fear, there is togetherness through hope. The Russian laughs heartily at this, and Harris can't react because he knows how volatile the Russian leader can be.

'Then we drop Tau. We say it's a new strain or a brand-new virus. The world has gone nuts. The new greatest threat to human life is not the atomic bomb. It is not chemical warfare. It is disease. The virus.'

'I still like chemicals and bombs,' the Russian says as an aside to the Brazilian. Half a smile.

'So, just a delay in the plan, then?' the American says. It sounds like a question but it's not.

'Why not?' Harris is almost ebullient. 'People accept these kinds of tragedies. A volcano explodes and it is the Earth answering back against our torment of the environment. An earthquake sucks half a city into the depths of hell and it is seen as an act of God.'

'People are idiots,' jokes the American.

'I know. I've been to Texas.' Harris laughs at his own joke and everybody joins in, just like he is used to. 'We can't create a tsunami but we can release a contagion. And we can drop it in China as planned. The goodwill of people being released from their homes will not last long. The rivers will get dirtier, Beijing will be covered in smog and the seas will gain tons more plastic. But we can pump a little money back into the economy for a fortnight. That's the shelf life on collaboration and thoughtfulness, I think.'

There is no talk of Haruto Ikeda other than to say that they have the best man on the job.

They now understand that it wasn't their virus that was leaked and that explains the low number of deaths, but they have no idea what came out of the institute in Wuxi. They are oblivious to the fact that Haruto Ikeda changed everything with his kindness contagion.

The world media have reported certain stories but they don't seem to have picked up on the global situation around compassion. They have not noticed any links. The occasional high-profile charity donation is mentioned but is buried among the human despair and celebrity infidelity.

No reputable broadcaster is suggesting that the virus is a cover for a hidden agenda to make people nicer. The global conspiracy sites are still talking about the assassination of JFK and the Bermuda Triangle. They are saying that the smoke coming from the first tower was black, which indicates that it was not hot enough to melt the steel beams holding the building up. That it was a detonation. That there was a second gunman on the grassy knoll. That a flag would not ripple on the moon. That the autopsy was performed on a model. That two old men with a wooden board attached to a piece of rope are making all the crop circles.

But a virus that turns its host into a better, kinder version of themself? That sounds like science fiction. Only three people would even think that and they only think it because they know it's true.

Of course, these conspiracy theorists believe that vaccines are used to keep track of people, to catalogue them, that microchips are being injected into the body. And 'sane people' deride them for believing that a secret cabal of leaders are working above government.

But they will never *know* that.

Jackson's collective understands that this virus wasn't theirs.

And they know what they want to do next.

They know more than they did two days ago but they only *think* that they are beyond reproach. They think that, with everyone locked away in their homes, miserable and drunk and longing for human contact, they can wander the world with impunity.

But one man, one beautiful, slender, Chinese man knows about the group.

He knows about the virus.

He knows about the schedule.

He knows about 'They eat dogs.'

And he knows that they should all be held accountable – and they will – but there is something about Harris Jackson that bothers him the most.

A DIFFERENCE HAS BEEN MADE

In 1989, the Chinese government ordered the massacre of ten thousand protesters – largely made up of students – in Tiananmen Square, Beijing, as they peacefully demonstrated for political change. Soldiers shot and stabbed and ran over campaigners in their armoured vehicles.

When a line of tanks rolled in, one lone dissident, armed only with a bag of groceries, stood in front of the line and stopped. They tried to go around but the man moved in their way again. The tanks moved and he blocked them again. Eventually, they stopped and the man climbed on top to talk with the soldiers.

A picture exists but footage of the incident was censored in China. Eventually the man was pulled from the tank and they continued their journey. It is not clear whether he was removed by soldiers or other protestors, fearful of his safety.

His identity has never been uncovered and he is simply referred to as 'Tank Man'. He made huge strides in the direction of democracy and became a symbol of such. But nobody will ever know who he was.

Thomas Edison is credited with creating the lightbulb – one of the greatest inventions of all time. Until 1881, he had only been able to make the bulb light up for minutes at a time. It wasn't until Lewis Latimer patented a method for making carbon-fibre filaments that could burn for hours that things really took off.

Latimer also helped Alexander Graham Bell file his patent for the telephone before inventing a device that cooled and disinfected hospital rooms, reducing infections acquired while in care. But you have to dig deep to discover his name and huge contribution to the world.

Charles Darwin is the father of the theory of evolution. But the idea of natural selection could have been called 'Wallaceism' as Alfred Wallace appears to have written about the idea first.

He was an anthropologist and explorer but had a keen interest in many things, including the spiritual world and the possibility of life on Mars. This meant his credibility as a scientist was called into question.

He sent his ideas to Darwin, who was working in a similar field, and hoped he might help get the papers published. Darwin wrote his own version of the papers. Both were read by the Linnean Society, who wanted nature to be understood and protected, but Darwin's connections ensured that his was read first, and was quickly followed by a book on the same subject.

Both men were published in the Linnean Society journals but, while Darwin continues to be remembered with great reverence, Wallace saw out the rest of his days travelling and writing about a plethora of subjects that interested him.

Some people say that they want to make an impact on the world. A few actually do just that. Fewer than that are content to know that they made the difference without everyone else patting them on the back for their efforts.

Haruto Ikeda is one of those very few.

He developed a vaccine for a virus that no human was ever subjected to. That is not something you are remembered for. It was something that never happened. No change was made.

Following that non-event, Ikeda created a mutated version of a coronavirus that attacks the body in such a way that it imitates the symptoms of SARS, then affects the brain, causing acute pain, and then the deepest of empathy.

And nobody noticed.

They noticed the SARS-like symptoms and the unfortunate casualties, but the positivity stayed under the radar. This very phenomenon of focussing on the negative is one of the reasons Dr Ikeda released his virus in the first place. He wanted to pick the world up.

Help it back to its feet.

Give it a hug and tell it that everything is going to be okay.

The planet's most successful and well-known meat-loving chef swore off causing suffering to any living thing. One of the richest men in the world has his heart set on providing free energy to all. An influential Canadian couple are ending homelessness in their home city and they won't stop there.

These are the people who will be remembered for the difference that they made to the world.

But then there are the ones who pay for a struggling mother's shopping or stop to help somebody change a tyre or volunteer their time to help those less fortunate. They may not do one large thing, one grand gesture, but their small kindnesses add up and they snowball and get paid forward.

And nobody will know why there was a global shift in attitude.

And Haruto Ikeda does not care.

He is just pleased that a difference has been made.

Perhaps Dr Bauer will see fit to understand and carry on Ikeda's work. Perhaps develop it further and find a more ethical way to administer the virus. It could end up with a name that people remember. Bauer could be the Darwin to Ikeda's Wallace.

Ikeda could live the remainder of his days back in Japan. With Kimiko. Reading. Cooking. Swimming. Philosophising. And not worrying that the world will never know his name because the world in which he was living was so terrifying and self-centred and destructively apathetic, that he would not have wanted those people to remember him.

People have died and he will bear that burden but he made a positive impact. He may not have saved the world, but he made a difference.

And that's enough.

GIVE A MAN A FISH

Ikeda decides to focus on the positive. He searches for stories of kindness rather than the smear campaign against compassion.

Freya Hely-Hutchinson went viral. She was interviewed on several wellbeing podcasts before appearing on morning television, talking like a professional about a subject that she has no formal qualification in. She draws it back to herself and her panic attacks. She says, 'Before you can be kind to others, you need to be kind to yourself.' It's not a bad message but it's muddled. So, when it gets paid forward, it gets warped even more. Until, eventually, the message is 'kindness is bad for you'.

Someone says, 'Forget compassion fatigue – when James Ritchie sees how much his restaurants are losing, he'll get so bored of being poor he'll only serve meat.'

Somebody else comments with '#CompassionBoredom'.

Beneath that, another hundred negative responses.

But Ikeda avoids this talk. Freya's message may be spreading but so is his virus. And he can only focus on that which he can control.

He sees that another online influencer has pledged to clear the oceans of plastic. He is using the millions of subscribers to his YouTube channel to push for clearer waters. In his videos he gives away large sums of money to his subscribers and then he donates to his favourite ocean clear-up initiative. His last video had 150 million views in the first three weeks. He donated a million dollars.

Over the next year, he will provide over thirty million. The clean-ocean initiative aims to get rid of ninety percent of ocean surface plastic by 2040. But with this kind of cash injection, they could take five years off that target.

Ikeda reads the article that profiles the young humanitarian, and he doesn't know whether the kid has been infected by CompX or he was always thoughtful and benevolent. But it doesn't matter, it's an example of kindness. A kindness that has impact.

The only problem Ikeda sees is that he had to find the article. It's much easier to get hold of bad news. It's easier to get into an argument than a debate. But these are the things he is hoping will change.

He finds another story. Two young women had their drinks spiked at a bar. They ended up in a car, believing it was a taxi taking them home. When one of them said she was going to throw up, the driver kicked both of them out and drove off. They were left in the cold for hours, drugged and scared. An Uber driver stopped and helped them back to their home.

He did it for nothing. He paused his jobs and drove out of his way, saving the girls from a potentially dangerous situation. He didn't know that, he just knew it was the right thing to do.

Ikeda smiles. It is a story of compassion that does not have the reach or dramatic impact of the clean-water initiative but these small acts mount up. This is the way to build a movement. And better yet, it is something that can go undetected. Millions of small acts of kindness. Ikeda will never get found out.

A quote from the Uber driver, later in the article, says that he had not been feeling well for days, he thought he might have the flu. He had been struggling to see straight because of a migraine, but he is self-employed – if he is sick, he doesn't get paid, so he pushed through.

The young girls said it was fate, that luck was on their side. But Ikeda knows exactly what it was. It was his virus.

It's working. And, in his mind, it is stronger than the Freya Hely-Hutchinsons of the world.

Doctor Haruto Ikeda sees only the good. In his haste, the idea of compassion fatigue never even occurred to him, he was only thinking about how he could save the world, how he could make people better.

People will get better. Their bodies will find a way to fight off the virus. What happens then? Will they go back to their apathy? Will it all be for nothing? A flicker of compassion?

This was never supposed to be the cure. Ikeda wanted to provide humanity with the tools for survival, to show them a better way. Give a man a fish and he can feed his family for a day. Give him a fishing rod and he can feed his family forever. But he could also use it to hang himself.

IT COULD MAKE CHINA LOOK WEAK

Tank Man was nothing.

The Publicity Department of the Central Committee of the Communist Party of China is something of a mouthful. As an acronym would also pose to be. It is more affectionately known as the Central Propaganda Department. There's no disguising it. It may as well be called the Chinese Disinformation Office or the Department for Spin and Indoctrination. It is responsible for spreading the ideology of the party, and its inner workings are as secretive as Harris Jackson's Megalomaniac Boys' Club.

There may be a billion people in China and hundreds of layers of bureaucracy but, when the video drops, the Propaganda Department works seamlessly with the State Council Information Office and the Ministry of Culture for one purpose.

Censorship.

They call in the big guns, too. The Cyberspace Administration of China. Forget the seven wonders of the modern world, this is The Great Firewall of China.

Nothing gets into the country that they don't want to get in. And if you find a way to do it, they can find a way that makes your site run at less than dial-up speed.

The video is devastating in its content but it is potentially more harmful to China in terms of how the world will now view its strength. There could be economic instability. Manufacturing and supply around the world could be massively impacted. But worst of all, the video could make China look weak. Like it needs help.

Unseen videos and images of Tank Man, halting the military with one hand while the other held his shopping bag, have surfaced over the decades since the event. They have fallen through the net.

This video will not.

It cannot.

The people of China will not see what is happening. They will think that everything is fine. The world is as it was yesterday. People are heading back into their office jobs, though there has been more of an openness to the occasional day working from home. Restaurants are opening fully. The markets are trading. Public transport is moving. Cars are being driven. Bikes are being cycled by people in face masks.

China is no longer locked down. But only internal flights are running, for now. Nothing foreign is coming in on a plane or an ethernet cable.

The only thing coming in is that gas. That yellow cloud, the size of Ireland, which has sprung up from somewhere unknown and swept across one of the most densely populated areas on Earth.

It is the hail.

The boils.

The darkness.

A plague, worse than any virus. It is fast-acting and brutal. There are videos that appear to be taken from mobile phones and there is professional news-camera footage. And none of it can be seen by the Chinese people.

But while it cannot penetrate the wall of security around China, it can travel to the West.

First the footage.

Then the gas.

There is a bang on the door of Harris Jackson's office but they do not wait for a response before pushing through the door.

'What the hell? I never said to come in.'

But Delaney cuts him off. It's before lunch so it was unlikely that the prime minister would have his trousers around his ankles and a new starter bent over his oversized desk.

'There's no time to stand on ceremony, I'm afraid. You have to see this.'

Delaney logs into his phone and swipes to the left a couple of times before tapping the screen. He hands the phone to Jackson.

'What the hell is so important that you would just barge in here like that?'

'Please. Harris. Just...'

Harris Jackson watches the first video. It's around thirty seconds in length and appears to be from a CCTV camera. It looks like a Chinese street market. There are vendors on stalls. Meat hanging from hooks. Large metal trays filled with different kinds of fish. An elderly woman uses two long wooden sticks to stir a boiling pot filled with around thirty eggs. Fruit. Spices. Dried flowers. Cakes. It's colourful and vibrant, and there are lots of people in attendance.

'Where is this?'

'Suzhou.' He pronounces it *Sooz-hoo*.

Jackson continues to watch. People walking, talking, shopping bags in their hands. It could be used as a tourism video for the area.

Then it comes.

In the distance, a yellow cloud starts to move down the canal. Within seconds, half the screen is covered in what seems like a dense smog. Nothing can be seen behind. The buildings disappear. They are swallowed up.

Another two seconds and the entire screen is flooded in swirls of ochre. It lasts for another ten seconds before clearing and showing utter devastation.

Whatever animals that were hanging from hooks on one of the stalls seem to be dripping. As do the faces of the people leaning against shop windows or lying on the floor. Anything that was once flesh is now some kind of viscous, gelatinous consistency. One woman, who was buying a turquoise beaded necklace moments before, has a hand on her face as her cheek slips through her fingers.

'Some Japanese horror film?' Harris says, showing his ignorance.

'Suzhou is in China, Harris. And this is taken from a security camera.'

'Or it's made to look that way. Come on, Delaney, are you telling me a deadly gas just wiped out a market square in China?'

'Swipe left. There's another one. This time with sound.'

This time it shows hundreds of people walking on a zebra crossing with skyscrapers behind them.

'This is not the same place,' Harris points out.

'Shanghai. Also China.'

'I know where bloody Shanghai is.'

Car horns and footsteps. People talking loudly on mobile phones. A porcelain-skinned woman waves at somebody across the street.

Then the sound.

You would think that a moving gas would be silent. Nobody hears clouds travelling through the sky. But this cloud is not like that. There's a buzz. A thrum. A constant humming like a billion locusts swarming and digesting everything in their wake.

The same thing happens as it did in the market by the canal.

First, the air turns a dirty yellow, almost brown.

Then the building disappears.

Then everything is covered. But this time, there is pain and torturous screaming. It's a different language but they are begging for their lives. At one point, a man is heard gargling and fighting for breath. Those closest to the camera swipe at the air, but to no avail.

When it clears, maybe three hundred people are lying in the middle of the road. Some are still. Dead, it seems. Others are crawling or trying to move. A car horn sounds continuously, as though somebody is slumped against their steering wheel.

'This is disgusting.' Jackson blows out his cheeks as if to signify he has thrown up in his mouth. 'It can't be real.'

'We have phoned the Chinese government to verify and nobody is picking up. Emails are bouncing back.'

'Okay. Get me the home secretary. I'll need MI6. And let's see what we can do with our diplomatic channels, too.'

Harris Jackson spends a lot of time preaching about 'fake news' even though the newspapers are generally correct in the things they print about the behaviour in his personal life. And he certainly isn't afraid to run his mouth off and spout things that he has made up on the spot. He knows that a lot of the information out there has been edited preferentially or somebody has employed artificial intelligence to make a point. The Chinese could be using the video as propaganda. But to what end?

For once, Jackson does the right thing and checks the information before opening his mouth on national television to respond to it.

He will not like what he finds out.

Churchill is regarded as a great wartime prime minister for his leadership during World War II.

Clement Attlee ranks high in the list of greatest prime ministers after inheriting an almost bankrupt post-war nation, but is praised highly for his welfare-state reform, involvement in NATO and, of course, the creation of the National Health Service.

Harris Jackson, much like Haruto Ikeda, will not be remembered. And, even if he could be, it would not be as the prime minister who restored the country to prosperity after the pandemic forced it into complete lockdown. It would be as the coward who bent over and surrendered.

SAVE YOURSELVES

Social media does what it does best: it causes hysteria.

The videos of the gas attack spread throughout the West. Clips of close-ups surface. People start posting reaction videos where they throw up. On some occasions, these videos are seen more times than the footage of the massacre itself.

There is panic.

Worse than with the virus.

Nobody is wearing their mask anymore. They don't care about hand sanitiser, it isn't going to save them. They need to go into hiding.

There is a run on towels and bedsheets because somebody said that they need to be soaked in water and placed at the bottom of all the doors.

It's trending.

And everybody wants masking tape and parcel tape because, apparently, doubling up is the best way to stop the gas from getting through gaps in the windows. It's mayhem in the supermarkets and the corner stores, and the online retailers are hiking their prices for next-day delivery.

Somebody is beaten up in Oslo for trying to take a pack of pillowcases when all the sheets had run out. There are hundreds of videos of women pulling at each other's hair because they want to stock up on tinned goods for the apocalypse. These images appear at the top of people's feeds instead of the news articles about China.

It's a mess.

Men scrapping in parking lots. Car crashes. Scared children.

Instead of stories of empathy for the huge loss of life, people in the West are worried about how this will affect them. And it doesn't take long for that to become the message.

Save yourselves.

None of this filters through to China. It's blocked. It is not going to help.

There is not much that the leaders of these countries can do at this time, because their people are scared, even if the gas feels like it is a million miles away.

They are afraid.

And it is the wrong kind of fear.

It is immediate. Instinctive.

That is not the kind that can be controlled.

FAMINES, PESTILENCE AND EARTHQUAKES

Edmund Whittle is what is known as a cultural attaché. He can travel where he wants, when he wants, with diplomatic privilege. He even has one of those brown, leather cases, like he sent off for a diplomatic kit when he obtained the role.

He has been an ambassador for the United Kingdom for over two decades but he has not been able to set foot in China for months. While nobody in the government seems able to make headway with contacting a representative from the East, it falls into his more-than-capable hands.

Whittle is good at his job. He's steady but firm. Ideal for diplomacy. A few feathers have been ruffled during his tenure but relationships remain intact.

He understands how difficult it can be when China decides to hide something or spin a situation. It's difficult to get in. Everyone thinks they have a contact that will help them breach the defence but they don't.

Whittle does.

'Thanks for taking my call,' Whittle says, but there is no voice at the other end. He understands the need for discretion more than most. 'We have seen a video.' Still nothing. 'Two, in fact. One that looks like low-quality CCTV and the other was maybe filmed on a phone.'

At some point during this conversation, Edmund Whittle is going to need a confirmation or a denial. But he can't force it. So he talks some more.

'It seems unreal. Brutal. Devastating. So is it a hoax that you are trying to keep under control, or did it really happen and a country has been ravaged by something the world has never seen before?'

Another long pause and then a voice at the other end of the phone line.

'Worse.'

'I'm sorry?'

'Ed, it is worse than you could possibly imagine.'

Whittle's contact goes on to explain the extent of the terror in his country. How he would long for another virus because it could not compare to the way the gas is ravaging his beloved China into ruin.

'God. I don't know what to say. Where is it now? Can it be contained? Stopped? What is it?' Whittle feels himself choking up. An unfathomable loss of life.

'We are advanced in many ways that the rest of the world is unaware of, but we do not know how to stop this. We hope for rain. Perhaps that can help. But it continues. We shut down to not cause panic. We can, at least, contain information, as you know.'

Now Whittle is the one not speaking. He nods along in agreement at his old friend's words.

'Do you have flights in the UK yet?'

'Um, no. They're supposed to start in the next week, perhaps.'

'No foreign travel?'

'There may be lorry deliveries through the tunnel with France but that is it.'

'We are friends, yes, Ed?'

'Many years.'

'Then hear me. Use all of the tools you have available to you to get out of the UK. Don't wait. Just go.'

He hangs up. Edmund Whittle knows that he will not be able to get through to his contact again, now. The call was a courtesy. He will have much work ahead of him.

Whittle sits in silence for a while, the telephone still in his hand. Shocked. Upset. And worried about the warning. It feels like the end of days.

For nation will rise against nation, and kingdom against kingdom:

and there shall be famines, and pestilence, and earthquakes in diverse places.

All these are the beginning of sorrows.

What feels like signs of the end can also be construed as birth pains.

Whittle is not a particularly pious man but he understands a sign when he sees one. He is a diplomat, it is his job to pick up on subtle cues or tics. Like a poker player spotting somebody's tell. This is the Earth saying that she is angry. That mankind will have to pay.

And he knows a thing or two about advice, whether it is genuine or it cloaks a different meaning. What he received was neither of these. It was an order.

Get out.

Now.

Find a way.

He snaps out of his pondering and puts in another call, to Delaney, and tells him everything. Everything but the fact that after he has hung up, he will not be contactable because he is going to call in every favour he is owed and barter with everything at his disposal to get him off this God-forsaken island.

LOOK AWAY NOW

Fox News reports on the video before verifying whether or not it was taken from the set of a Hollywood blockbuster.

'Horrifying scenes from Suzhou in China today, where a mysterious gas was unleashed on an unsuspecting public as they innocently shopped for their groceries. The yellow dust cloud moved down the canal at great speed, smothering those who were out to pick up a quart of milk and some potatoes for dinner. Discretion is advised. Some of the scenes in this video may be unsuitable for younger viewers.'

The anchor sits back in his chair, feigning concern before the tape rolls.

It's the same as the CCTV footage that Delaney showed to the prime minister but from a shop on the opposite side of the street.

'Nobody has come forward yet to claim responsibility for this most heinous act.'

The Americans want to get there first. Seem like they discovered the incident. They call it 'horrifying'. They say the Chinese are 'innocent'. They want the viewer to feel sympathetic.

And then they go straight for the fundamentalist angle.

The war on terror.

Make America Great Again.

Russian TV opts for an angle of relief. They could have been affected but it seems that the 'giant ball of poison' is moving in a southerly direction. Away from Russia.

Their news anchor doesn't bother pretending to be emotionally invested in a town full of Chinese people he never knew. He sits back while the graphics switch to a satellite image depicting the travel of the cloud.

The Germans report on the speculation by the Americans and the Russians. But they do not validate the footage they have seen – though they still show it.

Eventually, Britain weighs in.

They collate the information they have gathered and they allow their most esteemed and beloved BBC newsreader to deliver the information to the people.

'We have, today, learned of the devastating news that China has been the victim of a horror, the likes of which has never before been seen. Understandably, the country has been rocked by events and it has been almost impossible to speak with appropriate representatives, but we have been reliably informed that this was not something that affected only Suzhou and Wuxi. We also do not believe that this was a terrorist attack against China but more of a natural phenomenon like an earthquake or tsunami.'

He pauses here, not because he thinks he should. Not for effect. But because he needs to digest the magnitude of the situation.

'While many of us here were resting in our beds, peaceful in the knowledge that our release from the confines of lockdown are imminent, China was being subjected to an horrendous ordeal from the emergence of a mysterious gas that, from the footage you are about to see, appears toxic to the lungs and caustic to both hair and skin. If there are children or people of a nervous disposition watching, please make sure they look away now.'

Adults across the land are so enthralled that many forget to avert their children's gazes. It doesn't matter, though, because they can still hear the screaming and crying for help. It is harrowing. There are tears and vomiting, particularly from those who have been infected by Ikeda's virus.

The newsreader goes off script.

'These are, indeed, dark times. I have never, in all of my years of service to journalism, seen anything quite like this. I have covered wars and terrorist atrocities. Elections and sporting triumphs. This defies all logic.'

He stops for a moment, rests his elbows on the desk and places his hand in a prayer position, his chin resting against his thumbs, the tips of his forefingers against his brow.

'Organisations around the world are reporting on this. They show footage of Suzhou and they talk of Wuxi as if that is the extent of the damage. A source in China has reached out to the UK government, against the information lockdown currently under way, to inform us that things are much worse than that.'

Deep breath.

'It is with an immensely heavy heart and absolute disbelief that I have to say, the gas started in the north-east of China and travelled diagonally towards the south-west, which encompasses the majority of the most densely populated areas of the country. Conservative estimates suggest that ... that ... half the population has been affected in some way by this mysterious phenomenon, most of whom have died. The population of China is approximately half of what it was when you went to bed last night.'

The United Kingdom is brought together again. This time in shock. Parents stare at their television screens while their children cry in the background at the horror movie they just witnessed.

Viewers pour a glass of wine.

They call their loved ones.

They check in on friends that they haven't heard from for a while. Everything seems to pale in comparison to what China is experiencing. Nobody cares about the stupid virus anymore. They want to hug their friends and their neighbours.

This is a massacre.

'With air travel still limited due to the pandemic, it will be difficult to provide aid to the Chinese people, and their government is denying access to their air space for any foreign aircraft. We should respect that. We will report more, as and when information becomes available. The Met Office is trying to determine the origins and whereabouts of the gas. Please stay tuned for a message from our prime minister, Harris Jackson.'

THE UNITED WORLD

He is clean cut. Not handsome, but pretty. He's a pretty man. Tall. Slender. Athletic. Crease-free suit.

And he's alive.

He's in Beijing and he is alive.

The room is dark and he is alone. Images of dead Chinese people with blistered skin and burnt scalps circulate on every kind of screen in the West, and this man looks perfectly coiffed. Dark hair parted neatly on the left. A tailored suit that is deliberately short in the leg to allow more freedom of movement.

The Chinese premier cannot even access a web page that is not hosted in his home nation, but this manicured man sits in what looks to be a bunker and watches Harris Jackson make a speech of sympathy.

'It is with deepest condolence that I offer my sympathy to the people of China, who have lost loved ones today in this terrible unnatural disaster. Such a gigantic loss of life and time. So sudden and unexpected, and on a scale which has never been seen in all human existence.'

Jackson wanted to compare it, mathematically, to the Jewish holocaust, but was advised against pairing one tragedy with another, particularly in the light of recent antisemitic allegations within his own party.

In China, a man looks on from the comfort of his technological underground suite and forces himself to breathe slowly.

'...such a strong nation, a proud nation...'

He shuts his eyes and grips his left hand into a fist.

Breathe.

'Half a billion people. Half a billion lives cut short. It is so difficult to comprehend such a bleak and merciless statistic. Now is a time to come together, not just as the United Kingdom, but as a united world. We must put aside our differences. Look out for each other.'

He then goes on a long diatribe that seems to say that he wants an end to fighting and war because existence can be over in a split second. Without warning.

Jackson says that London has knife crime and America has gun crime. Nine countries have nuclear weapons. It feels like he is putting his name in the hat for a Nobel Peace Prize. That what he wants is the same thing that Haruto Ikeda wants.

'Because there are forces unknown to us now. Deadly viruses. Killer gases. We don't know where they come from and we don't know how to stop them.'

Cue another few minutes on the environmental damage that man has caused. Polar ice caps melting. Methane gas. Drilling for oil.

The one person in China watching Jackson's speech turns it off part way. He can't listen to the pontificating liar a moment longer. He sits in the gloom, just the red LED on the front of the screen for light and he pictures Harris Jackson, the man he blames for this. They would not be in this situation if it were not for him.

He is not a genuine man.

He is not a man of thought.

Bravado.

Libido.

'They eat dogs.'

He is a monster and proof, if it were needed, that there can be no God, for no god would allow such a buffoon to avoid the justice he deserves.

Someone else will have to make him pay.

A NATURALLY OCCURRING CATACLYSM

Russia is first.

Harris Jackson suspects that the 'gas' that is ravaging its way across one of the most densely populated territories on Earth may have been deliberately released. Some kind of biological weapon that the world is just not ready for.

Russia has led the way in this area and has been suspected of releasing a nerve agent within a UK pizza-restaurant chain, not with the view of harming British citizens but for poisoning a former intelligence officer, who allegedly sold state secrets.

The Russians have nuclear capabilities but are shrewd enough to know that the world has moved on, and the real threat is from chemical warfare or cybercrime.

Jackson puts in a call to his secret ally. Russia shares over four thousand kilometres of border with China, so it would be easier for them to launch a surprise attack than it would for the US. And the Russian leader has made no secret that his preferred method of politics is brutality.

'If I had that kind of capability, Harris, I would not stop with China.' He laughs, but Jackson knows that he means it. It seems to make sense.

It wasn't the Russians, he decides.

It wasn't the Americans, either. The president is insulted that the question should even be raised.

'It's just a case of doing my fact-checking. Due diligence. This is scary, we need to find out where it came from,' Harris bats back. Then ruins it by saying, 'We're not just going to run with the first thing we hear, like Fox News.'

He receives a spikier response from his German contact. And the French president, far from shrugging his shoulders, launches a tirade of abuse towards the prime minister for his lack of sensitivity. Jackson is tempted to call the Canadian prime minister, who would probably find a way to apologise for causing any inconvenience, just to have an exchange that didn't end in acrimony.

If nobody from his secret group is claiming responsibility, that leaves only two options: it was an act of terrorism from elsewhere or it was a naturally occurring cataclysm. Neither of which is ideal. But at least if it is North Korea or Iran or Guinea Bissau or anywhere, there is a target that everyone can launch bombs at.

If this came from somewhere inside the earth, if it seeped out of the ground or flew in from space, there would be no way to stop it. The thing has already taken seven percent of the world's population. There's no saying what further damage it could cause.

At his desk, Harris Jackson rests on his elbows and clenches his hands together. And he prays. He begs a God that he only pretends to believe in at Christmas or on Remembrance Day or when he has to address the nation after a tragedy and deliver the platitude, 'Our thoughts and prayers are with ... whoever.'

With hands clasped and face to the heavens, Harris Jackson begs God that this cloud was an act of terrorism.

EVERYONE IS WATCHING. EVERYONE IS SCARED

The gas turns.
Met Office satellites have worked out the route that it has taken

so far. It is not conclusive but there is a faint sign that it first gathered shape either in Choibalsan, in the north-east of Mongolia or north of that, in Chita, Russia.

The image really starts to 'thicken' in the north-east of China, around Harbin and Changchun, which could mean it started near Khabarovsk before working its way down. Oddly, as it travels towards Shenyang, it does not even cross the border into North Korea. Not even by one centimetre. But that is something for the intelligence community to consider, not the Met Office. They are just plotting the path of the gas.

And it turns.

Beijing. South towards Nanjing. Hangzhou and Wuhan. Then it hits the sea and veers of course, saving Vietnam and Laos, which seemed the natural trajectory.

It turns, still strong. Vast. It swirls over the South China Sea and manages to squeeze between Taiwan and the Philippines, where no casualties have been reported, so far.

Then it just disappears.

Perhaps it dissipated into the atmosphere or was swallowed by the sea. These are things that have to be investigated, but, for now it seems the gas has gone.

Every country in the West is monitoring the skies and the weather. They are replaying the route the gas took and the wind directions and temperature. They have to think about themselves. Harris Jackson may have given a stirring eulogy for the Chinese people, invoking the need for a global community, but nobody knows what this thing is, where it has gone and whether it's coming back.

Maybe it is a Chinese thing.

When it comes to natural disasters, the US and Canada hold all the records for casualties as a result of wildfires. The States dominates on winter storms, too, with the exception of a freak blizzard in Iran in 1972.

Indonesia features highly in both volcanic eruptions and tsunamis, despite Japan being more associated with the latter.

Tropical cyclones: Bangladesh.

Tornadoes: also Bangladesh.

Europe starts to get involved when it comes to heatwaves.

Then China comes into its own.

They've got floods all sewn up. Four million deaths in the 1931 China floods. Another two million on the Yellow River in 1887. Throw in the Banqiao Dam Failure for the hat-trick.

The Great Chinese Famine killed nearly forty million people. And it's only called 'Great' because they had already had the Chinese famine of 1906–07, which *only* took twenty-five million lives.

The Tangshan earthquake is the most fatal in history.

And the top three deadly landslides of all time occurred in China, either as a result of an earthquake or flooding.

Now they have whatever this gas is.

That's going to be hard to beat.

Every other country has empathy for the magnitude of the loss of life, but they also have their fingers crossed that this is another thing that China will be known for. Perhaps the winds will disperse it neatly over the Pacific. Or there will be smaller incidents in Japan or New Guinea before it fully dies down.

Everybody but China is watching.

And everyone is scared.

Because it looks as though it is gone, but, with any great plague, there is a moment of darkness. The only thing that can follow is the killing of first-born children.

ARMCHAIR PSYCHOLOGISTS

Bring on the trolls.

The nuts.

The conspiracy theories.

The armchair scientists.

And the influencers.

A disgusting social-media account, @RuleBr1ttania, often spouts racist rhetoric dressed up as patriotism. The things they post are more and more demeaning to ensure that they get the airtime they crave so much.

They say that God did this. Something about cleansing the Earth. They pretend they are proud to be English. God Save the Queen. But these wife-beater-vest-wearing, overweight, shaven-headed morons haven't set foot in a church since their ignorant parents had them christened because they wanted presents and a party.

They quote Nostradamus. Something about a Muslim Armageddon. Something else about 'yellow people'. And they say, 'Whatever the gas was, it didn't work. It only got half of them.'

This type of clickbait does not get through the Chinese firewall. Nobody there is seeing it. Otherwise Haruto Ikeda would consider himself a complete failure.

He is still finding stories of kindness. Somebody was talked down off a bridge in Seoul. A woman in New Delhi was complimented on her style twice on the way to work and it made her day. In Tokyo, a family with a bunker in their garden realise they have enough room for the neighbouring family. They have never really spoken but they could not leave them out there in fear. Levels of kindness that are met and cancelled out by levels of nastiness. Ikeda doesn't want balance, he wants compassion to win, but he knows it takes time.

The nuts and the conspiracy theorists overlap. Some are saying that the Met Office images make it look as though it came from Russia. Somebody else says that the Chinese did it to themselves, that they were testing a weapon and it went wrong. Then there are others who say that it never happened at all. Or that aliens were involved. Or crop circles. Or that it gives them a reason to go to war with the West, which is what they have been building towards.

Of course, there are people who have Googled 'deadly gases' or 'natural poisonous gas examples' and then paraphrase an article, inaccurately, that they have only half read but fits the theory they already had in their heads before they hit the search button.

All of them get people talking.

And the point is that social media should be sociable. It should provoke debate and constructive discourse, but it also encourages righteousness and the idea that something is either right or wrong, with nothing in between, and it gives people an elevated sense of self-worth.

All the things that Haruto Ikeda was fighting against.

Bring back the days when people were only worried about a virus.

But it's not all about the gloom-mongers and narcissists – it's just that they seem to get the most views because they are divisive.

Charlie Eckhart is a stand-up comedian. Observational humour. Topical. Political at times. He had never been on television or had a Netflix special. He doesn't get asked to appear on panel shows. But, during the lockdown, he streamed half-hour bits to keep people laughing.

And it took off.

His following grew exponentially as people looked for any way to gain some relief from their prisons. Sure, he started making money out of it, because, all of a sudden, a million people were watching his videos on YouTube rather than a few thousand.

He isn't one to punch down. He doesn't go for shock. He's anecdotal but relevant. He pokes fun at Harris Jackson. He's impudent but doesn't overstep the mark. He believes that a comedian can say whatever they want but they have to say it in the right way. And every funny, witty set he creates and posts ends with a final thought. Nothing too deep but certainly positive without being sickly.

It was difficult for Charlie Eckhart to watch the news about what happened in China. The subject matter was, of course, horrific, but he was also struggling with what he thought was a migraine and it was difficult to look at the brightness of the TV screen.

But that has passed. The migraine medicine he usually takes didn't help at all.

He doesn't like the internet trolls or the nuts or the armchair psychologists. He has enough followers now that he could legitimately refer to himself as an influencer. He doesn't. He is a comedian. But, before that, he is a human being.

He hits record on his camera.

'I know that you've clicked on this hoping that I will help you forget the world for half an hour, but, today, that doesn't feel right. I know that we may need laughter more than ever in the wake of the things we are seeing on the news, but there is something that we need even more. Each other.'

Eckhart is not solemn. He is pensive. Genuine. Serious.

A serious comedian.

'We arrive in this world the same. Naked. Confused. Desperate for air. Cold. Clamouring instinctively for our mothers. But we cannot get through life on instinct alone. Life is long and it's hard, and we have to endure the death of our loved ones and we have to have our hearts broken more than once. We have to work in a job that doesn't pay us enough money or give us enough respect or fulfil us in a meaningful way. It can be horrible. And it can all be over too soon.'

This is the point where a lot of people who have received so much joy from Eckhart's jokes over the weeks will switch off.

'These are the things that we tend to go through alone. We keep sorrow to ourselves and we don't talk as much as we should about the things that really matter. But here is the thing: along with despair and heartache, there is joy, love, happiness and hope. There is good. But for these things, we cannot be alone. We have to be together. Now is that time. Reach out. We are not meant to go through this journey by ourselves. It is not supposed to feel like this.'

It is a message of optimism and conviction. Charlie Eckhart had this in him from the beginning, but Ikeda's virus pushed him that step further. To put himself out there. Put himself on the line rather than merely online. Everything that Harris Jackson delivered so disingenuously in his last speech about a global community is said by a relatively unknown comic but in a more simple and endearing way.

And over half the audience switches off before the end.

This is what Ikeda was fighting. Not the crazy theories or the bigots or misinformation. It is the apathy.

Maybe Harris Jackson was right. Goodwill just doesn't have the same kind of staying power as good old-fashioned tragedy.

LIFE IS BACK TO NORMAL-ISH

It's brief but the Met Office picks up something that looks like the gas over Yagodnoye in Russia. It dances around the way that swallows fly but on a much greater scale, and then it disappears again. It is almost like the gas took a left at sea and was taken by the wind towards the Arctic Ocean.

But its presence is fleeting.

Like a storm began to brew and then just died.

It changed its mind.

Harris Jackson is alerted and decides that it should be monitored but that there is no sense in alarming the British public because it has been over a day now, and this morning is very important because the lockdown ends. It is just what the country needs.

Many companies are still cautious about workers suddenly returning to the office, but there are more cars on the roads and noise in the street. Market traders are calling out the price of strawberries and police officers are present in large cities. Coffee chains are bustling with life and people seem happier than ever to queue.

The trains are running but not at full capacity, and it will be another week before the airports are in any kind of shape to transport people to another country or accept tourists to give the economy a much-needed boost.

Julie Hibbert in Bolton reopens her hairdressing salon. The

government grant was helpful while she was closed, and it is going to be a slog to get herself back on top financially, but there are women waiting who are long overdue a trim. She can see bad home dye-jobs that will need correcting. Men have been cutting their own hair in the mirror and long to have things rectified because the YouTube tutorials could only show so much.

Shelly Douglas works for a builders' merchant in Essex. External sales. Her job is driving around the country selling manhole covers. She hates it. But today she can't wait to get out on the road, because teaching primary school mathematics at home to her two kids has sucked the life out of her more than talking about drains and getting whistled at on building sites ever has.

Black cabs and red double-decker buses complete the formerly empty London roads.

At lunchtime, joggers are back on the streets or they are filling up the gyms that managed to survive putting their membership payments on hold.

The supermarkets are open, but fruit and veg are at a higher price than usual because supply chains are not back to normal yet. Typically, this would cause outrage, but people just seem happy to be outside, breathing the freshly polluted air.

It's busy at the Met Office, which is continuing to provide weather- and climate-related services to the government and businesses but is also putting together a small group to delve into the gas that obliterated China.

Russia is on alert after their satellites picked up an intermittent swell of activity over the Laptev Sea. It was a fraction of a second but they are not taking any chances. It's an excellent bluff to put your country on stand-by if you are the ones who launched the bioweapon, but the Russian leader has assured Harris Jackson that the gas is nothing to do with him. And Jackson believes him, for now.

Food deliveries saw a roaring trade during lockdown. Some people were setting up their own pop-ups in an attempt to make some money while they couldn't attend their usual job. Thomas Pepper made a killing with his wood-fired pizzas in Truro. He made them to order, and his wife delivered them.

But not tonight. They are back to their nine-to-fives. The kids are at school. And they are all sick of pizza. They book to go out for a curry. And so do millions of others. They have had enough of online cook-a-longs followed by a countrywide quiz.

It was novel.

And now it is over.

Life is back to normal-ish.

Cinemas are open but only at half capacity because they have to leave one seat of space between each person to adhere to social-distancing rules. Luckily, there is plenty to watch. The lockdown in Hollywood will only have an impact on the films that are due out two years from now.

The country is happy, mostly healthy, and together. They faced a virus head-on and they prevailed. And they know how lucky they are because it could have been much worse. So people are grabbing at life with both hands. Even if they are worried about money, they tell themselves that they deserve to eat out or go to a bar and buy a decent bottle of wine, or watch a movie on a big screen, or simply go to a friend's house or hug their parents rather than faking merriment on a laptop screen.

The country is not hopeful, but they are happy.

Then the gas turns.

DOES SHUTTING THE WINDOWS KEEP IT OUT?

Governments around the world hold crisis meetings but several leaders and high-ranking officials require a meeting of their own. To pool resources. To spitball ideas. The secret cabal have to talk.

There are no flights. It would be a hassle but the American president could land Air Force One at Heathrow if he really wanted, but there just isn't time. They do what the world has been doing for the past few months and they set up a video conference. It's obviously more secure than a Zoom call but it is, essentially, the same thing.

Each member goes to a remote location and they log in at the same time.

They know what is happening. At 21:03 GMT, a dense cloud was seen flying low and heading west over the Komsomolets Islands towards the Kara Sea. Luckily, the islands are uninhabited and comprised largely of icebergs and tundra.

That is inconsequential. The thing that matters is that the gas is back. It appears to be moving with the wind or the flow of the oceans. It is almost like it is in orbit around Russia, making the country more suspicious to its alleged allies.

Maybe it's not the same gas. Maybe it has leaked elsewhere.

Maybe it is leaking all over.

Conversation becomes heated. Harris says something stupid about sticking the nuclear codes up his Russian counterpart's arse. The Russian, again, denies any involvement with what happened to the Chinese people. He then throws out some threats of his own.

You bomb me.

I bomb you.

America bombs us both.

'This is why we have the nuclear weapons, Jackson. So that we don't have to use them. So that we don't ever have to go to war against one another. So that we don't end the world. So let us stay calm.'

At 21:09, the gas looked to have hardly moved. It swirled and danced above the icebergs and then disappeared from view again. Jackson has his satellites zooming in on the islands to make sure there is no army base secreted there that the gas could have come from.

The leaders agree to share intelligence and military strategy should the gas reappear near a populated area. At its current trajectory, if it was still moving but somehow undetectable, it would hit the Norwegian archipelago, Svalbard, in a day or so.

Nobody wants that. There are people there. Only 2,500 or so, but they would be affected. They would perish. The cloud is large enough to wipe the area out. And, if it just reappears again, there will not be enough time to evacuate.

'We don't know how to stop this thing,' Harris says. 'Can we lock ourselves in a bunker? I've only just relaxed the lockdown. Does shutting the windows keep it out? We need intel and we need it fast. Could it be extinguished, perhaps, or combusted if mixed with the right compounds? We have to work together on this. There is too much to lose.'

After an hour of bluster and peacocking and hidden panic, these powerful men agree to serve the greater good rather than their own self-interest.

And all it took was the indiscriminate massacre of half a billion human beings.

This is the world that Dr Ikeda was trying to save.

JUST DOING MY JOB, MA'AM

The problem is gaining intel on something that cannot be seen. The Russians could scramble some jets over the sea and hope that they spot it. Then what? How do they collect a sample? How long will tests take to find out what it is?

And then how long to develop something that can neutralise it before any further damage is caused?

It would be useful to get a closer look at the after-effects, but the Chinese government has the country shut off from the world. No information gets in or out. And no people are getting in or out, either.

It's a mess.

But in the UK the mood is largely positive and optimistic for the future. Pubs call last orders at eleven and they're still full. They have taken more money today than they usually would over a weekend.

Customers are happy to be out. There are no fights. Strangers talk to one-another, they hold open doors, they take turns at the pool table.

Friendships are rekindled and new ones are made. People pair off to go home with somebody new or have a quick fix against a tree. Romance blossoms and conversations bubble with humour and gratitude.

Taxi drivers are happy to hear the same old questions they used to get, and restaurant staff are pleased that their feet ache because the tips have been generous. The kitchen crew don't mind cleaning all the surfaces and pans. Everyone is just happy to be doing something normal. Even if it is something they hated before lockdown. It is needed.

For hospital staff, nothing has really changed. The patients who were terminal before the lockdown are still going to die. The entire system is still teetering towards breaking point with the number of people affected by the virus, who everybody seems to have suddenly forgotten about.

Like it's over.

The Met Office is instructed to coordinate with other countries. For some, this doesn't sit well. This will have to be handled deftly so as not to give away what the UK might be observing from space that is not just related to monitoring the weather.

Harris Jackson gets home after midnight. He has had a few drinks and squeezed a few women's legs. Nothing has changed there. His children are fast asleep, but his wife is waiting up for him.

At first he is worried that news of his wandering hands has already made its way back, and he imagines who could have blabbed, but her demeanour is not one of anger. Quite the opposite. She looks relaxed. Grey joggers and a white vest, her feet on the sofa, glass of red wine in her hand.

'Good evening, sir,' she teases.

'Sir? Darling, what's going on?'

She stands up and walks over to him. Then she takes a swig of her wine, swallows loudly and licks her top lip.

'I hear that you are the man who saved the country from a deadly virus.'

He has heard this voice before. He knows the game she is playing.

'Just doing my job, ma'am.' He smiles. He takes the glass out of her hand and he drinks. She runs a finger down his chest.

'I just don't know if I could ever repay you for getting us out of this.'

'Well, you could start by getting yourself out of that.' He tugs at her vest and she obliges, throwing it on the floor behind her before moving in for a kiss.

Harris Jackson was not sure that he would be able to get back what was lost when his wife found out about his most recent indiscretion. But it appears that he's got away with it again.

She unbuckles his belt.

Damn, it's good to be the man at the top.

CRISIS HAS BEEN AVERTED

The good news is that the gas does not reappear over Svalbard. Jackson wakes up like he is a character in a Disney animated film. He can't stop whistling jaunty melodies that he makes up on the spot. He half expects some bluebirds to fly into the kitchen and sweep up the crumbs from his toast.

He is back in favour with his wife and his country. There were no calls in the middle of the night from the military or other world leaders. He has a meeting at 9:00 to debrief on the gas situation, but now, he makes himself and his beautiful, doting wife a mug of coffee.

The news about the gas is that there is no news, which Jackson takes as a good thing. The next subject is that Edmund Whittle, cultural attaché to China, has seemingly left the UK.

'What?' Jackson is confused. 'How the hell did he do that? Nobody can do that yet.'

It seems that Whittle used all of his diplomatic clout to travel through the Channel Tunnel. He was flagged up in France but is apparently on his way to Belgium.

'Get hold of him, will you? He's long-serving. I'm sure he is exploring avenues to get more information from the Chinese. I don't know what he has in Belgium that will help, but I probably don't have as many contacts as he does.'

Harris Jackson brushes it off as a trivial matter; there are much bigger things to consider.

Whittle is, indeed, a long-serving diplomat. He is old and he has seen enough of the world to understand that it is broken, and quite possibly irreparable. He plans to travel to Bruges and live out the remainder of his days eating *tartiflette* and chocolate while drinking unfeasibly strong craft beer and pairing Reblochon cheese with Côtes du Rhone.

He has earned it.

Now he just wants to live a little.

'Two hundred and six deaths from the virus yesterday, which is the lowest since the outbreak.'

Jackson nods along to the news like that is an acceptable number.

His military advisor speaks next, updating him on a Russian recon mission over the Kara Sea. 'They scoured an area the size of Switzerland based on their calculations of the speed of the gas and where it might be if still on the same trajectory.'

'What did they find?'

'Nothing. No remnants at all.'

'Could we get our own guys out there? I'm not saying that I don't trust the Russians, but I definitely do not trust the Russians.'

'I'll get on that right away, sir.' He seems excited, as all military personnel do when they know that they will get to use their favourite toys. They didn't get into this business to run around Sandhurst in their boots. They want to spy on other countries and drop bombs to assert their dominance.

Harris Jackson wraps up the meeting, saying that he has to leave for his weekly audience with the queen. For all his bluster, he takes this appointment incredibly seriously and considers it a great honour. It is not just a tradition, she has an astute mind and manages to remain entirely neutral on any topic they discuss, offering the wisdom of her years in power, during which she has already seen eight prime ministers come and go.

It feels like normality has resumed. Of course, this worry about the gas is distracting but terrorist dangers are silently thwarted all the time, otherwise the people would be living in constant fear.

And that is exactly what Jackson plans to do with this gas situation.

He will handle it.

That's what he does.

He takes a shit situation and turns it to his advantage.

He's Harris Jackson and he always comes out on top.

The remainder of the day goes by without incident. Jackson's meeting with the queen is a success. She has concerns about China, naturally, but her advice is to not loosen grip on the virus. If you take your eye off the ball, that will come back on you, and while the praise is being heaped in Jackson's direction, right now, if the number of deaths starts to creep up again, that will come crashing down on his shoulders.

He eats lunch at his desk and manages not to stick his angry inch inside any of his female staff. In fact, he calls his wife to discuss what they did the night before, relive some of the highlights.

Following lunch, he has an informal meeting with his new minister for education after the previous one resigned, citing a need for student grants to be reimplemented. They drink a whisky at the Strangers' Bar, now fully functioning, and the new minister agrees to 'no more of this grant nonsense'.

Jackson texts his wife. He is feeling powerful today. Invincible, even. He suggests meeting in an hour for a 'nooner'. She tells him it is a wonderful idea but that he could try being less vulgar about their love-making. Besides, the children are playing up today and she couldn't even spare thirty seconds for one of his famous knee-tremblers.

His afternoon is filled with managing the opposition and the governments of Scotland, Wales and Northern Ireland. Then he has to chair the cabinet and set its agenda, focussing on the message of social responsibility now that lockdown has lifted.

At 18:21 he speaks with the Met Office, as that is the time the gas would have hit Svalbard at its previous speed and trajectory. Nothing has shown on satellite imagery. Svalbard is intact. Everyone is alive. There's nothing in the sky.

'We will continue to monitor, sir, but it seems that crisis has been averted on this occasion.'

Harris Jackson returns to his family just after eight. One of the kids is already in bed. He goes in and kisses them on the forehead, gently. He's exhausted and hungry, but a hard day's work has not dented his libido in the slightest.

His wife is in the kitchen warming through a carbonara she made from scratch.

'Here you go. Keep your strength up.' She kisses him on the top of the head and takes the other child upstairs. 'I'll be back down after story time. Eat up. Keep your strength up.'

Harris Jackson smiles as though there was some kind of hidden flirtation in what his wife said. He will need every ounce of stamina in two hours when he receives an urgent call from British intelligence and defence services, saying that the gas is back.

It's bigger.

It has turned again.

Heading south-west.

Straight for Great Britain.

There are not enough thoughts and prayers.

REASONS THAT NOBODY CAN FATHOM

The Western world falls into a spin. The Norwegians take a moment to rejoice in the fact that the gas missed them but then drop back into hiding, knowing that it can seemingly disappear and reappear wherever it wants to.

None of this message penetrates The Great Firewall of China.

They have their own problems to deal with, anyway.

Germany has been in full lockdown for days. People living in their cellars, huddled with their families, watching the BBC World coverage of events. They wear their face coverings inside and they have gas masks for if the time comes.

If the wind changes direction.

If they are next.

And every country starts to worry that it could be their time that is up. There are so many people gathered in prayer at the Vatican that it has more than doubled its usual population. The only people in Rome who feel safe, right now, are the altar boys.

Even France goes along with the majority. The people have been instructed to remain at home until further notice unless they are already at a wine bar or restaurant, then they should absolutely remain there.

The Russian people are on high alert because they appear to have narrowly escaped the deadly gas that ravaged half the population of China. There are riots in Belarus. In Estonia, they are letting off fireworks for reasons that nobody can fathom.

The Americans should feel safe because the gas doesn't seem to be able to move that fast, so they have taken to the internet to call out government conspiracies or blame the Mexicans for reasons that make the Estonian fireworks look like a viable deterrent.

Whether it is fear or the need for self-preservation or concern for others, it amalgamates into something that can only be identified as hysteria. And that's the only thing that makes sense. Because a poisonous gas that kills half of the Chinese people then disappears out to sea, before making a beeline towards the United Kingdom, sounds like science fiction.

The world may have grown kinder recently, but kind people can still get scared.

Fear is what Harris Jackson and his cronies wanted in the first place.

But not like this.

IT'S MRS ADAMSON

The gas doesn't disappear this time, which fills the general with positivity, because it, at least, gives him something to aim at.

A select committee meet to discuss ways in which they could stop the gas reaching the British shores.

Dropping containers of seawater on top of the gas – like they do with forest fires – was a popular initial option. But the size of the cloud is so immense that they could never scramble enough helicopters over it even to make a dent.

Perhaps a well-timed nuclear explosion near sea level could drench the gas from underneath. Scientists are getting to work on the numbers.

An even more precisely timed explosion within the cloud could potentially raise the temperature enough that it ignites the gas over the sea.

Is there a way to cool it down so that it sublimates and drops into the water below?

What about a barrier?

This is a time to panic. People around the table are losing their calm. This is the potential annihilation of the entire country. But Harris Jackson remains cool. Because he must, but also because, while he finds it difficult to implement the policies he promised during his election campaign, his greatest skill is getting out of sticky situations.

He's always done it.

Jackson is invincible.

He remains calm and clear, as a leader should. But even he cannot see a way out of this one. That cloud is heading in a straight line of utter destruction. He can throw everything at it that the army has to offer. He could tell the country to lock back down and hope for the best, shut the doors and windows. If there is a cellar, get into it. All of those conspiracy nuts who invested in an end-of-the-world bunker could be laughing at him in a couple of days as they eat cold beans from a tin while Jackson's eyes melt out of their sockets.

They could risk letting the Russians take a sample. From the video of the China incident, the burning of eyes and hair could indicate an abnormally large concentration of sulphur dioxide. That means it could be neutralised with sodium bicarbonate. Again, there is the difficulty of how to administer this, but it is something else that can be thrown into the mix of ideas.

Along with the prime minister, handfuls of top scientists and the best military minds in the country, Jackson's deputy, Henrietta Adamson, is also present.

And she is unshakeable.

'There is no time to get people away from here. It would be absolute pandemonium to orchestrate a mass exodus. The planes haven't run for months. And who is going to go to work knowing that there is a giant, poisonous cloud on its way towards us? You think that Jackie from Sussex is turning up at Gatwick to get trampled to death and die outside a Burger King for £6.20 an hour?'

She is talking straight and talking sense.

Nobody can deny that.

'We can throw everything we have at this thing, and maybe we should, but we don't know what it is. We send a bomb into it, it could ignite and incinerate the whole of Scotland in seconds. We just don't know. I understand that you like to blow stuff up, General, but that doesn't sound prudent without the intel to make such a decision.'

A few 'hear hears' ring out around the room.

'What do you suggest, then, Ms Adamson?' The military advisor is clearly put out.

'Firstly, it's Mrs Adamson. If you can't get that right then we shouldn't trust you with the codes to our nuclear arsenal.'

Cue nervous laughter.

'Honestly, I am English. And I am proud. I was thinking of addressing the nation – stiff upper lip, cup of tea – and advise everyone to meet with their loved ones and hunker down. Wet some towels and put them at the bottom of all the doors. Tape the windows shut. Take our chances.'

'That's your great plan? Sit around and hope our skin doesn't melt away from our bodies? Keep our fingers crossed that we don't have to endure an immense agony?' The defence secretary is livid. 'Sir, I beg of you, let's shoot something at this thing. Give us a chance at winning.'

The room erupts. Shouts across the table of 'madman' and 'coward'. Hands slamming down on wood. Fake laughter. Eyes rolling. Spilled drinks. Chair legs scraping against the floor.

'Quiet.' Jackson raises his voice.

Everyone stops.

They look at him.

'The situation is dire. And we are at a loss. We can unleash the fury of the British army, navy and air force, but this is not a conventional enemy. We could not have foreseen such a grim and dismal end. But make no mistake, that is what this is. It is the end. And I am afraid I side more with Mrs Adamson's view. We have had too much time away from our loved ones recently. We should allow people one last moment together.'

The room is in shock.

'None of us can leave. We cannot suggest that we are more important than anybody else. I think that we should continue to brainstorm ideas and perhaps try to find out what this thing is. But there needs to be a contingency. Perhaps there is a chance. But I do not expect any of you to continue in your role if there is somewhere you would like to be and somebody you would like to be with.'

Nobody moves.

'Mrs Adamson, I do believe that you have done it again. You would have made an excellent, no, formidable prime minister and I'm sorry we may not get to see you in power. I do not think that we should risk the suffering of sixty million people. Therefore, I am invoking the Kevorkian clause.'

This would not be the Haruto Ikeda approach. They should try something rather than waiting on intel. Doing nothing and doing the wrong thing has the same outcome.

Everybody dies.

Jackson is no Ikeda.

SIXTY MILLION PILLS

It could have been called the Shipman clause, but his name conjures up the image of a murderer rather than a campaigner or human-rights activist. When Dr Harold Shipman was bumping off his elderly patients, he was not assisting people through empathy, he wanted to kill and he wanted to pillage.

Both men did the same thing, they helped people die. They even share the same dark moniker: Dr Death. But Jack Kevorkian was more philosophical in his approach. He believed that a doctor's primary role was to ensure that patients did not suffer. Even if that meant they died. He did not see death as a crime.

Though he was jailed for euthanasia practices he gained notoriety for his crusade to allow people the right to die if the quality of their life was so low that it seemed like a mercy.

The Kevorkian clause is buried deep within the legalities of governing a country. Much like the way that certain laws change or come into effect in times of war, the Kevorkian clause is reserved for a situation that nobody dreamed would ever be required – the painful and barbaric death of an entire nation.

It is something that every prime minister is told about upon their appointment and something that they never discuss with anyone else for the duration of their premiership.

Nobody would ever need it.

Nobody would ever use it.

Harris Jackson wants to use it.

He has to explain it. That it will be an unprecedented rollout of free medication. Sixty million pills. 'We will call them dignity tablets or something that sounds more positive,' he adds. 'Everybody in the country will be allocated one that they are to use on themselves when the time comes. A tone can be delivered to every mobile phone or landline to signal the beginning of the end. We've already tested this a month ago because of the virus.'

Nobody says a thing.

'One final night with loved ones, eating their favourite meals, drinking, smoking, doing drugs, whatever. Making love to your partner or playing cards with your grandparent. You can take your chances at a gory and excruciating death, or you can choose to go your own way. No pain. Just the dignity that you chose your own end rather than some poisonous gas or biological terrorism.'

Nothing.

Then, 'Are you suggesting that we tell everyone to kill themselves?' A voice from the crowd.

'We give them a choice. It's a back-up. A mercy. If they want to make a swim for it, they can. If they want to go underground, they can. But we should show more solidarity than ever on this.'

Henrietta Adamson has swallowed Harris Jackson's bullshit for years. But she will not swallow a goddamned suicide pill.

'What about kids?' she asks.

'Parents will have to ensure that the kids go first.'

And there it is.

The final plague.

The death of the first-born children.

THE THOUGHTS OF A GRAVE MAN

The government has to get on this quickly. The message has to be right and the product has to be available. So they take it to the top. The queen. She will deliver a nationwide message of hope. That the people of Great Britain are not part of a mass suicide but are merely being prepared. That the military and scientists are trying to come up with a way to destroy the cloud. Disperse it. Sink it. Explode it.

They are on a deadline, though. The alarm is scheduled, so that's how long they have. If it sounds, it's too late. Take the pill or take your chances. But, if the gas killed half a country the size of China, the UK will be swallowed without any effort. If the gas continues on its path, Portugal, part of Spain and Morocco are the next in line.

They will have their own protocols. That is not the concern of Harris Jackson. He cannot make the initial announcement. While he seems to be in favour, right now, he has been divisive in the past. But the queen is beloved. Even those who oppose the idea of a royal family have warmth for the queen.

It should be her.

Jackson's team have prepared the script, and the announcement will be filmed at Buckingham Palace. The queen has to put it across that she will also have access to the dignity pill. This is not for a select few. This is for everybody. This is to prevent suffering.

There will be people who will not take the news lying down. Crime will rise and police will not care. And the queen will be responsible for reassuring the nation that, if there was any other way, they surely would have taken it.

Jackson is talking with experts all the time. Trying to think of anything that can stop the country from swallowing that pill, hoping that he can perform his greatest escape act to date.

He watches as the queen makes her way through the prepared speech and he admires her. She is the essence of poise and graciousness. He can't help but think about things he may have done differently since worming his way into the hallowed and cursed position of prime minister. He has to stop himself. These are the thoughts of a grave man, of somebody who knows that he is beaten.

The queen finishes her recording.

'Well, Mr Jackson, this is not the way I thought your leadership would end, I must say...'

He doesn't know what she is trying to say here and he doesn't really want to ask.

'It's not over yet, Your Highness.'

'Oh, dear boy. Do what you can do. Try what you must try. But there will come a point when you must be with your loved ones. I am going to call my family here today. I would like to see my grandchildren, and then I plan to walk my dogs and drink sherry to Mozart. If things don't work out, I shall be seeing my husband sooner than I thought.'

She gives him a smile as if to say that she is not scared. And she doesn't look it.

Things are different with the dignity pill. The UK has the lowest suicide rate of all seven member states of the secret cabal and they went straight to that resolution. But then, the deadly gas seems intent on mounting British shores.

The rest of the Western world will watch as the once great empire opts to annihilate itself rather than go through what they saw in China.

Again, each country deals with it in their own way. The Germans hunker down, bury themselves. Board up windows. There is no dignity pill rollout but it is available, though only eight percent of people collect, and only as a precaution.

Australia continues as it was. The gas that was heading in their direction from China has moved across the globe. They watch the news in bars. Strangely, it brings people together. It forces kindness.

In Brazil, they dance on the beach. They drink and party, and will take whatever is coming to them. In France, they follow the poisonous cloud and they watch what the rest of the world is doing, and, even though they are the nearest country to the UK, they somehow manage to go against everything that every other country is doing.

Russia seems surprisingly bashful about the entire incident, as if it makes them appear guilty of something. Like they unleashed this thing. First on their neighbours in China and then on the country of the most irritating world leader they know.

In America, the president makes some adjustments to his campaigning message.

Harris Jackson is downtrodden. This is supposed to be a global event but it feels like it is only happening to him, such is the ego of the man. He is getting hourly updates from the Met Office and the military. He wants to believe that he is doing everything he can to avoid this but it feels hopeless. His lifelong privilege has kept him from experiencing such an emotion, even if he did lose both parents in one evening.

Jackson wishes he could be more like the queen but he can't. He has to get back to Downing Street for the fallout while also overseeing the logistical side of the country's death and hoping that the army can come up with a better solution than a Kamikaze pilot armed with a nuclear warhead.

And he thinks about the Chinese and how they could potentially save everyone if they would just pick up the blasted phone. They have first-hand knowledge of the gas. There may be something that they could say to help. But they prefer to keep themselves insulated. Separated.

Harris Jackson thinks to himself, *I hate the Chinese. It's their fault that we are all going to die.*

A MOVEMENT

Dr Haruto Ikeda wakes up. Kimiko is fast asleep next to him. She looks peaceful. He watches her for a few minutes, appreciating her. Then he places a hand, gently, on her shoulder and shakes.

'Kimiko. Would you like some tea?'

She nods, almost imperceptibly.

Haruto gets out of bed. He is wearing blue cotton pyjama bottoms and a white vest. He is humming a tune he does not know the words to.

In the kitchen, he boils the water and prepares the sencha. Even though he now lives in the tea capital of the world, he prefers his first hot drink of the day to be Japanese. And so does his wife.

When he returns to the bedroom with two hot cups on a tray, his wife is sitting up in bed watching the news.

'It has been a slow few days, Haruto, have you noticed?'

'What do you mean?'

'The news. It is almost like nothing has happened. Isn't that strange?'

'What do you want to happen?'

'Nothing. I don't know. It just doesn't sit well, and I can't put my finger on what it is.'

'We should be happy that nothing is going on. Nobody is suspicious about the virus. Nobody asking questions.'

A story plays in the background about how China's Gansu province is owning the beef-noodle industry. Neither of the Ikedas is really listening to it because it's nothing. It's filler. They turn it off and sit back in bed with their tea. It's comfortable silence.

The blinds are slightly open and the sky is blue in Suzhou.

Haruto showered last night but he still does the same in the morning. It is his ritual. Like the tea in bed. Like kissing his wife twice, once on the cheek and once on the forehead, before he leaves the house. Or like picking up his favourite sandwich on the way to the lab.

He likes to take the bus now because he has longer to watch everybody. It gives him time to see the changes. Offering seats to others. Not just the less able-bodied, to anyone. For no other reason than kindness.

The incident where a stranger paid for somebody else's shopping was not a one-off, it has become a thing. A movement. A trend. Easier than most would imagine to be nice to somebody else. It is not something that has been picked up in the news – it is almost like its own contagion. For the first time in a long while, there is no sign of the sandwich that Ikeda usually has for lunch, so he picks up a bottle of water and he walks up and down the aisles to soak up the goodwill.

He walks the last part of his journey so that he can see the lake and the grass and the trees. It does not look as though a deadly gas has passed through this part of the world. It looks lush and bright and welcoming.

If anyone had melted on the path or while crossing the road, there is no sign of that. Ikeda does not step in melted skin or liquid eyeball on his way to the lab. The media has been so closely controlled that anyone who'd survived would not even know that it had happened.

The news has been filled with the melting of glaciers in the northwest and how no country should be accepting a visit from the Dalai Lama and how Tibet is becoming more separatist, yet continues to teach Mandarin in its boarding schools.

A poisonous gas that has killed half the population of the country?

No chance.

Ikeda walks slowly. He likes to take his time. He is as deliberate in his movements as he is with his speech. The breeze in the trees and the cyclists passing him fill him with joy. Fewer people are hunched over a mobile-phone screen and, like him, are taking in their surroundings.

He starts to wonder whether this is it, this is what a saved world looks like.

It does feel different on the streets of Wuxi today, and like Kimiko, he can't quite put his finger on what it is that makes things feel so unusual.

Wuxi is magnificent.

And kind.

The lab is eerily quiet when Ikeda arrives. There is nobody around. There is usually somebody at the front desk, but it's empty. Ghostly. He scans his card at the door and lets himself through. He is not a visitor, he doesn't need to sign in, it doesn't matter that nobody is manning the front, right at this moment.

Ikeda does as he always does. He walks the length of the corridor until he reaches his office, he goes in, drops his bag by his chair, then he goes into the communal area to make his morning coffee. And that's where he finds people.

That's where he finds everybody.

'What's going on here? I walked in and thought the world had ended and somebody forgot to tell me,' he quips.

Bauer appears. 'Good morning, Dr Ikeda. We have heard something disastrous. In fact, it does sound somewhat apocalyptic.'

Ikeda does not like cryptic talk. If you have something to say, say it plainly and succinctly.

Over Bauer's shoulder he sees that the woman from the front desk is in tears.

The 'news' that they have heard was no accident. Information can easily be kept from the people but it is even easier to spread it. The Chinese have this down to an art. They know how to stay on message.

Nobody is talking about the virus anymore.

'It's a gas, Haruto,' Bauer continues.

'A gas?'

'A cloud of poisonous, lethal gas. Huge. Millions of lost lives.'

'What? Here?' He wants to speak with Kimiko.

'Gosh, no. I think we would all be somewhere else if we knew there was a giant gas cloud heading to China. It is currently near Sweden, apparently, and it is hurtling straight for the United Kingdom. The details are hazy, but somebody said the queen has told everyone to take a cyanide pill, or something, because the effects of the gas are so painful.'

'This is not a very nice joke, Dr Bauer.'

'It's no joke. The entire country is going to be wiped out unless they can find a way to stop it, but I just can't see that there is enough time.'

On a screen in the background, Ikeda sees the image of the queen of England. She looks as demure as ever. Not like she is telling her people to kill themselves.

Ikeda walks out of the communal room without saying anything. He goes back to his office and locks the door. His breathing is heavy and he needs to sit down. All of the work, all of the sacrifice to try to make the world a better place, and it all gets wiped out in a day by some natural gas.

There you go, Kimiko, he thinks, *there's your news.*

WARRINGTON TO PLYMOUTH

Tony Aitken has been taking migraine medication but it doesn't seem to be touching the pain in his skull. He knows that he shouldn't complain, though, not when Betty, two doors down, has lived in constant agony since her accident. And all her family live on the south coast, so she doesn't have as much help as she needs.

She's on her own, and so is Tony.

He knocks on her door and waits. He knows it takes a while, she has two sticks to help her along. The wheelchair is supposed to be temporary but, it turns out, she'll never know what it's like to walk without them.

The gas is coming.

Tony was going to grab a box of beers, a pizza and watch his DVDs of the first four Rocky movies. He figured that combination would make him brave enough to swallow his pill. He was going to die alone. But, as the pain in his head began to fade, he could not bear the thought of old Betty doing the same.

'Betty? It's Tony,' he calls through the door in case she's thinking about not answering.

He doesn't want her to be alone.

Eventually, the lock clicks. Betty has placed a stool by the front door because the trip from the lounge always tires her out.

Tony is going to ask her, in the nicest way possible, whether she would like to see out the remainder of her life with some company. He thought he might open up by asking how she feels about Sylvester Stallone.

He pushes the door open.

'Betty, you're in a coat.'

'I'm going out.'

'What do you mean?'

'I'm not going to sit here and bloody die on my own, Tony. I'm going to see my daughter. I'll put up with that idiot husband of hers if I have to. And my grandsons are so big now.' She stops talking because she's getting upset and out of breath.

Tony's heart breaks.

'What were you going to do?'

'Get a train, of course.'

'Betty, there are no drivers. Nothing is running.'

'But ... how am I ... What about..?'

She gives up. Tony sees it in her. His headache has gone and he can't allow this to happen.

'Have you even packed a bag?'

'My sticks and my purse. What more do I need?'

'Wait there.'

'Where the hell else am I going to go?'

But Tony is already walking down her path and away from her house. Then he is jogging back to his own place two down. He runs into his kitchen and picks up his wallet from the counter and the cable that charges his mobile phone from the drawer beneath the cutlery. Then he runs back to Betty.

She is sitting in the same place he left her.

'Right. Up you get.'

'What are you talking about?'

'Stand up with your sticks, make sure you have your purse and come with me.'

'Tony, you are a nice neighbour but if it's all the same to you, I'd rather wallow here with a bottle of sherry.'

'Well, I have a full tank of petrol and a phone that also works as a map so that I know the directions to your daughter's house.'

'Warrington to Plymouth? It's three hundred miles away.'

'Well, we'd better get going now then. Come on.' He puts an arm around her back and helps her to her feet. Betty goes along with it even though she doesn't quite believe it.

She still doesn't believe it when Tony buckles her seatbelt for her. But, by the time they pass Worcester, Betty understands that Tony was absolutely serious. For some reason, he is driving the length of the country to drop his neighbour at her daughter's home so that they can die together. Betty knows that Tony is alone. He doesn't have any family around. But she doesn't understand why somebody would do something so kind for somebody they only know on a surface level.

'It's not that I'm ungrateful or anything, Tony, but I don't understand why you're doing this for me.'

'What else am I supposed to do? Sit at home in my pants and get pissed?' He laughs.

'I don't know what's in it for you.'

'Should we only do things for others if there's something in it for ourselves? Look, I've lived. I've seen things. I loved somebody and she died. If this is going to be the end of the world, what use is there in wanting anything? It's too late for all that. If the last thing I do is something nice, then I think I've done okay.'

For every story that Ikeda can find of his virus doing what it was designed to do, there are even more that he does not hear about, that nobody really hears about – that impact people in a lasting way. Betty's forever won't be that long, but she is forever changed because of the kindness and selflessness that Tony has showed her.

He has inspired her.

This is the point behind CompX.

This is what Ikeda wanted.

ACTION

Roger Pett has been a news man all his life. He is not a creative man. He is driven by facts, by presenting accurate information. For Pett, news broadcasting is not about flair or embellishment, it is about delivery. It is about honesty, and integrity.

He ran a news segment on his university radio station and landed a job on regional radio straight after graduation. From there he moved into television, again in a regional capacity, before landing a job with the BBC, where he has remained since.

Pett is not a tenacious reporter. He is not out there on the ground, working all the angles. He's not an investigative reporter, he's not breaking stories as they happen. He's solid. Dependable.

He's the same in his personal life. He's not the kind of guy who whisks his wife away for a spontaneous dirty weekend, but he has never strayed, he rarely raises his voice, he provides. And his kids don't have wild stories about their crazy father, but they also have no tales of abuse or frustration.

Roger Pett is a good guy. He's not the life and soul of a party, but people are never sorry to be around him.

And this workhorse moved his way up and up until the only place left to go was presenting the early-evening news. A coveted position. Everybody in the country knows who reads the early-evening news on the BBC, and Roger Pett has sat behind that desk for decades, covering royal weddings to lost football finals to terrorist attacks and landslide elections.

He's seen it all.

Until he was told that a giant cloud of poisonous gas was going to wipe out the entire population.

He is not a brave man or a man that takes risks, but he is a proud man, he is an ethical man, and, while only one junior producer turned up at the studio today to help him set up, Roger Pett will soldier on. He doesn't want history to go undocumented. That's what he does. That's who he is.

He has been there for his family, and they have their own to look after on this day. His wife has not recognised him for years. He used to hang around for the occasional glimmer of the woman she once was but her brain has let her down.

It's not that he has nothing to live for, in fact, it's the exact opposite of that. He has to do this. For himself and for everyone who has switched on their television before dinner to hear him deliver the latest news stories.

He is not special or gifted, but he is the nation's security blanket. And somebody has to be there to show what this gas does when it arrives. Somebody should be there to relay the information, the truth. It doesn't matter that it is a disaster. It doesn't matter that it's not good news, it's still news.

And Roger Pett is going to cover it.

The junior producer sets Pett up with everything he needs to broadcast. First, a statement from the studio and then a live segment from the Thames – Pett wants the viewers to be able to see London.

'Thanks for everything, Elaine,' he tells his producer. 'Now get the hell out of here and spend some time with the people you love.' And he smiles.

Elaine hugs him and leaves. He hears her crying.

Pett sits down to make his daytime broadcast. He has to count himself in. Before he does so, he looks over at the pile of equipment he has to get down to his car when he finishes. Two video cameras, a still camera, tripods, a laptop, microphones. It will take him five trips.

There's only one other thing he can't forget.

Roger Pett taps his inside jacket pocket to make sure that his dignity pill is still there.

Then he counts.

Five, four, three, two…

Action.

THE
BEGINNING

THE POSSIBILITY OF AN AFTERLIFE WITH DENNIS

Humanity is a quandary.

Everyone in the country should be with somebody they love, somebody who loves them back. They should be eating their favourite food and drinking the most expensive wines in the cellar, and kissing and hugging and fucking. Maybe they play some music that means something to them or takes them back to a time in their life when there was hope and prospects and a future.

There is no future now.

Pepsi cans litter coffee tables and kitchen islands across the UK because it's so easy for these large corporations to dominate the media and social platforms, they have told people the best way to swallow their dignity pills is with their drink.

Jane in Swindon is scrolling through her Facebook page. Friends are saying goodbye. Her estranged father apologises in a direct message. She looks at photographs of her children when they were toddlers. There are videos of them singing along to that Disney song that everyone learned to hate but now looks back on with nostalgia.

Dennis and Andrea in Rotherham haven't slept in the same bed for two years. And they're not going to start now, just because the world is about to end. But they can, at least, be civil, as they have been for the majority of their marriage.

They turn on the television news, so they can witness the imminent destruction. You'd think that there would be no live reporting, that all of the journalists would be at home with their families, but a few hold on to the importance of their job, of being there to document these historical events, even if nobody is going to be around to know.

Andrea pours two glasses of red wine in the kitchen and opens the pack for the two pills that are designed to send the unhappy couple into a peaceful slumber.

But Andrea doesn't want to die with Dennis. She's been dying with him since they first got together. So she drops both pills in his glass and swirls it around until they dissolve.

She's going to take her chances.

Better to fight a plague than submit to more nothingness.

Better to be eaten alive by locusts than surrender to mediocrity.

Better to have the skin melt away from your face than risk the possibility of an afterlife with Dennis.

Some rich dick in the Hertfordshire countryside hopped into his helicopter, thinking, *How hard can this be?* He got the thing off his roof and into the air for a few minutes before plummeting out of control onto the carless, still A10 road, which he planned to follow to Norfolk, before heading out to sea and avoiding the encroaching cloud.

The news is not covering panicking millionaires.

Again, it's too late to do the right thing.

The tipping point went by without a care.

The newsreader tells anyone who is watching that the unknown gas appears to be around thirty minutes away. That the dignity pills should have been taken by now.

And he says that he loved his mother.

And he says that he loved his job.

And he says, 'God help us all.'

THE NEEDS OF THE COUNTRY

'I'll be here when the time comes, I promise,' Henrietta Adamson tells her husband in a whisper.

'How many times have you said that, Hen?' He taps his foot on the floor while waiting for the kettle to boil.

'That's not fair. I'm the deputy prime minister of this country. The job is different every day. And it's hard.' She wants to say how wonderful their home is because of the money she earns, but she's not a spiteful woman, and she hasn't got to the position she is in by being more antagonistic than she has to be. Besides, she is incredibly grateful to her husband that he put his own dreams on hold to raise their children in a way that her parents view as untraditional.

'I know, I know. I'm sorry.' He always backs down. 'It's just, this really isn't one that you can miss, you know?'

He's right. It's not the end of the world but it is almost certainly the end of their world. It doesn't look like there is anything that can be done to stop this gas from breaching Britain's formerly impenetrable coastline.

'I am going to have to work until the last minute. If there is a way of stopping this thing, then I am going to find it.'

Henrietta Adamson's husband believes this. If anyone has the fortitude to find an answer, it is his wife. It doesn't take a lot to be smarter than Harris Jackson, but she has proved she is time and time again. And he knows that she has been carefully biding her time to take the helm at some point. She has the support of the party, too.

When it comes to politics, Henrietta Adamson means what she says, it's just that she doesn't always mean it when she says that she will be home in time for dinner. Or to say goodnight to the kids. And she rarely follows through on her promises of intimacy these days. It's work. And it's the most important thing in her life, it seems.

'I know all of this.' He stirs the coffee. 'You cannot miss this time. They could be our last moments together as a family. We are going to have a decision to make.'

He leaves this hanging in the air. Henrietta doesn't want to take the pills. She doesn't want to give them to her kids and know that she killed them, even if she only knows this for a few minutes before she dies herself – it's too long to live with that sort of heartache. But her husband doesn't want any of them to suffer unduly.

There has been no resolution. They stuck a pin in it. Both are hoping that the deputy prime minister will save the country again while Harris Jackson takes all the credit.

Henrietta Adamson closes the lid on her coffee flask and looks at her watch. She wants to get into the office as soon as possible, but she considers sitting herself on the kitchen countertop, pulling her underwear to the side and giving her husband a couple of minutes of pleasure. It might be the last time they get to be close like that.

She bites her lip, looks at her watch again, and decides that the needs of the country come above the needs of her partner.

'Wish me luck,' she says, kissing him on the cheek, her expression looking as if she is going to a job interview.

He doesn't answer.

And she doesn't stick around long enough to hear one, anyway.

ONE LAST MOMENT OF PLEASURE

Harris Jackson weeps. He's overweight. His hair is a mess. His nose is large and crooked. His bottom lip is bulbous and heavy and makes him talk in that annoying way. He knows he only got laid as much as he did because of his position, because of his power.

Because of his empty promises.

He was a glutton for fine wine and women and food, and maybe that's why the pill is taking longer to affect him than it did the rest of his family. Mentally, he is a coward, but physically, he's a little harder to be taken down.

So he cries as he looks around the bedroom of his prime-ministerial residence. His wife looks peaceful on their king-sized bed, hugging their eldest child. Both dead. He wants to be taken, too. Not because he thinks that he will be with them, he is not like his father in that respect, he just doesn't want to see this. He doesn't want to be alone.

He makes his way downstairs to his office and takes a bottle of Scotch from one of the cabinets. He pours it into a glass – he may be about to die but he's not going to be uncouth enough to drink from the bottle. He's not a tramp. He's Harris goddamned Jackson, for crying out loud. It's an odd time to opt for manners and dignity but it doesn't last long.

Next, he is opening his laptop and looking for a file. A video of his secretary bent over the desk he sits at now, being taken from behind.

One last moment of pleasure.

A final sordid orgasm to sign out on.

Jackon hits play, swigs at his drink then pulls his trousers and boxers down to his ankles. It says everything you need to know about the man that he would choose a video of himself to masturbate to for the very last time.

But he can't do it. He's limp. He can't get excited when he's this afraid.

He punches himself between the legs.

'You useless fat idiot.'

And then he is startled when the telephone rings.

Who the hell is calling at this moment?

Now Jackson gets excited. It could be the military. They've found a way to divert the catastrophe. But he's already taken his pill. Maybe he should try to throw it up.

He doesn't even pull up his trousers to answer the phone.

'This is Jackson.'

There is a short pause.

'Mr Jackson, this is Zhu Jian. I am the minister for science and technology of the People's Republic of China.'

'I'm afraid this isn't the best time to call.' Jackson shakes his head in disbelief and sips more whisky. He adjusts himself, sticking to the leather of his office chair.

'If you are busy, I can arrange a time to call back.'

Jackson is dumbfounded.

'Are you serious? Do you have some information from your president?'

'Not quite. The premier asked that I contact you. We are a constituent part of the state council, based in Beijing, with an annual budget of fifty-one billion dollars.'

'Why would I care about that now?'

Rude to the end.

If only he were kind.

'We are interested in how much of your science and technology budget is dedicated to nanotechnology.'

'Are you insane, Mr Jian? An unknown gas is heading towards my country to wipe out this great nation, and you want to know how much of my budget is wasted on nanotechnology. Hardly anything.'

'So you allocate it to developing bioweapons, viruses.' This is not a question. It feels, somehow, backhanded in its delivery.

'Who the hell do you think you are, talking to me like that?'

'I'm Zhu Jian, the minister for science and technology in the People's Re—'

'I know where you are from,' Jackson interrupts, 'and I'm sorry that half of your people are gone, but my entire country is almost dead.' He's not sorry, and that comes across.

'Ah, yes. You are quite the expert on Chinese culture, I hear. We eat dogs.'

The man calling himself Jian lets the sentence hang in the air for a moment. Jackson blushes instantly. How the hell does this guy know that Jackson said that? It was a closed meeting. It had the highest level of secrecy. There were seven people in that room.

His mind races.

The Russian? No way.

American? Surely not. It's a *special* relationship.

Jian continues. 'It wasn't so much the fact that you wanted to release a virus in our country or even that you wanted to blame us for the leak. It was the comment about the dogs. You are a buffoon, Mr Jackson. But it will all be over soon. Perhaps you should have a cup of tea.'

Jackson can almost hear Jian smiling.

'You sent a poisonous gas here.'

'Fifty billion, Mr Jackson.'

'What? What are you talking about?'

'Fifty billion out of the fifty-one billion budget. That is how much we have dedicated to nanotechnology this year.' That doesn't include the American money syphoned from the Wuxi Institute of Virology.

'Why are you talking about budget again, you fucking mathematical psychopath?'

'Sleep well, Mr Jackson. The intelligent will rebuild and start again.' He hangs up.

For the entire call, Harris Jackson's trousers were down by his ankles. He pulls them up aggressively, his face still red with embarrassment, turning crimson through anger.

He stands by his window. It seems to be getting darker.

It's coming.

The gas is coming.

He drinks.

He thinks.

Fifty billion dollars.

Nanotechnology.

He drinks again.

Thinks again.

Realises.

There is no gas.

Harris Jackson gulps down as much whisky as he can. From the bottle. Like a commoner. Then he sticks two fingers down his throat as far as he can. He has to get rid of that pill.

He could call someone.

A doctor.

Military intelligence.

But Harris Jackson tries to save himself.

NOBODY CAN KNOW EVERYTHING

If you stood in one spot and the population of China queued up – six people deep – then walked past you, the sheer number of beings and the rate of births would mean that the queue of people wandering past would never end.

It would go on forever.

There are twenty-two million people in Beijing alone.

More people in one city than there are in Sri Lanka. Or Romania. Or Cambodia. Or the Netherlands.

Even in a country like Chile, with a population of under twenty million, it cannot be expected that the education minister knows all the business of the environmental agency. There has to be delegation and trust. The president is the head of state and government and national congress, but he is not aware of every judiciary matter. There are people for that.

So, in a country the size of China, the layers of power and influence and information are as long and complicated as the never-ending queue of people that walk by.

The premier is the head of government and leader of the state council. This post is still beneath the general secretary of the Chinese Communist party, who is also known as the paramount leader or president. Throw in a chairman to the National Committee or the Central Military Commission or the National Supervisory Commission. It's already a lot of overlapping, wires tangling.

Too many cooks.

What about Chinese intelligence? The Ministry of State Security has to be across everything. They don't have enough time in the day to brief everyone.

Sometimes, things happen and decisions are made without going through every channel.

Because there is no way of getting to the end of that queue.

The president does not have to know that his intelligence community has sleeper agents. He doesn't need to know the location of every operative who has been sent overseas or is working within the country, hidden in big business or the health service or religion. He has to trust that what needs to get done will get done.

If a meeting of world leaders is being held in secret to disseminate a virus among Chinese people, the secretary for education does not need to know.

If a rogue operative at the Institute of Virology is planning to infect the world, even if his plight is honourable or well meaning, there are people who can deal with that who need to be known by nobody. It's not worth alerting the president, because it will be handled.

Information is closely controlled. No Facebook in China. Sure, you can set up a VPN to get around it, but *they* still know.

Whoever they are.

In fact, *they* could create a video of people dying in Wuxi, being ravaged by an airborne plague, and the Chinese people wouldn't even see it. Especially if it is only meant to be seen by the West.

Effects could be created in a film studio or in the editing suite. It could look real. They could say that half the population have been affected and almost all of the Chinese population would be clueless that this false information, this fake news, travelled west.

And Zhu Jian would have required somebody higher to sign off almost his entire budget if it was to be allocated to nanotechnology. But he also does not have to tell Harris Jackson the truth. He just needs to make a point, get a message across.

It may not have even been Zhu Jian that called Jackson on the telephone.

Zhu Jian may not even exist.

Nobody can know everything.

And that works well for deniability.

But certain sections of Chinese influence did know about the secret meetings of Harris and Co. And other people are aware of Haruto Ikeda's quest for a more compassionate planet. Some know about the virus found deep in that cave and somebody else understands how much more advanced the Chinese are when it comes to nanotechnology. That they have the capability to work with organisms on such a minute scale, in such vast numbers, that they could seemingly control the speed and direction of a gas that could sweep through an island the size of the United Kingdom.

And, with a phone call, there is now one person in England who knows that the deadly gas, which most of the population have decided to dignifiedly avoid, will not cause any harm at all.

He'll also know that it's too late.

LIKE ANYONE ELSE

The queen has been around so long that she has earned the right to be quirky in her old age. While her husband was still alive, she allowed him to take control of inappropriate comments in public.

She didn't take over from him when he died but she didn't hold back, either. After the period of mourning, her personality started to shine through. A sideways glance caught on camera during a visit from the US president. A roll of the eyes at her granddaughter's outfit choice. A deliberate slip of the sword during the ceremony for her recent honours list.

One newspaper suggested she was senile, but the people know. She is a woman who managed to change the face of the monarchy from stuffy pageantry to something more down-to-earth. Normal. Relatable. The royals had always been well liked by foreigners, and the tourism alone brings in more money to the country than people can fathom, but opinion shifted at home.

And with a poisonous gas heading straight for her proud nation the queen remains strong but with a stiff upper lip and a sense of humour. She's going to sit it out like anyone else. She has her pill, like everyone. But she also has a room buried deep underground where she can sit alone, watch the news coverage and drink a pot of tea or glass of sherry and pray.

She can pray that her bunker holds and she isn't forced to take that damned dignity pill because what she wants, almost more than anything, is to outlive that idiot Harris Jackson; she can't stand that bumbling fool. She hasn't felt well over the last week but one thing that has kept the queen going is the motivation to avoid Jackson presiding over her funeral and giving a speech.

She was hoping he might resign, but this gas should do the trick instead.

GOOD THINGS HAPPEN TO GOOD PEOPLE

Cellar Beach is quiet and secluded. The kind of place you could take a blanket, a bottle of wine and a lover, and watch the sun go down. Tony Aitken has a bottle of wine but he is waiting for a poisonous gas to swoop in and melt the skin off his body.

He dropped Betty at her daughter's house. Her grandsons were so pleased. Her daughter was shocked. She cried. Her son-in-law could not turn up the corners of his mouth. But he did invite Tony to come inside for a drink.

Tony declined. He had realised somewhere near Bristol that his dignity pill was back in Warrington on his coffee table. He probably wasn't going to have time to drive all the way back up the country before this thing hit the UK shores. He was just going to have to brave it out. On his own. Like always.

'I cannot thank you enough for what you have done, Tony,' Betty said, on the doorstep of her daughter's home. 'If I went on to live for another twenty years, I would never forget this.'

'It's quite alright. Go. Be with your family. It's been nice knowing you, Betty.' He smiles.

'What are you going to do?'

'You know, I thought I'd grab a bottle of wine. Probably for free because nobody is manning the tills. So, a really good bottle of wine. I'll take the car down to the beach, try to find a quiet cove. I'll drink. Take my pill. And maybe get to see the sun disappear into the sea one final time.' He's trying desperately to be gallant but he knows there is no pill and that his lonesome ending will be a painful one if the Chinese video is any indication. He wants to be strong for Betty. He wants her experience to be a good one.

They embrace. Then Tony does exactly what he said he would do.

He puts more petrol in his car and drives off without paying. He finds a supermarket and wanders around the aisles. He stops at the red wines and sees one for £65. He takes two bottles. He finds a bottle opener on a different aisle. And he drives around the coast until he happens upon Cellar Beach, finally stopping at a spot where he thinks it might be nice to die.

There's nothing on the radio. All the DJs are with their families. Classic FM has left a playlist on repeat, but there is no news. He doesn't know how close he is to the end. And maybe that's better. Hopefully, when it comes, it will take him quickly. The first bottle of wine was delicious and it's starting to make him feel sleepy. Maybe he'll catch a break and pass out.

He opens the second bottle.

Tony recalls moments throughout his life. The first time he went on a plane. Meeting the woman he loved and then losing her. That Rolling Stones concert. Being drunk in a Canadian diner at breakfast because he'd gone through the night.

He hopes the end is quick.

He hopes that Betty has enjoyed her final day on Earth.

He thinks about that dignity pill on his coffee table.

He thinks about his mother. Petite. Demure. Such a kind face. Such a caring woman. 'Just remember, Anthony,' she would say, 'Good things happen to good people.' And, now more than ever, he wishes that were true.

Then he hears a humming noise. Like a swarm of bees.

He drinks and looks out over the sea, the sun nowhere close to setting.

IT'S A MESSAGE

The cloud rolls in.

Millions and millions of nanobots, swarming, dancing around with the grace of a flight of swallows. It is beautifully choreographed.

They are controlled, but artificial intelligence allows them to move independently, within certain parameters.

It looks natural.

Like a gas.

Millions upon millions of particles, orchestrated to fly across the sea and wade through the British Isles, starting at the North-East and Scotland, travelling diagonally until emerging off the tip of Plymouth and dispersing. Touching streets and houses and trees, playing among parked cars, bouncing off shop fronts.

And doing absolutely nothing.

No burning. Itching. Scratching.

No melted skin.

No coughing. Wheezing. Spluttering.

The gas is inert. It isn't even really a gas.

It's a message.

Carol in Lincoln doesn't feel a thing when the nanobots stream through her living room. She doesn't hear her dog barking. She is deep in her eternal slumber, sitting in her reading chair, her right hand still holding an empty can of Pepsi. She thought about splitting her pills and putting something in the dog's water bowl, but she couldn't bring herself to murder her companion.

Grant in Middlesbrough used his time well, downloading an app that would help him hook up with a man. Something that had always held some curiosity. He fucked a stranger, loved him for one day and died next to him in bed.

The Portsmouth University football team went to the beach. They took a couple of barbecues and a few cases of beer. They ate and drank and kicked a ball around before swilling their dignity pills in their final bottle of lager and chugging it. John, who plays on the left wing, is a lightweight. He passed out after drinking the first few beers too quickly. He will wake up to find the tide coming in to wash away the dead members of his football team.

Eddie in Feltham didn't take his pill. He didn't even go to the surgery to pick up the one that had been allocated to him. He wasn't buying any of it.

The same thing with Cheryl in Glamorgan.

And Terry in Woking.

And Janet in Solihull.

James in Wigan just forgot. He was playing his guitar and writing a new song, and time just went by. He only remembered when he saw a yellow 'gas' zoom past his bedroom studio window on its way to Field Farm.

He turns on the television to find a BBC reporter on Westminster Bridge.

'If timings are correct, the gas should be somewhere over Newcastle by now. It's moving fast. I'd imagine, for those who are still watching, it will appear on your screens in minutes. If, by some miracle, somebody makes it through this, the video showing what happened here today will be automatically uploaded to my YouTube channel. This will, undoubtedly, be my final report. It has been an honour to bring you stories over the years. Now, I guess, we wait.'

It's morbid. Pockets of anti-pill-takers are watching and waiting for a man to be killed on live television, but James in Wigan knows that he's going to be okay, that the gas flew right past him with no effect. That somebody, somewhere, got this very wrong.

He wants to contact the reporter somehow. Give him some relief. Let him know that he's doing a great job and that his video is going to document a cruel hoax. Perhaps he could get in contact with him through social media. The reporter is so brave. So gracious. So selfless. He's something of a national treasure. It seems like only a few weeks ago he was taken ill. But he bounced back and was nicer than ever.

If only James could tell him that.

Everything is going to be okay.

The news reporter gazes upriver in contemplation. James is transfixed. Then the reporter opens a can of lager, drops in his pill, swirls and swallows.

TIRED AND PAIN-FREE

Harris Jackson's eyes are open. There's vomit on the breast pocket of his shirt. He is lying on his back, next to the window of his office on Downing Street. An empty bottle of whisky next to him. Some has spilled, the rest was poured directly into his mouth.

As soon as he realised he couldn't make himself sick enough, he decided to make himself drunk enough. The cocktail of diazepam, morphine and phenobarbital started to kick in. He thought it was the booze making him drowsy. There was no pain. The constant ache in his lower back was not there anymore. He could no longer feel where he had punched himself in his useless flaccid dick.

He began to drift.

Human curiosity meant that Jackson wanted to see the deadly gas that he alone knew was fake. He wanted to look at whatever the hell nanotechnology was. His cuckolded wife upstairs, dead in their marital bed, holding their dead children. He wanted to be sad at what he had allowed to transpire.

He wanted to feel sorry for trying to get a grip on the world through fear.

He wanted to feel angry at the Chinese for forcing the British public into a mass suicide of such scale that it makes the Jonestown Massacre look like a cub-scout jamboree.

But he just felt good.

He felt tired and pain-free and then he felt nothing.

He drifted entirely.

And when that yellow cloud came through London, sounding like bees and wind, disturbing the silence with its thrum, Harris Jackson did not hear a thing, he did not feel the vibration. He was dying in his sleep. The cardiac arrest shocked his eyes back open, but he didn't feel a thing.

Spencer Compton – natural causes.

Henry Pelham – natural causes.

Charles Watson-Wentworth – flu epidemic.

William Pitt the Younger – natural causes.

Spencer Perceval – assassination.

George Canning – natural causes.

Henry Temple – caught a chill that turned into a fever.

And today, the eighth prime minister to die in office. Inebriated, soiled, bloated and shamed. Impotent, scruffy and sitting in his own sick.

Harris Jackson – suicide. With all the dignity that he could muster.

WHAT DO YOU WANT IT TO BE?

In East Sussex, a group of free-thinkers gather in a garden bunker and watch as a mysterious gas rolls down the Thames towards a beloved newscaster who just took a pill that will kill him on air. It envelops the man on the television. He tries to convey what is happening but the buzz of the yellow cloud drowns him out.

And then it's gone.

The newsreader is left on the screen where he was standing only moments before. His hair is a little dishevelled but it is not falling out. His eyes are red but they are not boiling in their sockets. His skin is not melting. His fingernails are still attached. This is nothing like the video that circulated showing what happened in China.

'Holy shit, Duncan, you were right.'

Duncan nods. He runs an underground magazine that focusses on conspiracy theories. He actually believes that man went to the moon in 1969; he does have some questions about the 9/11 attacks; but his particular area of interest is ancient Egypt. The rest of the group consists of crop-circle enthusiasts, astrologists, scientists and philosophers.

They're not your regular whack-job keyboard warriors, posting outrageous theories on their social-media platform of choice. They are unbiased. Anyone is welcome within their group. It is not about fighting the power. It's not about proving people wrong. It is about the spirit of enquiry and the freedom of expression. It's global awareness, once a month at the local scout hut with drinks afterwards in the pub across the road.

They didn't take the pills. Duncan put across his point that it would go against everything they believe in just to trust that this is the only solution. They should question it. There wasn't a lot of time to question it, but that is exactly what they should do.

He has a buried bunker in his back garden that he bought from a Norwegian subterranean spaces company that allows you to configure your area with their modular pods. He edits his magazine down there. It has power and lighting and air conditioning. It stays cool when it's warm outside and warm when it's cold outside. There's enough tinned food in there to last the group for a few months.

'Millions of people are going to be dead for no reason,' Ginny – the astrologist – cries.

'We need to get word out, see who else is out there.'

'Will the socials still be up and running?' the philosopher ponders.

'The people stopped. They gave up. But they didn't turn the lights off before they went to bed. I still have reception on my phone and the wifi seems to be working,' Duncan explains.

And then he convinces the group that they shouldn't go outside. Not yet. Just because it looks safe, doesn't mean that it is. Best to watch what happens on the news. Get online and observe the chatter. Will someone claim responsibility for whatever that was? Was it a natural phenomenon? Where will it travel once it has swooped across the South-West?

Duncan points at the television. 'He looks okay now but he could be a puddle in twenty minutes. Whatever that was could blow back in this direction. Let's sit it out. There's food, water, a shower. We have space to meditate. There are computers. It's the sensible thing to do.'

The group nods in unison.

One of the crop-circle guys, Barry, is in the kitchen area opening a tin of food. There are some shop-bought items in the cupboards, but Duncan also purchased a pallet of 'compo' from an ex-soldier who had lots of product left over from basic training.

All gold tins. No labels. Many with a simple black text on top that gives an indication of what might be found inside.

'Hey, Duncan, what's this?' He tilts the tin so that Duncan can see what's inside.

'What do you want it to be?'

'Er, I don't know, maybe some kind of lasagne?'

'Then it's some kind of lasagne.'

The philosopher laughs.

Duncan pats Barry on the back. 'Just a couple of days, Barry.' He smiles.

Barry shrugs and pours the contents into a saucepan.

It's clear to everyone that Duncan is the leader. It's a democratic group, an ensemble, but he does emerge slightly ahead of everyone else. He started the group. He is the creator and editor of *Focal Point* magazine. If he says to stay down here for a couple of days, they stay down here for a couple of days.

And they will need a leader because, when they open that hatch, they will be in a country with no prime minister. No government. No monarchy. Once a global superpower. A former empire whose tentacles spread into every corner of the planet. Left in the hands of a group of weirdos who refused to drink the Kool-Aid.

ALL THE DOCTORS ARE DEAD

It's not just them. There are pockets of people around the country who, for one reason or another, did not take their dignity pill. Who either didn't believe what the government was telling them because they lied so often, or had formed an alternative theory about the killer cloud. Or they were lazy. Or drunk. Or on drugs. Or sick in hospital. Or in a coma.

Vashti works at the hospital.

She's an angel.

A slightly overweight, smokes-like-a-chimney, fucks-like-a-trojan, nurse angel.

She couldn't leave her patients.

The highly paid doctors and specialists left. They went back to their country houses or four-storey Victorian terraces. They drank from their wine collections and smoked Cuban cigars. They ate a bowl of ice-cream before they ate their steak.

They indulged.

They were selfish.

They ignored the Hippocratic Oath.

Primum non nocere.

First, do no harm.

Vashti isn't like that. She can't do it. She can't neglect her responsibilities.

Everybody left. Everybody. They went home for one final night of love or pleasure or debauchery. They took a day to pretend that they didn't care what tomorrow would bring, blissfully ignorant that they are in this mess because they have spent their lives not really considering the future of the planet. Confronted with certain death, a person re-evaluates.

Vashti kept calm and carried on. She filled a rucksack with dignity pills and she went around every bed that she could. She gave people a choice. She would provide them with a pill that would make them sleep and never wake up – it wouldn't hurt them – or she would continue to care for them the best that she could.

A lot of people were weak. They were fighting for something. To see the birth of a grandchild. To watch their child grow up. To get strong again and quit the job they hate so much and open their own nail salon or consultancy business or move to the country.

Many gave up the fight.

If their child wasn't going to grow up, what was there to hang on to?

If their pregnant daughter would never give birth, why wait around?

Give me the pill.

Vashti did as they requested. It wasn't like she was euthanising pensioners. She wasn't administering lethal doses of morphine. These pills were in the government guidelines.

Some patients were so ill that they couldn't be bothered with the pill – they were happy to be taken by a poisonous gas or shot by a disgruntled postal worker. It all ends in death.

Parents took their sick kids from the hospital so that they could die at home. And others with terminally ill offspring simply left them hooked up to the machines that were helping them breathe. It was a real shit show for anybody who stayed around to watch.

But there was only Vashti.

Making the occasional executive decision to turn a machine off as she went around delivering pills, giving people one last taste of wine with a dash of digoxin and amitriptyline. Cheap cabernet and a heart attack.

She sits alone at the nurses' station, exhausted, her emotions heightened. She was so busy, she forgot that she was scheduled to die.

Shouldn't it have happened by now?

She calls her home but there is no answer. Her partner was devastated that she chose strangers over one final evening with him, watching their favourite film, laughing, pretending. He watched the film alone. Didn't laugh. Took his pill.

Vashti waits. The hospital has wards filled with corpses, but she is still alive. There are three guys in oncology who chose to roll the dice in the face of an unknown gas because they'd already come this far against their varying cancers.

Where is it?

Vashti takes a long walk down the corridor to the hospital entrance. It's so quiet. No sirens. No vehicles on the road. Nobody is being wheeled in on a gurney after being stabbed at the cinema in

Newham. She can hear birds. Maybe they could fly high enough to be above the gas and avoid it. Maybe it only affects humans. How would she know? She's not a doctor.

All the doctors are dead.

But she's not.

Shouldn't she be dead?

The air seems fresh, not like something toxic has passed through. It's been so much clearer since people were locked down. She looks up at the sky. No planes. No vapour trails. A few grey clouds, of course, this *is* England, but, somehow, it doesn't feel the same.

Then, a man appears from the right, speeding down the empty road on his bicycle. He passes quickly, double-taking when he sees Vashti in the doorway of the hospital, the automatic doors opening behind her. And she hears a crash.

Vashti stubs out her cigarette on the wall and runs, on instinct, towards the road. The cyclist is on the floor. He's scraped his leg and banged his head. Luckily he was wearing a helmet, even though he was expecting to see nobody.

'Are you okay?' She crouches down and checks to see if anything is broken.

'I'm alive. Which is more than I can say for the rest of this place. How ... how are you here?' He sits up.

'Be careful. Don't move too quickly yet. Don't try to stand up.'

'I'm okay. Honestly.'

'I've been working for thirty-two hours. I didn't take the pill. I mean, I guess I thought that people needed me. You didn't take it, either?'

'No, I did. Well, I thought I did. My girlfriend said she put it in my wine, but I woke up this morning and she's fucking dead and my parents are dead and my brother is dead and ... and ... and you're not.'

'No. I'm not.'

'It's like that fucking millennium bug thing that I read about.' This guy looks to be in his twenties. Hell, he may have even been conceived on New Year's Eve of 1999.

It's a lot for either of them to process.

If this was a romantic comedy, it would be the strangest meet-cute. Neither really knows what their story is yet. If it's a tragedy, it doesn't feel like one. Perhaps it is theirs to write.

The cyclist stands up.

'This is some real *I Am Legend* shit, here. We could go to Harrods right now and take what we want. Food. Clothes. Board games. Whatever.'

'Look, before we go ransacking the capital, come into the hospital so that I can clean you up and get that leg dressed, okay?'

He nods and they walk back together.

'I'm Thomas, by the way,' he tells her.

'Vashti.'

Thomas wheels his bike and leans it up against the wall. 'You know, Vashti, we could be the only ones left. We don't know what's happened out there. We don't know if there is anyone else that's like us. I've been riding my bike for twenty minutes, not knowing where the hell I was going to go, and you are the first person I have seen.'

The idea never even entered into Vashti's mind. She's been so preoccupied with caring for others that she hasn't had the opportunity to think about herself.

That's not how she operates.

But what if this guy is right? She doesn't even know him. Is he a mature student? Is he a courier, a bike messenger? How can they leave the fate of the country in the hands of some drop-out and a nurse? What if another country wants to come and claim the UK as its own? That Russian guy is crazy. She hears things about North Korea.

Vashti thinks the worst.

But they can't be the only ones.

There have to be others.

It doesn't matter if there are five others or five hundred. There is one person that cares. Who has compassion. Who is kind.

This wasn't how it was supposed to go but maybe, in the end,

Haruto Ikeda's plan will work. Small acts of compassion coming together around the globe. Larger acts of philanthropy and benevolence to inspire the masses. And the biggest change of all in the United Kingdom: an entire country filled with kindness and consideration and gratitude.

A LESSON TO BE LEARNED

The newsreader, Roger Pett, loses consciousness and falls out of shot.

For a short moment, the camera is still, looking out over the river towards the South Bank. There's no cameraman. There's nobody in the studio to cut transmission or fade to black. The beloved anchor is lying on the floor, drowsy, in and out. He knows what is happening and that he is powerless to stop it, but he has a remote control in his right hand. He didn't drop it when he fell.

He presses the button.

He had hoped to do this at the very last moment, so that there was a document of this skin-eating gas that had ravaged the East and was now devouring the West. He wanted to hold on as long as he could. And that is still what he is doing.

As he feels himself fading, he squeezes his thumb down, which cuts the footage and immediately starts to send it into the cloud. It will take sixteen minutes to upload. The camera continues to broadcast a view across the Thames.

The video will receive millions of hits.

Nobody is really interested in what the reporter has to say, they just want to skip to the part where he gets swallowed by the yellow cloud. They want to pause it and zoom in to see if they can spot something that nobody else has seen.

Governments across Europe who had locked down their countries (again) will understand the tragedy that has unfolded in the United Kingdom. There will have to be talks of a clean-up. Of salvage. Of possible survivors. There may be somebody alive who was once sixty-millionth in line to the throne that can legally stake a claim on Buckingham Palace.

It may be easier to let the island rot and mine it for resources in the future.

There may even be a lesson to be learned.

But, at this moment, with sixteen minutes to go until the video of the wreckage makes its way to the web, where it can exist forever, an unlikely group of people have survived the cruellest of pranks.

A magazine editor, three crop-circle enthusiasts, a philosopher and an astrologist are hunkered down below the earth of an East Sussex garden – it sounds like the start of a joke. They are eating tinned food and continuing their 'work'. Asking questions. Striving for a collective consciousness.

A twenty-year-old student sits on a beach, surrounded by the dead members of the Portsmouth University football team. He is quiet. Solemn. Seems he is the best player on the team, all of a sudden. Hell, he's probably one of the best players in the country.

He has more followers on Instagram than the population of the United Kingdom, though he should expect very little engagement.

He sits still and quiet. The tide has come in and has pulled the left back and attacking midfielder into the sea. He doesn't know what to do, and he is sad that all of his friends are gone, even the ones that weren't really his friends, but he is glad to be alive – whatever that means now.

And the musician who forgot about the impending apocalypse because he was laying down a new track.

And the guy on the bike who will never know how much his girlfriend wanted to end things that she took both of their pills and decided to let him melt to death. Not because she hated him. Not because she wanted to cause him pain. Because she was worried that one pill would not be enough for her. She had valued her own life more than others and, as such, she valued her own death more, too.

She was how far humanity had come.

She was the shocking indictment of civilisation.

She was everything that Haruto Ikeda was fighting against.

Thomas hasn't had enough head space to mourn her yet, but he dodged a bullet.

And then there's Vashti. She itches at the scars on her shoulder blades that are burning from the days of work, hunched over hospital beds, administering pain relief. She cleans another wound, this time on Thomas's leg and wraps it in cling film.

'It's not serious, I just don't want it to get infected,' she tells him. And she smiles.

The world has ended, and Vashti smiles.

She is one of a small number of people still alive. Of all those people, she cares the most. She's instinctively compassionate. And she is still paid the least.

All of these people will be forced to consider what is best. How things will move forward. They are responsible for what happens in the future and they are more aware of this than they were yesterday.

This is an opportunity.

To do it another way.

To make things better.

Or find a new way to screw it all up.

GENESIS

LET THERE BE HOPE

It turns out that saving the world isn't easy. Haruto Ikeda cannot fathom that even one person would not want to do that, but the ache in his heart tells him otherwise.

His newsfeed is inundated with stories of kindness and compassion across the planet, but it also shows that the United Kingdom is now without form. And empty.

Where there is compassion, there is also despair.

If Tau had been released, it would not have made anyone kinder, but it would not have killed this many people, either.

Henrietta Adamson picks the wet towel from the floor in front of the bathroom door. She leaves the tape around the windows. The humming has gone.

In the lounge, her husband is lying on the sofa with his giant headphones over his ears. The fucking coward. He didn't like his wife's plan to see it out. To risk it for a chance at life. A life that one could appreciate on a different level having almost had it taken away.

He had arrived home before her. They had planned a meal and games with the children. And the expensive red wine they had been given on their wedding day but had never found the right occasion to have. A full-bodied, oaky Shiraz that pairs perfectly with the end of the world.

He let the kids have a fizzy drink, which was usually against the rules. A Pepsi. He told them to go to their rooms for a while. He was going to listen to some music and relax before Mummy got home.

He didn't believe that she would make it back from work in time.

She did.

Henrietta Adamson can hear the tinny sound of Carole King's *Tapestry* album on loop. She sees her dead husband, seemingly peaceful but clearly having made the wrong decision.

It's too late.

She knows Harris Jackson took his pill, so technically, she is now the prime minister. She may be the *only* minister. But the minister of what?

She is too afraid to go into her children's bedrooms again.

No mother should have to witness that.

But, from this tragedy, Henrietta Adamson will emerge much stronger. Formidable, even. An agent for change on a global scale.

Vashti and Thomas walk the streets. They could go to Harrods, like he suggested. They want to find others. And there will be others. Like them. Who don't want to be left in the country alone, and are already imagining what they can make of it. Can they rebuild it to be equal or democratic? Could this situation be transformed into something positive? Could there be hope?

The Sussex bunker group are biding their time until they think it is safe. Wondering what the hell happened, why they are still here, what they can do with this new freedom. They eat and they sing and they talk. Philosophising about whether this means a clean slate or whether the truth will trigger a war, or something worse.

There are smatters of grapeshot around the country where people have survived, either by accident or through laziness or, better still, the strength to stand and fight. They have a journey ahead of them.

There are survivors at several churches and mosques and synagogues. People who chose faith and now believe that they have been rewarded by their God for such devotion.

There are more groups who moved underground, who will emerge with the opportunity to fight for control or fight for democracy. They will still have their queen, whose wish to outlive an incompetent prime minister came true. His replacement has one hell of a job ahead of her, but she's up to the task. She will not have sixty million people demanding retaliation.

Perhaps it is time for an alternative narrative to war.

The start of a new story.

And on the south coast, in a secluded cove of Cellar Beach, Tony Aitken savours the taste of his second bottle of wine and waits for the sun to go down. His mother was right.

Good things.

Good people.

There are not that many left in the UK, but they all have that in common.

And in Wuxi, China, Haruto Ikeda sits at his desk and he wonders how his silly little virus can compete with a deadly gas that has killed millions. The story being broadcast in China is similar to the one that the Western world reported a few days ago.

Neither were true. But the entire world sees this one.

'Haruto. There you are,' Bauer says, walking into Ikeda's office, uninvited.

'I needed to be alone.'

'This world is brutal, that's for sure.' Bauer tries to use few words, like his mentor.

Ikeda is happy to sit in the silence, but he sees that Bauer is not.

'Did you need something from me, Dr Bauer?'

'No, no. I just wanted to make sure you were okay. You had the right idea with your virus, but perhaps it is a battle that cannot be won.' He expects Ikeda to concede but his belief goes deeper than that. 'Here,' Bauer pulls something out from behind his back. 'I was getting a coffee, early, and I saw that there was only one of these sandwiches left. I know that you get one each day, and I was worried that somebody would take this before you managed to get to the store.'

Ikeda smiles.

A kindness, he thinks.

It works.

It continues to work. It may not stand a chance against Mother Nature but CompX stands a good chance in a fight with human indecency.

'Thank you, Dr Bauer. I shall meet you in the labs shortly. I just need to have a few moments alone.'

'Of course. Of course.'

Very little work is done at the Wuxi Institute of Virology before noon. The receptionist has not stopped crying. Studying disease seems futile when a gas could wipe out an entire country in moments.

The roads in London are empty. Henrietta Adamson does not pass a single car. She sees nobody walking around, no faces in windows. By default, she is now in charge of the country – whatever is left of it. She can't sit at home with her dead family and cry but she needs to know if there is anyone still alive out there.

She speeds past Downing Street, knowing that her predecessor is in there. He's dead. Really bringing down the tone of her new home. She hooks a left and drives to the bridge. He's there. Lying on the floor, a can of beer next to him on the ground. The beloved Roger Pett. But Henrietta Adamson has no time for nostalgia. She is here with one purpose.

The camera is still on its tripod. The red light is on. She unhooks the lapel mic from dead Roger and holds it in her hand.

'Hello. This is Prime Minister Adamson. I am hoping that this is still broadcasting and I am hoping that there are still people watching. This is a monumental tragedy. A freak of nature. An act of God. Call it what you will. It will take a long while to unravel the devastation to our country but we are not done. I made it, so I know that there must be others who made it, too. If you are seeing this, I want to know. In a moment, I am going to give you my telephone number and email address. I don't know what is working, so please try anything. Get on your social media and message me there. I am going directly to parliament after this; if you are a minister, please get there as soon as you can. In fact, if you are alive, get there as soon as you can, whatever it is that you do.'

She gives out her personal contact details on the air. And she hopes that somebody sees.

She hopes.

There will be time to grieve but this is not it, she thinks. Now, in the wake of such misfortune, there is, in fact, an opportunity.

When Haruto Ikeda has finished with Bauer in the labs, he returns to his office for what will be his last day in Wuxi. When he gets there, a young, attractive, slim man is sitting at his desk.

'I'm sorry. Can I help you?'

'Ah, yes. Dr Ikeda, please come in.' He is calm. Scarily polite.

'Yes, this is my office.'

The man stands to vacate Ikeda's chair. He is tall. His trousers seem too short. His hair is perfect. His hands are smooth. Like he has never done a day of work in his life. But his dark eyes tell a different story.

Ikeda sits in his chair, perhaps to show some authority.

'How may I help you?'

'I would first like to say that it is an honour to meet you, but I should add that it is very rarely an honour to meet me. I am an admirer of your work and, for that reason, I am here as a courtesy.'

The doctor doesn't know whether to feel threatened or intrigued.

'Sir, the world is in two halves. That is how it works. East on one side and west on the other. You are right, there should be more kindness in the world.' Ikeda baulks at this. 'And it could do with a little more. But we are not here to meddle with nature. We should not upset the balance. You keep good company with your friend Lao. He shares your ideals but he sticks within the lines.'

'Who are—' Ikeda starts but is cut off.

'You are a great man, Dr Ikeda. But now is the time for you to go to the place where great men often have to go. Into the ether, unknown.'

'You're here to kill me.'

The man in the suit laughs quietly to himself.

'I do not need to do that, Doctor. If that were the case, it would already be done, we would not be talking. You should listen to your wife. She is always right, you know? When Dr Bauer's father died, Dr Bauer had nothing left to lose. This kind of person is useful for certain organisations. They can be used. But they do not contribute much to the world because they have lost their ideals. They have had everything taken away from them, so they know only how to take. I would suggest that you throw that sandwich in the trash.'

Ikeda looks at the packaging on his desk then back at the man standing on the other side.

He will visit Dr Bauer later this evening.

It will not be as courteous.

Ikeda is told that he should leave. He should return home. Or perhaps it would be the time to take Kimiko to London – she has always wanted to visit.

'Thank you for trying, Doctor.'

The man walks out, and Ikeda is left at his desk with a poisoned sandwich in his hand. He throws it into the trash with three other identical packages that have not been emptied from the basket this week.

It is time.

He and Kimiko will leave.

Henrietta Adamson is in her car for a minute before her mobile vibrates. Joseph Reed. The secretary of state for environment, food and rural affairs. The message just says, *On my way*. Not necessarily a senior minister but he is on her side. And, more importantly, he is alive.

Then things blow up. Message after message. Emails. Social-media mentions. The video of her impromptu speech is being shown on news channels across the globe. CNN. Al Jazeera. Mediacorp. Canadian Broadcasting Corporation. Everywhere.

Then her phone rings. She answers. A woman says, 'Please hold the line for the president.' Then a different voice.

'Prime Minister Adamson,' he says. It sounds odd. It felt odd when she said it herself on the broadcast.

'Yes, Mr President.'

'Looks like you're going to need some help.'

Just as a butterfly flapping its wings can set off a chain of events that will eventually cause a tidal wave, Haruto Ikeda's chance stumble across a spreadsheet catalysed a series of episodes that resulted in a global epidemic of compassion, and the death of sixty million Brits.

His kindness virus may not have changed the world in the way that he hoped, but it may just have done enough to restore some balance.

The man in the suit may think that it has to be equal – light and dark, good and evil – but Haruto Ikeda is an idealist. The positive can outweigh the negative. The world can be better.

It is an unknown world, today, and it is a different world.

Ikeda made that happen.

There was no time for testing.

Sometimes you just have to take the risk and move straight to a treatment. Because no treatment and the wrong treatment have the same outcome. Death.

Everybody dies.

But a treatment, even if it doesn't fully heal, can buy you time.

It can give you the opportunity to try something else.

To get it right.

In the UK, there is a chance for a new start, with a strong and moral leader. And people who understand kindness. And people who have triumphed over tragedy. It is the base of something good. Something right. Something to appreciate.

It's huge.

Elsewhere, it is smaller.

In Boston, a man travels on a bus to a dinner party with a bunch of red roses he bought for the host. He sees a woman, on her own, sad, deflated. He reaches his stop and gives her a rose from the bunch before he gets off.

In Toulouse, many people are frightened, still. They want to remain locked down. They want their own dignity pill, just in case. But at a fast-food restaurant, a young man does not have enough to pay for his order. An elderly couple behind offer him some money. He says no but they place it in his hand. Anytime he sees somebody on the street needing money for food, from this day, he will help them.

In Bogotá, an eight-year-old boy, who has been sick for three days, asks his father if he can offer to pick up groceries for the elderly couple a few doors down.

Russia is still run by a madman and China is in possession of the deadliest weapon in history. And, while there has been death, and while there is still fear and panic in many countries, something has shifted in the collective consciousness. Ikeda has not fixed the world with his virus but the world has changed. He has made a difference.

It feels like the beginning.

And he said, 'Let there be hope.'

And maybe there is hope.

Maybe it is better this way.

To start over again.

On Friday.

Over seven hundred people make their way to the Houses of Parliament by the end of the night. They come from across the country on empty roads where they can drive as fast as the Germans do, and they are greeted, personally, by the new prime minister, Henrietta Adamson.

Nurses, firefighters, school teachers and café owners. No doctors yet. Two lawyers who could prove incredibly useful. There are so many homeless people who did not see the broadcast but who also did not get a dignity pill. They are going to be given a second chance at life.

Support comes in from everywhere that light touches. Statements are issued from the United States and Burkina Faso, Russia and Tuvalu. New Zealand to Kiribati and everything in between comment on the tragedy that has befallen China and the United Kingdom.

There are thoughts and prayers and disbelief, but the overall message is both gentle and thoughtful.

True compassion.

Not an ounce is spared for Stefan Bauer, who takes two bullets to the chest and one to his brain without a word of courtesy from his beautiful murderer.

China are yet to comment, and nobody is pressing them to.

There is still panic but there appears to be a ceasefire on selfishness, for now.

Ikeda sees it. The firewall allows these stories through. He does not know whether this is a response to tragedy or it is his virus taking hold, or a combination of both. It doesn't matter. It is how people should treat other people. It is what he wanted, though the methods do not necessarily justify the outcome.

He takes the bus back to Suzhou. There are not many travelling this evening. But he watches them as he always does. And, this time, nobody is watching him.

Ikeda does not stop for a tea before returning home, he is too hungry today; he did not have his usual sandwich.

Kimiko greets him at the door. She hugs him as he kicks off his shoes. She kisses his cheek. He does the same to her and then gives her an extra peck on her forehead.

'Dinner will be twenty minutes. I have put a glass of wine on the bedside table. You have time to shower.'

Haruto nods. His wife moves off towards the kitchen and he heads to the bedroom. The wine is there. As is a mixed-up Rubik's Cube on his pillow. He smiles at the normality of the gesture and solves it quickly before taking his shower.

He eats with his wife. Tempura cauliflower with a soy-sauce broth flavoured with horseradish. They drink wine. It is quiet. They are waiting for Adamson to make a statement.

She gives a rousing speech on global community. On an end to war. On a focus on the planet because there is no defence for Mother Nature. She talks of rebuilding the country. She says more people are showing up and that she will make sure that everyone who is alive will be found and accounted for and that, going forward, they will count for something.

The Ikedas both find it moving.

'She is the right person for this job, don't you think, Haruto?'

'A strong woman. A good person.'

Kimiko nods.

'What is our plan? We cannot stay here, I understand that.'

'No, that will not work. I once heard that great people often have to disappear. Into the ether.' He lets that hang for a moment.

'There is still no air travel. Are we safe?' Kimiko looks out of the window at the apartment opposite.

'Yes. I believe we are safe. But we must leave.'

'Home? Are we going back to Japan?'

'Wherever you want to go, my dear. As long as we are together. But, I was thinking we could finally take that trip to London. Everyone there seems so kind.'

ACKNOWLEDGEMENTS

I did not have a book published last year. I don't like that. It doesn't work for me. It was a dark time. There are usually a lot of people to thank, and I know that I will be grateful to many. The journalists and bloggers who review and share thoughts and make sure people know about my book. The booksellers who champion it – particularly Fourbears Books and Bert's Books, who always have my back. My publisher for jumping up and down about the things that I write and making sure that other people get excited, too. The fellow writers who read advance copies and say nice things that we can put on the cover. I know this and I am always grateful for it because there are a lot of books out there and not a lot of time.

I have a new agent. The wonderful David Headley. This is our first book together and I am sure that there will be many more. I already know that our hunger for success and love of the written word is in alignment. I also thank you for saving my year by publishing my short story in Goldsboro's *25* anthology. I'm really proud of that story and I'm excited about what we have ahead of us. (I also hope to be able to buy that first-edition Hemingway at some point.)

Steve Watson, our little podcast project has kept me creatively buoyant and our weird friendship has brought me great joy. (Even though I do most of the work in both.)

West, we had a proper humdinger with this one. It's usually so quick and smooth but we had to dig deep this time. We did it, though. We still worked brilliantly together to get the job done. This is as much yours as it is mine. I thank you for your diplomacy and directness. (When needed.)

I know that writers fill these things with thanks but I didn't like not being published and only one person really had to deal with how that made me feel. That's Kel. You don't realise that you get me through. You remind me that I am a writer when I don't feel like one. You support me in trying to live this dream and inspire me by trying to live yours. We are trying to make things happen and we are doing it together. I love that. We'll catch a break soon.

And to you, the reader, I give thanks. Because there are lots of books out there that are being thrust in your face and you chose to read mine. It won't be like those books and it may not even work. If this is your first Will Carver story, I was less experimental about five books ago. If you keep coming back for more, you'll know that sometimes I nail it and sometimes I go too far. And that's half the fun. I hope.